MAN–MACHINE INTERFACE

Something—something was coming, moving like a cockroach, crawling and stopping, darting and stopping to watch him again. It carried something on its back. Something disk-shaped, flat as it was.

The disk was shining. The light let him see where he was. The floor was circular and huge. The ceiling was high, but he found a bundle of thick cylinders like the trunks of close-spaced trees climbing toward it from the center of the floor. Everything was dark, aged metal, and he knew he must be inside that immense space machine.

The moving thing was metal, too, but gold-colored, like the gold-filmed seedship and his own body. Darting and stopping, darting and stopping, it came on from toward the clustered tubes. He knew it meant nothing good for him . . .

* * *

"In Manseed Jack Williamson ventures into unfamiliar ground, the melding of humans and robots. Tied to this is the more familiar theme of colonizing alien planets, but by a method no other writer, to my knowledge, has ever used. The concepts are joined with masterly characterization, close attention to dramatic development and a warm sense of humanity. Jack continues in the old tradition—the telling of good stories with a deft, sure touch."

Also by Jack Williamson
Published by Ballantine Books:

with Frederik Pohl
UNDERSEA CITY
UNDERSEA FLEET
UNDERSEA QUEST
FARTHEST STAR
WALL AROUND A STAR

with James E. Gunn
STAR BRIDGE

JACK WILLIAMSON

MANSEED

A Del Rey Book

BALLANTINE BOOKS • NEW YORK

A Del Rey Book
Published by Ballantine Books

Library of Congress Catalog Card Number: 82–6824

ISBN 0–345–30743–7

Manufactured in the United States of America

First Hardcover Edition: October 1982
First Paperback Edition: October 1983

Cover art by Rick Sternbach

CONTENTS

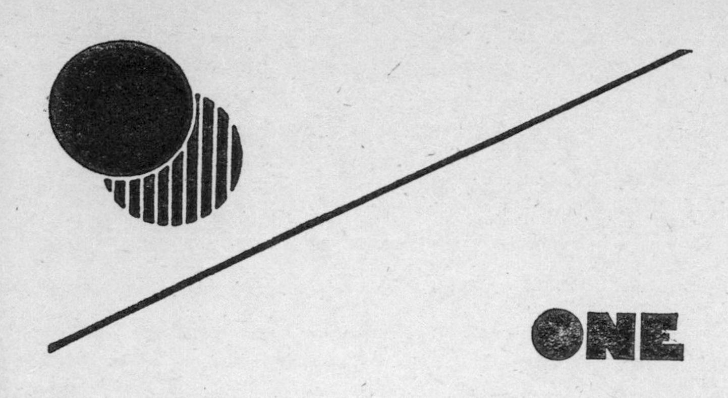

ONE

THE DEFENDER

In the nightmare, he had no body.

Frightened, he drifted forever in the empty dark, hunted by things that had no shape, that made no sound, that had no minds except their monstrous hunger for him. He tried to get away, but he had no limbs, no will, no clue to anything.

The alarm crashed.

He woke alone, chilled with sweat and shivering, clutching for Jayna until he remembered she was gone. Lying alone in the dreadfully empty bed, he tried to understand the dream. It must have come from the way he felt without her—desolate, helpless, still bewildered.

Trying not to hate her, he saw her in his mind. Nude and bitchily seductive, flashing down a white coral beach toward whiter surf, Crowler panting after her.

Groggily, he throttled the alarm and groped for things not so painful. His lecture at ten. The curriculum committee. The senior seminar. His pending research grant for the multilayer micromemory and the call to La Jolla to look at Tomislav's Biowand software.

A hunger pang, but he ate no breakfast now. Not since she left. Dressing, missing even her wry disapproval of his clashing shirt and necktie, he snapped on the morning news. Famine, riot, terror—the world had matched his savage mood, and there was no cheer anywhere.

He cut off the TV. Walking to the Kingsmill campus, he tried to savor springtime. Trees in leaf, a flower scent from somewhere, long-legged coeds blooming out of jeans and sneakers. A songbird mocked him, and he yearned for her. Since she had left, all the world was empty.

The phone was ringing when he reached his office door. "Martin Rablon?" His heart paused because the cool music of her voice could have been Jayna's. "The computer scientist?"

"I teach computer science."

"I'm Megan Drake. With the Raven Foundation. We need advice on a new direction in computers." Jayna had never even tried to understand them. "Professor, are you available for a consultation?"

"Sure." Another new escape, and he felt grateful for it. "After commencement—"

That black, never-ending nightmare chasm.

He sank into it, sank forever.

Who am I? Wordless urges ached and burst inside him. What place is this?

All he knew was darkness, stillness, bottomless infinity. That and a dull discomfort throbbing in his head. A tingling deadness in his fingers, in his face and his feet. Still he sank—or was he really somehow floating? Searching, he found no sense of motion or support, no clue to time or place, no glint of light, no hint of anything beyond that prickling pressure that wasn't quite even a pain.

It pressed and pressed, swelling inside him, heavy everywhere, until he thought he couldn't endure it. Yet when he tried to struggle, every effort seemed to close it tighter, its gray chill aching always deeper. He found no way to end it.

Still he sank or maybe floated through that soundless, stifling dark, touching nothing, all his body frozen—if he really had a body—without breath or even need for breath. That itself became a haunting riddle.

How was he alive?

The blunt throb beat, beat, beat, until he was glad to let it hammer him back into the vacant dark.

He sat with a margarita by the pool, his bad leg propped on another chair. Spray chilled his face when the fat man dived, and a sun glint stabbed his eyes. Turning to shield them, he saw the girl striding behind the sleek-haired manager through the mostly empty tables. They were looking for him.

"Señor Brink? Mees Drake."

"Megan Drake."

He liked her, even in the dark sunglasses. Vigorous and tall, her hair burnished red under the sun. She smiled to thank the manager, who had lingered as if for a tip. Waiting for him to go, she took off the glasses. Her eyes delighted him, greenish gray and very clear.

"You are Don Brink?"

Nodding, waving the manager away, he reached to pull up a chair. With a fleeting glance at his leg, she sat.

"The—the mercenary soldier?"

"Please—" He had to frown. "If you're media, I don't talk about my work."

"I'm not media." She seemed amused. "In fact, we've learned to be skittish about publicity. I'm with the Raven Foundation. Down here for a biogenics convention. I happened to hear about you, and I think we have a job—"

"Afraid you're a little late." With a wry shrug, he moved the leg.

"You've been wounded?" Sudden emotion widened her eyes. "We weren't told."

"A mortar splinter. Still lodged in the knee." Painfully, he grinned. "Dysentery, too, and recurrent malaria. The medics tell me I've fought my last war."

"Maybe not." She paused to weigh him. "We were told you command unusual fees because you earn them."

"I tried to. While I could."

"You'll do." A quick smile lit her lean, angular face. "If you want the job."

He shook his head. "In the fix I'm in—"

"No matter." He caught her scent as she leaned closer, something light and clean. Like the lilacs he remembered blooming in the untended yard around the parsonage in springs when he was still a child. "Not to us. If you can come to our Albuquerquc lab for a consultation—"

She was gone.

Again he was awake, at least half awake, still adrift in that boundless dark. Again he strained for sound, for any sense of place or time, but all he could find was inside himself. All he knew was that dull depression throbbing forever in his head and the stinging numbness that gripped him everywhere. When he fought to move himself, new needles of pain stabbed into his deadness.

But his fingers flexed!

His toes curled. Stiff wrists began to yield, and stiffer elbows bent. Painfully, he tried to reach out into the suffocating dark. His unfeeling fingers found something hard and slick and cold that walled him in, beside and above and even beneath. Something coffin close.

A wave of terror chilled him.

Had he been buried alive?

Not breathing, yet still with no sense of suffocating, was he even alive?

The phone caught him working late at the lab terminal, running Biowand programs to build and test model virus models, searching for one that might have saved his wife and Roger. Too late for them, but others might be cured. Absorbed in the dancing patterns of possible life and annoyed at the call, he let it ring.

It kept on till he gave up.

"What d'you want?"

"Dr. Tomislav?" A girl's voice, soft and clear as Olga's once had been. "The biologist?"

"Ivan Tomislav," he muttered. "I do biology."

"Well enough to win the Nobel." Recalling Olga and the Yiddish lullaby she used to croon when she was nursing Roger, he couldn't hang up. "I'm Megan Drake. With the Raven Foundation. We were warned not to bother you at work, but we're trying something very new in genetic engineering, and we need you urgently. Can you possibly come to Albuquerque for a consultation—"

Again, the icy, everlasting dark.

Still he floated in it, floated nowhere, still shut inside those narrow walls. Stiffly, fighting stabbing agony in every joint, he reached to feel for any opening, any clue, any device that might set him free. All he found was slick and seamless hardness. His tingling hands fell back, and he found his own flesh. His naked hips, his flanks, the flatness of his belly.

Himself?

All his body felt cold and slick as that coffin wall, oddly numb to his dull fingers. He groped again, lower. No balls or penis. Nor labia, either. Not even hair. All he found was smooth and strangely hard, more like metal than flesh.

What sort of thing had he become?

Recoiling from the shock, from the pain of loss and the riddle of it, he strove again for answers. All he could recall was those shattered scraps of dream. Megan Drake in all of them. Or had they been more than dream?

Still starkly vivid to him, they had the feel of actual recollection. He clung to Megan's image. Her fine lean features, her greenish-gray eyes, her vital eagerness. She must be, must have been real.

But—himself?

Was he—could he have been Martin Rablon? Or Don Brink? Or Ivan Tomislav? All of them? That made no sense. If she had really called them, or any of them, for a consultation at the Raven Foundation, what could that have been about?

Searching, all he found was the baffling dark.

His fingers strayed back to his naked crotch.

"Dr. Galen Ulver?"

Startled, he looked up from the half-assembled model rocket on the workbench and found her in the open doorway of the garage.

"Forgive me for breaking in." Her voice erased his brief annoyance. "It seems you have no phone."

"Nobody to answer it now."

"The fusion-drive man?" Suddenly doubtful, she was staring at the little rocket.

"Building toys." He shrugged a little ruefully, grinning at the bench. "They're better than alcohol or suicide. In fact, I kid myself that they're really more than toys. The best I can do since NASA scrubbed the fusion engine. To me, they're designs for starcraft that ought to be built."

He waited to see what she wanted.

"Megan Drake." In casual slacks, without makeup, briskly direct, she looked stunning in spite of herself. He wished he had been forty years younger. "With the Raven Foundation."

"What's that?"

"We're privately endowed," she said. "For a very special project. We've studied the research reports you used to publish. A shame your funds were cut off, but we're still interested in fusion propulsion. If you have time to talk about it—"

"Time? All I have left."

She leaned to study the model. He liked the way she moved. Her arresting eyes came gravely back to him.

"Wonderfully made." Her tone cheered him. "But I think we can get you a good deal closer to the stars." The promise took his breath. "If you can come with me to our Albuquerque lab for a consultation—"

He woke to the ache of haunting loss, fingers still against that hairless, sexless slickness. Shuddering, striving to understand, he groped for more of Megan Drake. He recalled no consultation, nor anything else. Why? Was the memory gone because he had loved her once and couldn't love her now, because the pain of his mutilation was too severe to be endured? He found no way to know.

Again he searched his prison. That first tingling numbness had eased a little, and his stiffened limbs moved more freely. Hands braced against those cold, close walls, he turned himself and found a break. A seam, almost too fine for his touch to trace, running straight as far as he could follow from above his head back toward his feet.

Escape?

Eagerly, he ran his fingertips once more along it, back and forth all across it. Nothing else. No knob or catch or lock or hint of any way to open it. He let his hands fall back and found another riddle.

A cable, a little thicker than his thumb. It came from somewhere below him, and his turning had twisted it around him. Hard and slick as metal, yet stiffly flexible, it felt oddly like his strange new skin. It was faintly warm, pulsing slowly where he grasped it.

His fingers followed it around his hips, on to his belly. It fastened to him there, where his navel should have been.

His own umbilical cord?

Was the cell no coffin, but a womb?

An hour out of Kansas City, a stewardess brought the note to him.

Captain Wardian, may I speak to you? At your convenience. About your career as an American astronaut. And about a very special project that ought to interest you. A moment of your time will be enough.

It was written in a firm but feminine hand on a stiff, buff-colored letterhead expensively embossed in indigo ink:

RAVEN FOUNDATION. MEGAN DRAKE, DIRECTOR. The address was Albuquerque. It was signed Megan Drake.

"You'll be sorry if you don't see her, sir." The stewardess grinned at him, a friendly malice on her sun-freckled face. "The type you like. She's in first class, by the empty aisle seat."

"Tell her when we're on the ground."

On the ground in Kansas City, he went back to meet Megan Drake. When she rose to offer her vigorous hand, he wasn't sorry.

"I think we need you, captain." He sat down to listen, pleased with the red glint of her clean hair and her lean grace of motion. "A moment will do. We've checked out your records, but I'd like you to confirm them. Physics at UCLA, summa cum laude. Masters in astronomy at Cal Tech. A NASA-trained astronaut." Her clear eyes grew graver. "How come you're flying now for Delta?"

"I've had my turn in space." He shrugged. "One's all you get since they've cut the budgets back, and I like this better than a Pentagon desk."

"If you still care about space—" She paused to survey him again, and he enjoyed the glow of her approval. "I'm pretty sure we can offer you something better yet. If you'd like to come out to our Albuquerque lab for a consultation—"

He woke with both hands loosely clasping the cord, as if to climb. It felt warm and alive to his fingers, pulsing as if it pumped something. Blood? Or did he need blood now? Blood or something stranger, it was his life. The reason, perhaps, that he felt no need to breathe.

But what kind of life?

Almost afraid to wonder, he twisted again in the dark to find that narrow seam. His touch, he thought, had become more sensitive, that prickling numbness nearly gone. He traced the mark again and found a slight bulge on the surface beside it.

Here, the way!

Without quite knowing why, he doubled his fist. He hit the bulge and thought it gave a little to the blow. He felt the seam. Still no wider. Shuddering, dimly alarmed, he struck the bulge again. Harder. Again and yet again. Still no sound, but he felt the fissure widen.

Light!

Bright points flashed and vanished. Diamond hard. Dimensionless. The slit grew wider, and they slid very slowly across it. He saw they were stars, the sky behind them queerly black. When he could, he pushed himself outside.

And fell into stunning wonder.

A night sky, black and blazing, with no horizons anywhere. Unwinking stars, in swarms he had never imagined, seeming strangely near. The Milky Way beyond them, a mighty wheel-rim of bright dust and black dust, rolling all around him. No up or down or sane direction.

Head spinning, he wanted the shelter of his dark birthplace, but it was drifting away. He clutched for its walls, but he had no weight, no purchase on anything. It slid out of reach. Dizzy and ill, he had to close his eyes. Panic chilled him.

For this was interstellar space. Airless, empty, alien. Any matter here would drop toward the absolute zero. Nothing living could survive, not without support equipment. Yet somehow, somehow not even breathing, he was still alive.

Grappling with that stunning riddle, he clutched at his belly and found the cord. Still attached, it trailed him out of that hard-walled womb. Still a little warm, still slowly pulsing. The secret of his life—if this was actual life. He let his fingers caress its hard, pliant slickness.

His foot struck something, clung.

He opened his eyes and found the ship. Most of it only a

shadow against the stars. The rest yellow, gleaming dully where light struck. A thin golden arrow. Maybe five times his own body length, so slender his arms would reach half around it. Its tiny size jolted him.

Too small. Too small for space. His own birthcell filled the nose, that vital cord trailing out of the blackness inside its glistening lips. The cord was golden. His own body was, when he looked. His flesh sleek, hairless as the golden hull, shining with the same dull gleam where the light struck.

The skin of his forearm felt stiff but elastic, yielding to his testing fingers. Neither warm nor cold. Somehow unharmed by the vacuum or the unshielded radiation he felt burning on him. A different stuff than—

Than what?

He shuddered, shrinking from the riddles of his being. He felt human. His hairless hand looked like a metal casting when he turned it in the light, but humanly patterned, complete with a strong-nailed thumb and four good fingers. It made a quick fist when he tried it, the pain gone now. Human? In those broken and confusing dreams in which Megan Drake had always been inviting him to a consultation at the Raven Foundation, he had always been normally human enough to desire her—

Chilled, he couldn't help looking down. The coiling cable shone yellow, but his crotch was in the dark. He turned his body to the light, to see the naked hairless gleam where his genitals should have been. Quickly, ill and trembling with the ache of loss, he looked away.

Looked at his feet. Human, five toed, bare to the bitterness of space, they shone like old gold and clung to the skin of the ship. Somehow magnetic. He could walk the narrow hull. Careful with his slender life line, he stepped toward the tapered tail.

It ended with a cluster of rocket nozzles on which the gold had tarnished blue. They were dead. He felt no acceleration. Yet the little ship was moving. Flying fast into the light. Knowing that, wondering how he knew, he looked to find the light.

A star, so near it shone brighter than all the rest together. He studied it and found his vision changing. The far white point became a tiny disk. He made out fainter points above and below it, four that formed one straight row. Planets. Planets of the sun?

Jupiter, Saturn, Uranus, and Neptune?

Could they be?

He shivered to a thrill of hope. Megan, in those shattered bits of whatever, had been promising not herself but space. Was the strange machine a creation of her Raven Foundation? A lifecraft, perhaps? And he—had he been a crewman on some lost interstellar expedition, his body somehow transformed to survive in space? A lone survivor now returning home?

He swung to search for clues. A giddy flicker; he had to wait for his telescopic vision to shift again before he could see the fainter stars. The galactic clouds of distant fire and dust looked just the same. The Pleiades—that wondrous jewel of luminous mist and burning points had to be the Pleiades, but its shape was strangely changed. Working away from it, he found a great red star that surely was Aldebaran but strayed far from where it should have been. He found the twisted Hyades, once so near it, and a ragged line of brighter stars—could they have been the Ursa Major cluster?

Peering behind, the way the little ship must have come, he searched for home. Again his vision shifted. Remote stars leapt apart, abruptly brighter. Blue stars, red stars, some of them doubles, most too bright or too faint, the yellow too yellow.

None looked like the Sun.

How long—he shivered again. How long had the ship been in space?

He felt afraid to guess. For the stars themselves had crept away from where he had known them. Seen from here, wherever this was, the constellations had reshaped themselves. With the time in flight unknown, even its first direction uncertain, the Sun was lost forever.

Earth was gone, with all he could hope to recall—if he could hope to recall anything sane. The builders of the ship would be dust by now, their science and purpose long forgotten. The world could have become a paradise, perhaps for evolving supermen. Or mankind could be a million years extinct. He could never even hope to know.

They were totally alone, falling into the bright star ahead.

Turning slowly toward it, he thought he had begun to understand himself. Whatever the science of his creation, whatever the energies that supported his awareness and his motion now, he was more than passenger or crewman. He was part of the ship, his duty to save and to serve it.

Their danger was shocking, now that his altering vision had begun to reveal it. They were shooting straight into that white and tiny-seeming disk, already moving far too fast and still accelerating to its gravity. Without control, the rockets dead, with nothing to be done.

Or was there something that might be done and doing it his duty now? Had his birth, his awakening, somehow been triggered by the danger? Perhaps by some sensor that detected the star's increasing radiation? Had he been born from that dark metallic womb to save the ship? Born perhaps with graver defects than his missing genitalia? And all alone, with none to tell him what he must do?

Very slowly, the hull was tumbling. Gathering the golden cord into loops to keep it from fouling anything, he followed the sunlight around the spinning hull, paying out the cord as he walked, looking for trouble. He found it.

A ragged hole punched through the shining skin at the waist of the ship, the metal burned black around it. A hole no larger than the ball of his thumb, but the gold-filmed metal was thinner here than at the nose; the wound had gone through into a dark cavity.

The meteor must have been tiny, perhaps microscopic, vaporized on impact. Stooping, he found a narrow seam that ran close to the hole. The edge of a hinged access door.

He turned five recessed bolts that secured the door, but still it wouldn't open. Welded at the edge, he decided, by that old explosion. He tugged again, failed to lift it. Scowling into nowhere, he somehow saw what to do.

Vaguely astonished by his own know-how, he slapped his left hand over the hole to make a ground connection. Drawing power from the ship, he touched the hull with one golden finger and drew it slightly back to strike a cutting arc. Its blaze dazzled him for an instant until his vision compensated. Moving the forefinger, he sliced along the welded edge until he could lift the door.

The space below looked black at first. When his eyes had adjusted again to the diffuse star-glow and the reflection from his body, he could see the circuit boards of the main computer, closely stacked to fill the narrow hold. Though at first he saw no damage, they must have been struck by fragments from the explosion. He pulled the top board for inspection. Rablon's close-packed supercubes looked unharmed at first, until his special senses sharpened. He found a ruined cube then, and another beside it, where hot metal droplets had splashed them. Microprocessors and memory cubes were dead. His missing sex organs—they must have been part of the loss.

Ignoring the stab of pain where his penis should have been, he groped for what to do and found a program of action emerging in his mind. With it, a dim recollection of spare microprocessors and spares for a few key memory cubes under a hatch in the floor of his birthcell. Almost machinelike, he followed the program, removing cubes, testing and replacing them, until that first board was functional. He replaced it and ran another test.

Still the ship was dead.

He pulled the second circuit board, the third, a dozen others, discarding ruined cubes until all the spares were gone. Some had been duplicates, but others were not. Thousands of lost kilobytes of memory could never be recovered. Maybe millions. Troubled, he examined the next board and the one below it. They, too, had been scarred by hot fragments, probably damaged, but he could replace no more. The ship was crippled beyond complete repair, though not yet entirely dead—

"Egan?" Megan's voice. "Where are you?"

He wondered how he had heard her because here there was no air to carry sound. Yet it was her voice, coming from somewhere, sounding small and frightened.

"Megan?" He whispered her name, or thought he did. "Megan?"

"You aren't Egan." He thought she seemed afraid of him. "Who are you?"

"I don't know who I am. Or what. I just woke up on a strange starship—a very little ship—somewhere out in space. I don't know where. Or when—I think a lot of time has passed. But I don't know—I don't know anything."

Terror touched him.

"Megan? Are you—are you here?"

He waited, trembling.

"Mister—" At last, she answered, uncertainly and faintly, as if from far away. "I'm sorry you're in trouble, but I don't know you. I never saw a spaceship, and I don't know who you are . . ." Her frightened voice trailed away.

"Megan, where are you?"

"At Uncle Luther's ranch. To stay till mother gets better. But Uncle Luther isn't here. There's only Jesus and old Dolores. They sleep in the bunkhouse, too far to hear us. The thunder woke me up, and all the lights are out, and I can't find Egan's room, and I stubbed my toe in the dark—"

He thought he heard her crying.

"Megan?" He tried to call again. "Megan, can you help me talk to anybody?"

He waited, squatting beside the access door. The little ship tumbled slowly, its hull a dark blot against the marching galaxy and then a golden glow once more. No answer came.

He was closing the door when another memory woke.

Megan Drake met him at the Albuquerque airport.

"Dr. Tomislav!" He heard her voice before he saw her. "I'm driving you out to the lab."

He picked up his bag and followed her out to a red sports car. She drove it fast but expertly, saying very little to him. Pleased with her, he sat wondering about the Raven Foundation.

Near the mountains east of the city, she took a narrow road that twisted south between brown and barren hills until they reached a tall chain-link gate. Grinning warmly at her, a guard there swung it open to let them through.

"The foundation." She nodded at a row of low buildings ahead. "We bought the site from Omega. A hush-hush outfit. They used to contract subassemblies for military nukes till something bigger swallowed them."

"Listen, Miss Drake." He turned in the seat. "You haven't said what you want to consult me about. If it's anything military, I've a rule of my own. Not to do it. Not for anybody."

"No problem." He liked her easy smile. "We aren't military."

She parked on a gravel drive beside a long building that looked like stuccoed adobe.

"Our guests stay here," she said. "A sort of barracks. Nothing plush, but we have security. Meals next door. Conchita cooks Mexican and American. Her Mexican's excellent if you care for that. Hope you do. The American—" She shrugged.

"I've got to know what you want," he said. "Why so much security if you aren't military."

"Nothing sinister." Her face grew graver. "I like to feel, in fact, that our project could grow into the grand climax of human evolution. At least here on Earth. If we can manage to carry it through. We don't talk about it outside the fence. The press would blow it into nonsense, and the backwoods are still full of fanatics who would accuse us of offending their tribal God." Her greenish eyes narrowed. "You'll remember not to talk?"

"Sure." She was moving to leave the car, but he sat still. "When I know what not to talk about."

"Okay." She settled back beside him. "I imagine you never heard of Luther Raven?"

"Not that I recall."

"My uncle. A financier—my brother used to call him an international gambler. Mostly in grain and oil and ships to carry them. Piled up his billions very privately and finally felt guilty about them. Endowed the foundation as a kind of atonement.

"To realize Egan's dream." Her eyes lifted toward the bare mountains, now turning red at sunset. "Egan was my twin brother. A crazy kid, but I adored him. Wrote unpublished poetry and loved the wrong women. Vexed our uncle because he never earned a dime or finished anything he started. Finally killed himself, climbing a difficult alp without a guide. But I loved him—"

He heard sadness in her falling voice.

"His dream—it can make up for everything."

Still she watched the high summit.

"Egan wasn't a happy man. I'm not sure he ever knew why. Went to shrinks and never believed what they told him. Quarreled with a lot of people because he got vehement with his own ideas and too short with skeptics. He met a lot of skeptics because his notions so often upset people.

"He used to say the whole human race was a kind of being. With a sort of group mind, existing somehow in the unconscious mind of everybody. He thought it had lived a life of its own since human evolution began.

" 'We're grown up now,' he used to say. 'It's time for us to seed.'

"That sounded strange till he explained it. He thought

we had outgrown the Earth. Thought we had a space instinct, driving us to leave it and look for new planets. He'd come to believe that most of our troubles—everything from mental illness to war and terrorism—were only symptoms of our racial frustration because we hadn't got away.

"That's how his dream began." Her grave eyes had come back to him. "Mostly he kept it to himself, because so many people laughed, but he always shared everything with me. He used to talk about colonies on the moon or Mars or out in space until he decided they weren't real solutions.

"What he saw at last was a way to sow the human seed on a larger field, farther off. On the worlds of other stars—"

She had seen Tomislav's growing doubt.

"Please." She raised her hand to stop his question. "I know the notion turns people off, because it's nothing they've ever thought about. Egan was no scientist himself, or he might have considered it too impossible. But Luther bought the notion—he was no scientist, either. A surprise to his lawyers and even to me when we found the endowment in his will. With a paragraph to say it was a payment on a debt he owed mankind.

"So here we are." Bent intently toward him, she gestured at the row of drab prefabs and then at the sunset sky. "Refitting the old Omega shops and labs. Designing the seed machines and the vehicles that will lift them into orbit and launch them toward new worlds.

"We're going to scatter our seed across the stars."

He sat blinking at her.

"It's not all that impossible," she said. "In fact, we're already writing contract specifications for a lot of the basic components. Though we've still got big problems ahead. That's why we need you."

"If you're talking about interstellar ships—"

"Seed." She shook her head. "They can't be large or very expensive because we'll be making many hundred. Thousands if we can. Nearly all will surely be wasted. Most will fall on barren soil, if they reach any soil at all. Maybe none will ever grow; we can't even be certain the right sort of planets exist anywhere. But we must try—that was Egan's vision. If we're able to replant mankind on only one new world"—her shining eyes were back on the mountain —"human evolution will not have been in vain."

He held his questions, waiting for her to go on.

"Seedships, we call them." She turned back to him. "Designed to survive flights that can take almost forever, searching the galaxy for habitable planets. The ship will be partly mechanical but also partly organic. A new invention in evolution if we can perfect it. We need genetic engineers to help us get the human genes into computer code and out again—"

The bright star had moved when he found it again.

A little wiser, he looked down at the small gold hull. That new invention, half machine and half alive, one of all those hundreds, built back on Earth he couldn't even guess how long ago. Dead since the meteor struck its computer brain center but revived—at least enough to bear him—by its approach to the star ahead.

His vision adjusted to let him study its four giant planets. Jupiterlike, they offered no possible haven. Even their moons, if they had moons, would be airless snowballs, with no fit soil for the seed of man. But perhaps, he thought, there might be an Earthlike planet, too small and near the star even for his telescopic eyes. A fallow world waiting for a new humanity.

If the ship could land. If the damaged seed would grow. If he could defend it from whatever hazards—

No longer feeling quite so strange, he walked back to inspect the Ulver engines again. They looked intact. He found the recessed fittings where the auxiliary mass-tanks had once been attached and then the inspection door just below them.

Opening that, he discovered an internal tank with a sealed cap he could reach. But no gauge, no indicator, nothing to tell him whether the little motors might ever burn again. There would be pumps and injectors to feed fuel through the lasers into the jets.

After the disaster, and so many ages since, would all that intricate gear still work?

"Ship to Defender." Speaking again in his mind, the voice was strangely changed. Still somehow faintly Megan's, it was emotionless, coldly precise. "Propulsion equipment undamaged."

"Megan—" Bewilderment chilled him. "Where are you?"

"Location in space, off unidentified stellar object. Coordinates unknown."

"Megan?" He tried again. "Aren't you Megan Drake?"

"Term Megan Drake not identified," it answered. "We are Ship Control Program."

"Then who am I?"

"Term I not identified."

He shivered. Staring down at the golden hull, clinging to the warm and throbbing cord that bound him to it, he strove to understand. Ship control must be the computer the meteor had hit, Megan's voice built into it—her voice and that scrap of frightened recollection from her childhood. Alive again since his effort at repair, yet still crippled. Vital memory cubes and circuits lost, perhaps forever.

He was the Defender, born of the ship, designed to serve and guard it. That at least seemed clear. His mind had come out of its computer, filled with bits of skill and power recorded to fit him for his mission. His life—a mode of life he had never imagined—still flowed from it, pulsing through the golden cord.

Yet in spite of all such wonders, he had been born defective. Naked, bare and slick and shining, where he should have been a man. And Megan—his longing for her was still alive, and he had heard her frightened voice. But what—where—was she?

Groping for her, all he found was numbing desolation. The ship wasn't Megan; she must have died back on Earth, perhaps ten thousand centuries ago. Anyhow, he was no longer designed for sex. He tried to shake that aching sadness off. Those old emotions were only faults in the Defender, chance hazards to his duty now.

He tried to gather himself.

"Defender to Ship," he asked in his mind, "can you get us to some planet?"

"Negative."

"But we've got to find a planet. A friendly world where we can land and plant mankind. There has to be a way."

"Negative."

"Why negative?"

"Drive power lost."

"Then we've got to restore it. What will that require?"

An image of Megan flickered in his mind. Lean features framed in red-glinting hair. Lovely for an instant, though stark with shock, the green-gray eyes fixed in blank bewilderment. Torn to shining shards an instant later, spun across exploding darkness.

Hearing nothing, he tried again. "How can we operate the engines to reach a planet and land there?"

"Computer malfunction." Almost Megan's, the whisper came faintly out of the dark. "Computer malfunction—"

"What is the malfunction?"

"Circuits interrupted."

"Interrupted where?"

Silence again while her troubled face flashed and shattered.

"Malfunction located." A dying breath. "Board E-One."

"Can it be repaired?"

When no answer came, he bent to open the access door.

He hated the cane, but he had to use it, limping off the plane at Albuquerque. He hated the bad knee when he had to let Megan Drake carry his bag out of the terminal to the little red car. Hated himself for getting too old and too slow for the game.

Megan looked very young and very lovely even in the casual tan slacks, and she handled the bag with athletic ease. The contrast hurt. Pushing to keep her pace, he wished bitterly that he could skip back to her generation.

"I'm driving you right out to the lab," she told him. "We've living quarters there—"

"Let's have dinner on the way."

He spoke on impulse. Because he wanted to forget the knee and his age and his own dim future. Because she was so wonderful. Distress swept him when he saw her head begin to shake.

"Couldn't we try the Penthouse Club?" he asked quickly. "A posh place, I understand. A client of mine gave me a card that ought to get us in."

Surprised, her eyes weighed him.

"A chance for us to talk." He urged her. "You've never told me anything about the war you're hiring me to fight." In spite of him, the bitterness shadowed his voice. "Or how you can think I'm fit to fight."

"Why not?" She shrugged, still warily intent. "We don't discuss our project outside the lab, but I do need to know you better, Mr. Brink."

"Can't you make it Don?"

She made it Don, and her impulsive smile warmed him. On the top floor of a downtown building, the Penthouse Club was posh enough but not too posh to let them in. Waiting for a table, they went into the bar. At first, she said she seldom drank, but she seemed to enjoy her margarita when it came. Though he wanted urgently to know her better, their talk began awkwardly. She was slow to talk about herself, and he felt naked when she wanted to know about him.

"Mr. Brink—" She paused, frowned at him oddly. "Don, if you'd rather—I've never known anybody like you. We talked at Acapulco, and of course we've checked you out. But I'd like to know how you got into—into your profession. Especially, how you feel about it."

"How I got to be a killer?"

He saw her shock. "You like the word?"

"I fight." He was deliberately blunt, testing her responses. "For pay. I fight men hired to kill me. Killing men gets to be a game. The most exciting and demanding game there is."

Her greenish eyes wide, her face was a study in appalled fascination. When she said nothing, he grinned and continued:

"Down at Acapulco, I was feeling pretty bad, thinking I might never be able to play it again. I'm anxious to know how you imagine I can."

"Later." Sipping her margarita, she paused to lick the salt. "I rather like it." When her eyes returned to him, he saw a glint of amusement. "I'll promise not to get you into the media if you'll tell me what made you what you are."

Her directness jolted him. .

"I—I'm not sure I know." He found his drink in his hand and set it back untasted. "Or if I do, it's something I don't like to talk about. It hurts."

She sat waiting till he went on.

"I was a preacher's son." He shook his head, flinching from the memory. "In a little Bible belt town. An only kid, in a tough situation. Because the preacher's son has to be a model. I took that for granted. Tried hard enough. At least through high school."

Enjoying her close intentness, he wanted her to like him.

"Sometimes it really wasn't all that bad. Class work was easy. I liked sports. Little League. Later, track and competitive swimming. Chess, too, after I learned to play. I always liked games I could win."

Her face changed a little, and she wasn't quite so close.

"My senior year, I fell in love. Puppy love, my mother called it when I tried to talk to her. But agony for me because I knew I didn't have a chance. The girl was named Virgie Ellen. A year older than I was, because I'd skipped a grade.

"Dazzling, to me—"

Eyes on Megan, he saw Virgie Ellen again; the creamy skin, the tempting swell of her breasts. Felt her in his arms at the senior prom, holding him so tight she took his breath. Felt the magic of her hair against his cheek and inhaled her strong perfume.

He found himself silent, Megan still intent.

"Not a chance—" Recollections were rushing back, and he hoped they wouldn't offend her. "All through high school, Virgie Ellen had gone steady with Walt Montalbert. His father was a deacon in the church and a millionaire banker. The wedding was going to be in my father's church.

"The night before, I was alone in the parsonage. My folks were away overnight, gone to a revival in the next county. Virgie Ellen woke me up about midnight, tossing pebbles at my bedroom window. When I got it open, she held up her arms for me to help her in. I—"

The surge of old emotion checked him until he saw Megan's understanding nod.

"I didn't know what to think. Too far overwhelmed, in fact, to think at all. I'd never dared tell Virgie Ellen how I felt about her, though I guess she must have seen it. A few times I'd found her looking hard at me, with a quirky little smile she had, and wondered what she was thinking.

"The room was dark, of course, except for light from the street. I remember that quirky smile and her finger on her lips. I don't think I had breath to speak, because she was stripping off her clothes. I'd never seen a naked woman, and I remember how stunning she was. Strutting a little when her bra and panties were off. Turning in the light to give me an eyeful.

"That twisty smile. Turning to a laugh as she spread her naked arms for me—"

He paused again, self-conscious and rueful; again Megan nodded.

"My first sex."

Leaning to listen, Megan looked as lovely now as he recalled Virgie Ellen. Wondering what her own life was like and how she could feel such interest in him, he had to fend off a pang of new desire.

"My first—" His voice had slowed. "Maybe the best. A night I might have dreamed if people hadn't taught me such dreams were sinful. She ripped off my shorts—that's all I wore to bed. Pushed me back across the blanket and fell on top of me. A sort of rape because I had no notion what to do. But I went crazy about it when she showed me."

In his mind, the experience was all real again. The budding magic of Virgie Ellen. The feel of her hot flesh. The creak of the old bed alarming till he recalled that his parents were away. The scent of her hair and her hot breath, of their sweat and his semen.

"I never knew why she came to me because she didn't talk. She wasn't drunk. Not that I knew about alcohol then. But she was in control. Cool when we began. Laughing at me for all I didn't know. Crazy as I was after we got going.

"We were still at it when my folks got home. They'd had car trouble and never got to the revival. Day just breaking. I'd seen the dawn and said we'd better stop, but Virgie Ellen wanted one more time. My mother heard that creaky bed. They opened the door and caught us at it.

"And I felt glad"—wistfully, he grinned at Megan—"because I thought we'd have to marry. That was what I wanted. More than anything. Till I found out what a fool I'd been. Virgie Ellen got her clothes on very calmly, not saying anything to anybody. She walked out the front door and married Walt Montalbert that afternoon. I sat in the back of the church and bit my lip when my father asked if anybody had a reason why it shouldn't happen."

He drained his margarita and held up two fingers to order again.

"After supper, he called me into his study and tried to scold me. I had fornicated. He wanted me to kneel with him and pray for God's eternal mercy. I lost my temper enough to call him a hypocrite. He said he had counseled and prayed with Virgie and Walt and even Mr. Montalbert. Virgie had confessed her sin and cried about it. He said Christ had forgiven her and Walt had. As He would forgive me. I told him they were all stinking hypocrites.

"That night, I thought it over. Lying in that creaky bed that still had the smell of Virgie and our lust. I didn't sleep much, but I saw what I had to do. When day came, I gathered up what I could take and got out of the house. I never went back or even wrote a letter."

Quizzically, he looked at Megan.

"If you want to know, I guess that's what put me on the road to what you call my profession. In the beginning, I got hurt a lot. Because I was still pretty innocent. Got knocked around. Sometimes hungry. But I joined the army when I could and found I liked it. Learned the game and learned I love it.

"Even if you want to call me some kind of rogue."

"Rogue?" Gravely amused, she paused to consider him. "Your own word." She nodded, and he saw he hadn't lost her. "If it means a solitary fighting male, I suppose it might fit you."

Their table was ready. The chef was French. Megan let Don order for her, though she declined the wine. Eating with relish, she wanted to know more about what she called his adventures.

"Your turn," he told her.

"Maybe so, if I had anything to tell about. But I don't. Nothing like your career."

"Anyhow, I'd like to know."

"Why not?" A wry little smile flashed and faded. "We were twins, Egan and I. Results of a bad love affair. We never knew our father. Mother was always ill, and she died before we were nine. Uncle Luther took us over. Kind enough but absorbed with business. Egan and I—we had very little except each other. He grew up unhappy. His analyst told him we'd been too close.

"Maybe we were, but I did better than Egan. Maybe because Uncle Luther always favored me. I stayed in graduate school when Egan quit. Took degrees in science and worked in research till the lawyers read me the will and I went to work with the foundation."

That, she said, had filled her life. She had never married.

Wondering if Egan had left her with some unconscious trauma, he wished again for a lot he had lost.

Women had always been part of the game he played, prizes or opponents or, often, both. The recollection of Virginia Ellen had sharpened his desire for Megan. Watching her, he thought she might be vulnerable. Recoiling from her image of the killer, she had somehow been caught against her will.

Yet longing to be liked—to be loved for more than that—he decided not to push his luck. He wanted her too much to risk offense, and he thought some better time might come. Anyhow, he couldn't afford to throw away an unexpected chance to get back into the game.

When they left the Penthouse Club, he let her drive him on to his quarters at the lab. She left him there without explaining anything except to say that most of the staff was out at the launch facility. The long dining room was almost empty next morning, but he found Conchita there. A friendly fat Chihuahuan, she served him peppery *huevos rancheros* and told him how to find *la doctora*'s office.

Megan met him warmly but still a little warily. She had him wait at a big table in the conference room while she gathered four men for his interview. Her brief introductions left him bewildered. Martin Rablon, computer expert. Ivan Tomislav, Nobel winner who appeared to need one of his own medical miracles. Capt. Mack Wardian, former astronaut and airline pilot. Galen Ulver, a spry little elf who had tried to build fusion rockets. All cordial enough but also sharply watchful. To judge him.

For what?

And what were they to Megan? All four seemed totally at home with her, and she with them. Rablon had longer hair than Brink liked but was nearest her own age, tall and striking, eagerly attentive to her. Tomislav looked haunted, half ill and a good bit older but craggily handsome and clearly fond of her. Wardian and even old Ulver were brilliant minds in leanly competent bodies, still fit enough. If she wanted lovers, she had them.

Megan brought coffee, and they sat around the table to interrogate him. About his skill with weapons, his experience in military planning and command. He saw Tomislav's disapproving frown at some of the causes he had served and Megan's reservations.

"I fight for hire." He let his voice lift. "Or I did when I could fight. For leftists or rightists. For legal rulers or rebels against them. Never found one side much better than the other. Or much worse, for all the slants you see in the media. Men don't fight because they're evil or because they aren't. They fight because they're human."

Feeling reckless, he challenged Megan.

"So do women when you know them. Because we're all human. Doing what we're born for. Animals if you like, after mates and territory."

He turned to Tomislav.

"Or tools of our genes, I imagine you would say, as they manipulate us for survival."

Scowling, Tomislav grunted.

"I'm a weapon." He had begun to enjoy the confrontation. "No more guilty than a gun. Or innocent. Except that I do have rules of my own, which I'll make clear if I'm employed. One of them is loyalty. I've been a useful weapon to a lot of people over too many years because I've taught myself how to survive.

"And I don't sell out."

Megan thanked him gravely and asked him to wait outside. Almost at once, she called him back. All four men stood up to shake his hand again. Even Tomislav, looking flushed and unsteady.

"You'll do," she told him.

"For what?"

She let the men take turns with the story. They were preparing to sow mankind across the worlds of other stars. Not with vast spacecraft carrying colonists on flights that must take many generations but with manseed. Tomislav's word when his turn came.

"Tiny devices"—he was heavy and soft, short of breath—"scattered toward every promising star within the light-years, the few light-years we can hope for them to cross. Half machines but half alive. Carrying the human genes—"

His wind had run out, and Wardian spoke.

"Our genes and our culture. All coded into computer memories and loaded into synthetic seed, designed to find root and restore the race. To plant a new humanity, designed to be a little better than ourselves, on any world where the craft find friendly soil."

Brink shook his head, more than ever bewildered.

"That sounds insane." He frowned again at Megan. "Even if it isn't, what use have you for me?"

"Interstellar space won't be friendly." Wardian again, his clipped accent faintly British, his manner one of half-quizzical yet grave detachment. "Any worlds we reach may be hostile. The fragile seeds must be protected in flight and defended when they land until mankind is well established. We are engineering them to create Defenders—special beings designed to deal with emergency or danger. We want to record some of your special skills for those Defenders."

"Nonsense—"

"Please, Don," Megan begged. "Just listen."

She looked at Rablon.

"If you're listening, Mr. Brink." Rablon was too loud and too blunt, hard for him to like. "Essentially, we want you to help educate a computer. The master computer, which each seed will carry. It will be programmed to create Defenders when circumstances require them."

Squatting over the access door, he looked for the nearing star. It was gone, carried out of view by the tumbling of the ship, and he had to rise to find it. His vision turned telescopic when he did, to let him see the dimensionless dots of the four giant planets and the star's own hot white disk.

Already looming larger?

He couldn't be sure, yet now he could feel its relative motion. Their own motion, really, for they were still rushing toward it, still at the top velocity of the long flight out from Earth, hundreds of kilometers a second.

With drive power lost.

If he could restore it, if the ship could be controlled and slowed, perhaps they could yet be saved. Perhaps they still could find a friendly world ahead, smaller and warmer than those gas giants, a fertile field for the human seed.

If he failed, if he let them flash into the star's vast gravitational vortex with no control, they would surely hit something. Planet or comet or another grain of meteor dust, perhaps the star itself. No matter which, almost any impact would kill the ship forever. Even if by chance they struck nothing, they would emerge on a random course toward nowhere, doomed to endless flight through interstellar emptiness.

He stooped again at the access door to pull the damaged board and inspect its close rows of cubes. They seemed perfect, so he let his vision go microscopic to follow the fine-spun golden tracery of its printed circuits. He found the broken circuits then, cut by a hairline crack. With no replacement board, he begged for aid.

"Defender to Ship. Damage discovered. How can I repair it?"

Megan's features shimmered and shattered in his mind again, but the far-off voice he heard held a nasal midwestern echo of Martin Rablon.

"Weld the breaks."

"Weld them?" His dismay came back. "Without tools?"

"You are the tool." A hint of Tomislav's Slavic accent. "Adequate capacities are engineered into your genes."

"I don't remember—"

But suddenly he did. The golden nail of his forefinger flexed and stretched into a needle-narrow tip, and the dark fissure swelled again to his shifting vision. He bent closer to the board. Blazing blue, the microscopic arc stabbed and stabbed again, down across the line of breaks. Metal shone and flowed and cooled. He pushed the board home again.

"Megan—"

"Term Megan unidentified."

"Defender to Ship. Can you retest circuit board—"

"The assembler lab," Megan was telling him. "Where we collect and organize the input file for the master computers."

He followed her out of the hot sun-blaze into the green metal prefab where two black-bearded technicians stood waiting. He hated their hurried abruptness, hated the thin chemical stink of the lab and all the tedious rites of preparation.

Stripped, he lay on cold rubber pads, trying not to mind the icy sensors they stuck to his scalp and his face, even over his eyelids. Around his throat, the things were chokingly tight, set to test for words subvocalized. The glaring light went out when they slid his head into the scanner. He had to lie there, motion forbidden. The needle in his neck stung like a desert scorpion, and he felt strange and ill from its radioactive trickle into his brain.

"Relax if you can," Megan said through the headphones, urgently insistent but cool and far away. "We don't want your soul. Just your space know-how."

"Relax yourself, Wardian." A man's voice, nasal, demanding, maybe Rablon's. "All we do—all we can do—is pick up physical data for computer analysis. Nothing telepathic. Dr. Drake will begin questions to guide your responses while we try to record unconscious indices. A less than perfect method because strong emotion interferes. Sometimes we get more than we want, often less . . ."

Recalling that, he knew more of what he was. A patchwork creation of advanced computer science and engineered organics, his mind put together from recorded bits of Brink and Rablon, of Ulver and Tomislav and Wardian, perhaps of others, too. Scraps half lost in that imperfect pickup process, worn thinner since by unguessable ages in space, tattered again by the impact of the micrometeor.

But he was the Defender.

Born from a narrow womb in this emergency to serve and guard the ship. That was all he had been made for. The rest of him was accidental, stray shards of feeling and being picked up when the computers read too much. His human emotion, his bleak and bitter loneliness, the pain of his missing manhood—all irrelevant relics of lives forever lost, totally meaningless now.

Moving like a machine, he closed the access door. Careful with the trailing cord, he walked back to the useless rocket nozzles and stood staring blankly at them. Slowly, the galaxy wheeled around him, dark dust and dust of dazzling suns. He scarcely sensed them. A dull despair had paralyzed him.

What was left that he could do?

The scraps of Brink's battle sense, of Rablon's craft with computers and Tomislav's genetics, Ulver's rocket knowledge and Wardian's spacemanship—how could anything serve the mission of the ship?

Yet he couldn't stop. Brink and Rablon and the others had done their part. It was his turn now. He was the Defender, with a function to perform. A function that needed no emotion and would never let him stop. Raising his eyes to the star, he let his adapting vision show the four gas giants.

"Wardian?" He spoke in his mind. "We need your know-how now."

"Wardian data recalled from memory bank." An emotionless monotone, Wardian's only remotely. "What does the ship require?"

"We're approaching target star. We require control programs for deceleration and search for target planet."

"Reaction mass exhausted." Wardian's troubled features flickered and faded into giddy blankness. "Deceleration impossible. Search maneuvers impossible. Landing impossible."

"Wardian, listen." They were the Defender; their functions did not include defeat. "Suppose we could secure reaction mass, could we then control the ship?"

"Supposition contrary to sensed condition of ship—"

"Never mind the problems." He overrode the gray computer-voice. "Show us a deceleration program."

"Impossible—"

"We require it."

Eyes fixed on the star, he watched its tiny disk swell again. He found the four planets, steadily brighter, spreading apart as his vision adjusted. Saw a sudden bright-green line stabbing ahead of the ship into black space.

"Indicating computed minimum-energy approach maneuver." The soundless voice held neither hope nor fear. "Computed for maximal safe deceleration through gravitational and frictional effects of close planetary passes."

Darting ahead, that bright line bent around the nearest planet, whipped around the star, stabbed back at another planet, grazed the third and then the first again, paused and thrust, paused and thrust, passing always nearer, creeping slowly back at last toward the star.

"Maneuver impossible," the voice insisted, "without reaction mass."

"Then we must find reaction mass." Trying to call Megan's name, he saw her wispy image, a blankly staring mask. "What sort of matter do the engine's require?"

"Fluids." That momentary mask shivered into darkness, and the quick computer voice lost its last hint of her. "Volatile fluids, with essential trace content of deuterium."

"What other elements?"

"Light elements preferred, in noncorrosive compounds."

"Give me an inventory of all fluids aboard the ship."

An instant of stillness.

"Reaction mass: main tanks zero, auxiliary tanks zero. Gas propellants: nitrogen zero, helium zero. Reserve gases: hydrogen zero, oxygen zero. Hydrocarbons: zero. Comment: all available volatiles exhausted in maneuvers to escape meteor swarm."

"Have we no other fluids?"

"None available as reaction mass."

"We have others? Not rated available?"

"We have feedstocks."

"Why not available?"

"Our feedstocks are an essential reserve required for the establishment of mankind on our target planet. They must be kept intact for that purpose."

"They won't be essential if we never get there. Give me a feedstock inventory."

"Hydrocarbons: one point two metric tons. Acids: point one six metric tons. Bases: point one three metric tons. Heavy metal salts in solution: point zero six metric tons."

"Do they contain deuterium?"

"Computing trace amounts." A moment of delay. "Hydrocarbons contain trace amounts adequate to support fusion."

"Then we'll burn the hydrocarbons—"

"Impossible. Design of tanks and pumps and tubing allows no feedstock transfer into laser injection system."

"Then we'll change the pumps and tubing."

A flash of Megan's face, ashen with distress, and that dead computer-voice.

"Impossible—"

When he called the Ulver data out of memory, the computer gave him a plan of the ship's internal plumbing. There was no access door to the pumps and tubing from the feedstock tanks, and he had to slice into the hull to reach them. The hydrocarbons were frozen, exploding into vapor under his cutting arc, but there were circuits from the reactor to thaw tanks and pipes and pumps.

He cut the hydrocarbon tubes, spliced them to the laser injectors, reset the valves, and tried to close the hole in the hull. His arc had left the cut-out slab too small to fit squarely, but he patched it back with waste metal from the discarded tubing. The wrong sort of stuff to endure the searing planetary passes, but he thought the refractory nosecone would get the worst of that. Perhaps his patch would hold.

Or perhaps—

It was not his function to dwell upon what he could not

control. Winding the throbbing cord on his arm, he climbed the bright hull again, back to the narrow door from which he had been born. Inside again, he tapped the smooth bulge that closed it.

Relaxing in the dark, he felt the gentle thrust of the rockets. The Defender's function had been performed. The engines were alive again, bending the ship's flight path toward that nearest planet, steering them into the deceleration maneuver that might take them safely at least close to the star, into a region they might search for a world fit for planting man—

He was happy in his dream because tomorrow would be wonderful. His birthday. Dad had promised to take him to the game. He'd found Mom baking a snow-white coconut cake, the kind he loved best, and discovered the shiny new trike they had hidden in the hall closet.

He would be five.

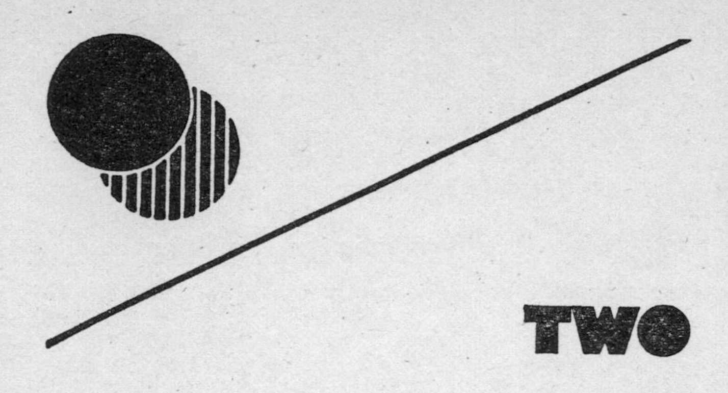

TWO

ATTACK COMMAND

The ship's computer broke into his happy dream of Megan Drake.

"Duty call, Defender!"

He hated the voice. Soundless, inhuman, yet edged with a mocking hint of hers.

"Ship in orbit around target planet. Your service now required."

He shut himself against the call, groping to recover his joy in the dream. They had been racing down the highest slope at Angel Fire. She had passed him, red scarf flying, her lean face aglow with cold and her skis singing on the snow, close enough to touch. The wind swept her laugh away, but he had seen the teasing glint in her greenish eyes before she bent to vanish in the swirl of flakes ahead.

Crouching lower, heart thudding, he raced to overtake her. She meant him to—he still felt drunk with the wonder of that, still astonished that she could be so different here, away from the Albuquerque lab and all the driving demands of the project.

Megan—weekending with him!

He strove to hold the dream, but it had shattered on hard recollection. Megan Drake was dead. A million years ago. Lost forever, with the human Earth and all he had ever known, somewhere in the bleak light-years and the measureless millennia behind.

"Attention, Defender." The computer's quick and brittle voice stabbed him again. "You will now survey target planet to determine whether landing is forbidden."

He couldn't reply. The dream still possessed him, the human Megan still alive in his mind. He wanted her again. The proud spirit and the sleeping passion beneath her cool reserve and all the wonder of her that he had only begun to discover. The magic sweetness of her hair and the taste of her mouth. Her joyous devotion to him—but that had been only in the dream. The ache of waking was still too sharp for him to bear.

In the dream, he had forgotten what he was.

Nothing human, but only a gadget. Half machine and half alive, a creation of computer science and genetic engineering, his mind—rather, his own controlling program —patched from bits of skill and know-how the Defender had been expected to require, his human recollections a haphazard mix picked up by lab accident.

Floating weightless in the dark birthcell, he explored himself again. The cold and hairless flesh, pliantly metallic. The throbbing umbilical, only slightly warmer, coiling out of darkness to his belly. Shivering, yet nerved with sudden hope, he reached to feel his crotch.

All he found was stiffly yielding metal, slick and cold and hairless. Nothing had grown while he slept. Still he had no reason to dream of any woman—

"Defender, alert!" The computer again, icily unfeeling. "Free oxygen detected on target planet. Interpreted as evidence of life. Our Master Control Program forbids planting on advanced planets. If we find native culture evolved to our own level or above, mission must be aborted. You will survey target planet for indications of advanced intelligence."

"Defender to Ship." Automatic words, spoken by the machine he was. "I will comply."

Fingers a-tingle as feeling returned, he searched the slick metallic wall of his narrow birthpod, found the seam where it closed. Squirming in the dark to reach the bulging opener, he hammered with his fist. Floating, waiting, he groped again for the source of that lost dream.

For it felt too real to be a dream, and he thought it might lead him to more of himself. A mongrel half thing, he yearned to be whole, hungered for humanity, longed to recover that lost instant of total happiness.

All his human fragments came from troubled men, trapped on a troubled planet, all in love with Megan—or at least itching for her. The project itself had been her only promise he remembered. A share in her eager hope for a new human start, a better human chance, on whatever worlds the seed might reach.

He wanted more. He wanted Megan.

Had any of them won her? Waiting for his dark cell to open, shrinking from the Defender's hard and bitter lot, he tried to follow the clue of the dream. Sifting again through those fragmentary bits of mind and feeling, he groped for any island of joy, any moment of untroubled love, any real recollection of skiing with Megan at Angel Fire.

He found another talk with her.

The day in the lab had been too long. Used to action, he had been forced to lie too still in the scanner, too cold and sick from the radioactives filtering into his brain, battered too hard by too many demands for all he knew of combat.

"It's all we offered." A glint of malice in her tone. "A way for you to fight again."

He hated the way, now that he knew what it was. Though, in fact, his bad knee didn't matter here. All the job took was lying passive while they pounded him with questions to get unconscious reactions Rablon's computers could record.

Too many questions, most of them painful.

What conflicts had he seen? How had he planned for them? How had he trained? What forces had he commanded? Who had commanded him? What weapons did he know? Where had he used them? What engagements had been decisive? How had they been won? How defeated? How much had he been paid? How little? With whose funds? What laws had he broken? With what consequences? Had he ever looted? Killed civilians? Worked with terrorists? With the CIA? With any other such agency?

He had never liked looking back. There had been more blunders than victories, more pain than elation. Perhaps there were secret selves inside him that he didn't want to meet. The moment had always been enough, and the lure of tomorrow—so long as he was fit to face it.

Why did men kill? Why had he enjoyed it?

Megan's questions, most of them, asked with increasing shock and revulsion. She wanted to despise him. Yet, in spite of all her idealism, she had been fascinated by his dedication to that oldest and most absorbing human game, played for life or death. And she had fascinated him, not through anything intentional but with the fierce emotion he could sense beneath her crisp control. Limping back from the shower after that hard session, he found her waiting for him in the lab.

"Buy you a drink?" He grinned wryly at her. "Something smoother than your radio cocktails."

"My turn." Her quick smile erased the ache in his knee. "With dinner. After all, it's Friday night."

She drove him to the Aztecan Temple, a shabby-looking little place off Central where the Mexican food was hot and the margaritas smooth enough. They talked. She asked for more about the elephant poachers he had fought in Africa and the *Izquierdista* rebellion. He relished her unwilling admiration. Nerved with the drinks and her clean loveliness, he begged her to come with him back to Mexico.

"I'll rent a plane—the knee's well enough for that—and fly you down to Baja." He saw her start, eyes almost frightened. "Most of the crew will take the weekend off," he urged her. "We'll be back Monday morning."

"Don—"

Her breath had caught. For a long moment, she looked at him across her salted glass, a flush of tangled feelings on her face. For a moment, she was about to yield, but then he saw her ripe lips tighten, perhaps with pity for him.

"Not that I've a lot left for anybody," he muttered. "And no harm intended. But—if I could love—I love you, Megan."

"I'm sorry, Don." Her fine head shook sharply, and she leaned across the table, eyes very grave. "Terribly sorry. Because I—I like you, Don."

"You forgive the killing?"

"Maybe—" She flinched as if to a stab of pain. "Maybe that's why I like you. But—" Her eyes fell for an instant, then rose to meet his. "I'm a virgin, Don. Egan and my uncle used to say I ought to see a shrink, but I never did. Seldom ever thought about it since the seedship project started. I've wondered if it somehow takes the place of sex.

"When it's finished—" She drew a long breath, and her hand reached for his. "Maybe—"

* * *

The long slit was widening. He saw the glint of stars outside, swept past by the ship's slow spin, but still she haunted him. Still he longed to know who—which part of him—could have been with her at Angel Fire. Not Don Brink. Even if she kept that uncertain promise in time for the event to get into the ship's computer, Brink couldn't have been the skier. Not with the mortar splinter in his knee.

Who else? Shadowy jealousies woke to spur him. If Megan had really been a virgin, all five men wanting her, who had been lucky? Watching the creeping stars, he sifted again through those scrambled scraps of memory. Few were clearly linked to any name, none of the rest quite so vivid as Brink's.

Martin Rablon? The computer engineer, maybe hoping for Megan to replace his wife—though the glimpses of his faithless Jayna revealed little likeness. No idealist, born poor but bright, she had been plain Jane Brown when he met her. His student in beginning computer science, failing till she began to pay for her grades with what she did best. Torn between his science and his business interests and her witchery, Rablon had no time for sports; he had probably never learned to ski.

Ivan Tomislav, the genetics engineer?

Searching through random scraps of Tomislav, he found skis and poles and boots, but they lay gathering dust in a bedroom closet at the La Jolla bungalow. Tomislav was aging, overweight, and on a diet. The gear had belonged to his dead son—

A burst of painful memory. Roger dead and Olga dying. Poor dear Olga, once fatter than he, skeletal and bedfast now, begging for the shots he couldn't deny, doomed by the same rare gene-linked malignancy that had driven Roger to suicide when it was diagnosed in him. Olga dying because his genetic science had been too slow with the synthetic virus that might have repaired those fatal genes.

For an instant, he was Tomislav, puffing off the plane at Albuquerque, a little troubled by the altitude and more by Olga's illness. Megan's voice calling his name and his wistful admiration when he saw her. As straight and strong as Olga had been when they met at Union. If he had only found the right research track ten years before—

But genetic clocks didn't turn back, and the happy skier at Angel Fire had not been Tomislav.

Wardian, the airline pilot and exastronaut? More likely. Young enough, well tanned and muscular, as tall as NASA allowed, he had an easy way with women. Angel Fire? He had known it most of his life. There with his dad when he was a kid. Later with Debbie, teaching her to ski while she gave him more exciting lessons—

They were sitting in the lounge at the lab, drinking canned Coors while they waited for Ivan and his crew to run down a bug in the scanner.

"Megan?" Wardian gave Brink a startled grin. "Not for me. Though she is a stunner. Could be, anyhow, if she ever lets anybody turn her on."

"I can't help dreaming . . ." He shook his head and eased the aching knee.

"Your lay." Wardian lifted his beer with a half-ironic flourish. "If she ever lets you make her, which I don't expect. As for me, I like to look, but I've got two rules for women. Never let 'em marry you. And never touch a virgin."

If Wardian had kept that second rule, if Galen Ulver had been too old and frail for Angel Fire—

The slit had widened, and the ship's slow tumble let a sun-blade slash across him. No clue found, he gave up the search for that lost instant of seemingly perfect love. Perhaps it had really been a dream. He would probably never know.

Not that it could matter now, because all those unlucky men were long gone to dust, their world forever lost. Shivering a little in the cold birthcell, he tried to brush their haunting ghosts away. He was all of them, none of them, more than any of them. Their wispy relics were random defects in the Defender of the ship, hazards to his duty now.

The opening door looked wide enough at last. Coiling the warm umbilical on his arm to keep it free, he squeezed his way outside.

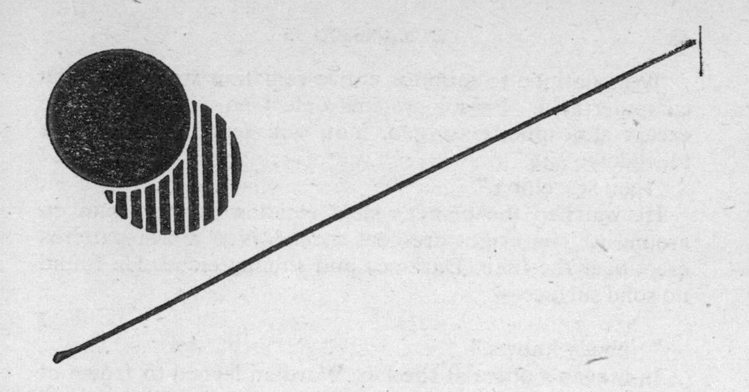

Black space and blazing metal.

He was blind for an instant, until his eyes adjusted to the savage sun. Magnetic feet clinging to the metal, he stood up to orient himself. The ship was still beneath him, alive again, still slowly tumbling, its gold-filmed skin crudely patched where he had tapped into the hydrocarbon feed-stocks, his slender yellow life-cord still trailing back through the slit behind him.

Searching, he found the planet.

Elation lifted him. Here at last, their long-lost goal! The new world where the seed of man might put out fresh roots and thrive again—if they got it safely planted.

Close below and more than half in shadow, the planet was a magnificent crescent, huge even before his eyes went telescopic. Dazzling clouds wound the equator in a snaky line that would be the zone of tropical convergence. Blue-black ocean reached north and south from that to meet white-swirling storms.

He saw no land.

"Ship to Defender." The master computer. "Requesting data as you observe it."

"Observation in progress." Trying to forget Megan's haunting overtones in the quick synthetic voice, he heard his own soundless reply, itself no more human. "Patterns of cloud reveal systems of air circulation which resemble Earth's, indicating strong Coriolis effect due to planet's rotation. Climatic environment should favor human survival if we can land."

"We continue to monitor entire radiation spectrum," the computer said. "Sensor systems detect no evidence of life except atmospheric oxygen. You will search for possible touchdown site."

"I am searching."

He watched the planet's slow rotation as they spun on around it. The bright crescent spread. New storm patterns crept over the limb. Dark sea and shining cloud. He found no solid surface—

"Nobody knows."

In Megan's office at the lab, Wardian leaned to frown at the big device he called a stellarium. Just installed, it still had a hot-plastic scent. The stars were tiny lights on thin rods radiating from the brighter central light that stood for the sun. A lucite sheet through the sun marked what he called the galactic plane. Two half hoops swung around it to show galactic longitude and latitude, and the monitor on Megan's desk displayed data on any star beneath their point of intersection.

Never data enough.

"Of course, we hope for planets."

Wardian shrugged. Just in from hang gliding off the Manzano slopes, he looked lean and dashingly intrepid in a trimly tailored yellow jumpsuit, a little too certain of what he could do, a little too ironic about everything else.

What did Megan think of him?

"Theory says planets should exist." Wardian spoke only half to him, fine eyes still fixed on her. "Planets enough like Earth to give the seed a chance, perhaps around every normal star. We do have uncertain evidence of a few gas giants, but our instruments aren't good enough to show the worlds we're looking for."

"We're shooting at planets we can't even see?" Brink shook his head at Megan. "What sort of chance—"

"Please, Don." Chiding him, Megan seemed almost hurt. "We've got good things going for us."

Pity for her stabbed through his half-unwilling worship. Standing tall beside that glittering gadget, she was framed against the window, her lean vitality in bright contrast to the desert vista beyond. Bold enough to challenge mankind's mortality. Lovely enough for anything, if she ever cared to be. But far too idealistic. Squandering herself on the project, her life a needless sacrifice to a goal most of the world would laugh at.

"The odds are terrible." She nodded soberly. "Against any single seed. But we're going to scatter them by the hundreds—thousands if we can—across a whole field of stars."

"If the authorities ever let Galen test his fusion drive." Wardian grinned wryly at her optimism. "If he can make it work when they do and build the units cheap enough. If we have time to launch the ships before our own world blows up."

"Problems." She shrugged. "We'll get them solved." Her greenish eyes came back to him, turning graver. "You're another problem, Don."

"You want me to fight for planets if we find them—"

"The problem is that you might do that a little too well." Wardian looked quizzical. "You've alarmed Dr. Tomislav. He's afraid your skills and your genes would turn the children of the ships into interstellar vandals, ravaging the galaxy. Which isn't what we want."

He looked at Megan.

"We need you, Don," she assured him. "Some of you, anyhow. The question is how much. I know how you love your old game of war, but modern weapons have made it suicidal. The new races have to be designed not to kill each other."

"If you make them pacificists," he said, "they won't last long."

"A thorny question." A needle of fear stabbed through him, fear that he wouldn't be wanted. "We're still looking for the answer."

She found him in the lounge at the lab, one morning not much later. Frowning at the program board, he was looking for his name. Again it wasn't there. Depressed about it, he turned to meet her.

"Through with me?"

"No, Don." He saw she wasn't sure. "I hope not."

"I've been waiting three days now."

Waiting for another session in the scanner. He felt baffled and bored. Still too lame for much activity, he had tried to read the tattered magazines on the rack, dry technical journals on computers and astronautics and genetics. Tried to read a paperback novel, a war story written by a romantic fool who had never been in combat. Tried to plan what to do next if Megan let him go.

"Let's talk to Ben," she was saying. "We took the problem to him."

"Ben?"

"Ben Bannerjee." He heard a special softness in her voice. "You haven't met him because he's too frail for the scanner. But he's the brain of Raven Foundation."

He followed her out of the lounge.

"Ben knows you," she said. "From editing your scanner pickups. Converted into audio, which he has learned to read. He says he wants to see you because you've done so much that he could only dream about. You'll admire him, Don, if you'll give yourself a chance."

He heard the admiration in her own voice.

"It's Benjamin Franklin Bannerjee." They were crossing the parking lot toward a building where Omega had fabricated weapon components. "A name he picked for himself because he never knew his parents. Born deformed, somewhere in India. He doesn't know the place or even his age. Maybe five or six years old when my uncle found him on a Calcutta street. In the hands of a one-eyed Fagin type who had him squatting there in rags and filth, playing chess against anybody.

"Winning every game.

"My uncle had never married. Or cared much for children, not even Egan and me. But he was taken with Ben from that first glimpse. Bought him from the thug who claimed him. Got him back to New York for medical care—nearly too late.

"He'll be a shock to you, Don."

She stopped on the walk outside the building.

"That's why I'm warning you. He does turn people off. His brains, I guess, as much as his looks. But I've known him since I was seven. And loved him as much as Uncle Luther did. So did Egan. Toward the end, I think he was Egan's only friend.

"Uncle Luther always trusted him. For business advice and finally about the seedship. Egan's idea, but Uncle Luther never listened to Egan. Ben saw how to make it real. Without him, we wouldn't be here."

He followed her inside. A white-starched nurse made

them put on surgical masks and wash their hands at a surgical sink before she let them into a windowless room in which the overheated air had a thin, antiseptic bite. He heard a queer screechy quavering and tried not to recoil when he saw Ben.

A child-sized thing in an odd-looking wheelchair.

A withered head, hairless, brown, and scarred. Its face narrow and dark and shapeless, a mask of long suffering, twitching strangely. The body too small for the head, grotesquely crumpled.

The nurse spoke, and the quavering changed. The powered chair spun toward him. He saw a single fleshless arm, the only useful limb. Dark, pain-haunted eyes peered up at him. Uneasy before them, he looked back at Megan.

"Ben—" Her easy warmth seemed strange in the lab-like room. "Here's Don."

"Hi, Mr. Brink." That gnarled mask had tried to smile, and Ben's single spidery claw scuttled across a computer keypad. Croaking from a speaker on the stark white wall, the words set a shiver in him. "Thanks for coming in. Miss Zorrilla will find you a seat."

The nurse brought a seat, and he sat uneasily before those disconcerting eyes, expecting to be grilled again about his life and his hopes and his ethics. Megan came to stand behind the wheelchair, one hand on Ben's shrunken shoulder, a tender smile behind her own white mask.

"Mr. Brink, I believe you play chess."

"Not often."

"Neither do I." The dreadful face seemed to grin. "Too many urgencies interfere. Have you time for a game?"

"Time's all I have."

Miss Zorrilla brought a board. Ben announced a two-minute limit, but that agile claw needed only seconds for a move. Though Brink tried to play a cautious game, in twenty moves he was beaten.

"Good game, Don." Those queerly brilliant eyes stabbed at him again. "I was asked for advice about you. I think we do need you in the Defender."

"Thanks—" The word came out with more emotion than he wanted. "Thanks!"

"I'm glad," Megan whispered.

"I've talked to Marty and Ivan."

Ben looked up at her, yellow fingers poised, that tragic mask transformed with love.

"They agreed?"

"We worked out a compromise." The fingers were flashing again. "The ships may need defense. The new colonies may till they can care for themselves. But we aren't launching conquistadores."

The haunted eyes came from Megan back to him.

"Marty's writing a new control program for the computers. A triple test, to protect any inhabited worlds the ships may reach. The first is technological, to turn them away from any planet that shows evidence of electronic communication or nuclear energy or space navigation. The second is economic and political, to protect any global social system. The third is cultural. It goes somewhat farther, intended to prevent the murder of any intelligent race or evolving culture. The program will kill the seed, even after landing, if any creatures simply say they don't want us there."

"You mean we can't fight—anything?"

"Our decision." Ben's skeletal head nodded unsteadily. "If you are challenged by anything intelligent, you will yield without resisting."

"Can't you—" That took his breath. "Can't you reconsider?"

"We did reconsider." The wheelchair was rolling away, and again the overhot room was filled with the audio chirps and squeaks and drones of the scanner recording. That electronic voice rang through it, inhumanly remote. "We've made the rules, Mr. Brink. The game's yours to play. We expect you to play it well—"

"But—"

"Thanks, Mr. Brink. Thanks for coming in."

The nurse waved them toward the door.

"Better than nothing, I guess." Unhappily, he followed Megan out. "But still a deadly handicap. If you build a suicide drive into the ships, what sort of chance is left?"

"Chance enough." She paused to take off the mask, looking back toward Ben with what he thought was wistful sadness. "We aren't setting out to conquer the stars. Just to keep mankind alive. If just a single seed finds a place where it can grow, that's all we need—and maybe more than we've earned, if you look at human history."

"I can't guess what enemies we'll meet—"

"But I've begun to know you, Don." She gave him an odd half smile. "I think you can cope with any handicap—"

Land!

A broken coast beneath the belted clouds, creeping over the world's bright curve. Brighter than the sea and softly tinged with green—which must mean chlorophyl or something very like it. Trembling, he watched its slow roll toward him.

A bright line shone along the horizon. He watched it climb, widen, become an enormous mountain mass that towered out of the clouds. A dead volcano, dominating the continent—in some remote tectonic past, it must have built the continent. His eyes went telescopic to study the icy dazzle of its vast caldera and the glaciers on its snowy slopes.

"Defender," the computer was demanding, "what do you observe?"

"All we could ask for. A land mass that reaches from the tropics nearly to the northward pole. Somewhere on it, we should find everything we need. If the program allows us to land—"

"Ship to Defender. We report all monitors recording. No negative input received. You will continue scanning for possible touchdown points."

Walking around the tumbling hull to follow the planet, he found the umbilical coiling to snare his knees. He pivoted back to free it. Shuffling again to watch the rolling world below, he found a second continent.

Not quite so large, it stretched from the equatorial clouds far toward the other pole. Not quite so high, it carried no visible ice. Drier, a vast waste of red-brown desert below the belt of storms. Older, perhaps, built by an earlier tectonic spasm and now worn low.

Scattered between the two continents, he found new patches of broken cloud. Formed, he thought, where trade winds were lifted by island chains—who had been the donor, he wondered, of his meteorology? Wardian, maybe. Pilots had to know weather—

"Defender, we request data for possible landing."

"The northern continent looked more likely. It should have a wider climatic range. Perhaps richer resources. But we'll need a long study of it before we can select any touchdown—"

"Defender!"

Still emotionless, the computer voice had changed. It spoke faster, with stronger hints of Megan. He caught another fleeting image of her face, turned rigid now and wan, eyes fixed and empty.

"Monitors detect radiation. We are under scan by wide-spectrum beams."

"Where?"

He turned from the planet to search the space around them. The hot sun-disk, a little smaller and a little bluer, he thought, than the lost sun of Earth. Two of the sun's huge gas planets, darting into view as his vision adapted. Nothing else. Not even a moon.

"Source not identified—"

The computer voice caught, came suddenly faster.

"Source located! Alien spacecraft following on our own orbit, close behind and closing."

Still he saw nothing.

"Can we signal?"

"We are transmitting initial contact code on every frequency available. Our signals are ignored."

"If we're attacked, can we fight?"

"Negative. We are unarmed. Control program forbids armed combat with anybody."

"Then we'd better dodge—"

"Defender, attention! We detect missile approaching."

"Take evasive action—"

"Evasion impossible. Our rockets lack adequate acceleration—"

Something hit him.

Struck his chest and knocked him off the hull. Whirling into space, fumbling for anything, he found it anchored to his flesh. A heavy metal disk that felt slightly warm. He clawed to tear it off, but still it clung fast. The ship spun away from him, a bright golden toy, still linked by his trailing umbilical.

The alien craft went by. A flash of bright metal and blue jets blazing. Something dragged him after it. A cable, perhaps, to the disk on his chest? Groping, he found no cable. Spinning, helpless, he felt the umbilical tighten.

"Ship!" He tried to call. "Defender to Ship—"

Agony dazed him, and his voice was dead. The hot sun dimmed. He lost the alien craft. Feebly, he slapped at his belly. The umbilical was gone, torn away, his life itself cut off.

"Ship!" He tried again. "Calling Ship—"

Megan's white ghost-face flickered in his mind, fixed and stricken. Spinning into space, he got one glimpse of the tiny golden seedcraft. Dull now, as his vision went out. Already tiny with distance and gone in an instant.

"Ship to Defender." The voice was almost Megan's, burdened with a bleak despair no computer could express, swiftly fading. "We report end of mission. In response to display of advanced technology, our master control program has canceled all landing plans."

"We can't give up—"

"Ship to Defender." A soundless murmur, dying. "We must obey. You will not attempt to damage alien craft or its masters—"

"But—somehow—can't we—"

His own voice had failed. Pain throbbed under the clutching hand on his belly, slowly easing. Dully searching, he failed to find the alien machine. The sun went out, and he slid into darkness.

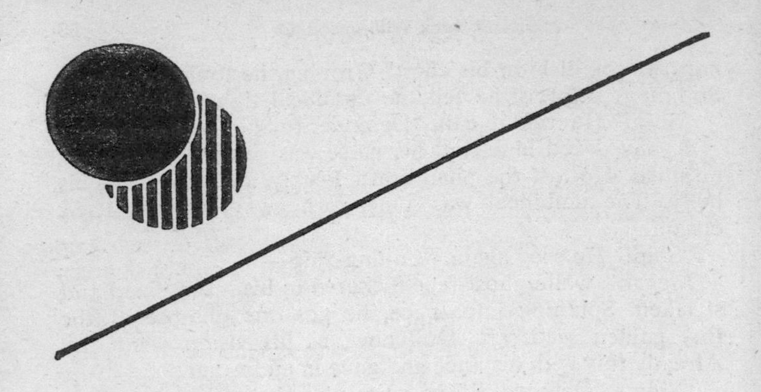

Sunlight revived him.

Still groggy from shock and the pain in his belly, he fought for awareness and found the thing against the stars ahead. A space toy at first, flying farther ahead as the missile hauled him toward it. In a moment, his perceptions shifted, to let it loom awesome and enormous.

Spacecraft or station, it made the seedship an inconsequential gnat. Never meant for atmospheric flight, its fantastic masses were not streamlined anywhere. Half black shadow, they burned where the sun struck, darkly rust-red.

Groping dimly to know what it was, he saw a wide strip of brighter metal, a long hollow down the middle of it. Brighter, perhaps, because its walls had been a shield against radiation damage. Inky shadow filled two others that lay parallel. All were trimly tapered, as if to fit streamlined machines.

One of them his attacker? Probably not; in his fleeting glimpse of that, it had seemed far smaller. No matter. The thing's very presense in orbit was enough to forbid the planet to them. With no fuel left to lift them toward another target, everything was over.

Ben Bannerjee's decision, and he knew he must accept it. After all, most of the seedcraft had been expected to die. A single cog in one machine, he shouldn't be upset about it. He had been engineered to obey the Master Program, not to feel emotion.

But—

In spite of himself, in spite of the program and his own gray despair, he found both golden hands grasping and wrenching at the missile on his chest. A thick metal disk, it was still stuck fast, still dragging him toward that monstrous starcraft.

Numb and clumsy, his fingers slipped off the clinging thing. He tried again, weaker still, and found awareness washing out. A little energy, he thought, had somehow come from the sunlight, but too little to replace the umbilical. His feeble struggle had drained too much.

Cursing silently, in a bitter fit of unengineered and useless human rage, he felt darkness strike. A dazing blow. Dimly, he knew he must have been hauled into the shadow of that great space-thing, but all he knew was the pain from his belly—

He ran to hide in the closet. They wouldn't find him there because Sharon would want to look outside, in the shed or maybe behind the hedge. If anybody found him, he hoped it would be Penny. She had a nice smell, and she would scream and be glad. He liked Penny.

It was dark in the closet when he pulled the door shut. Something silky hung against his face. It had a smell he didn't like: mothballs and old perfume. His heart was thumping hard. He leaned against the door, listening.

Nothing. He waited. The house stayed very quiet, and he knew they were looking outside. The silky thing tickled his face. When he tried to push it away, it fell down over his head. The old perfume was too strong in it, and he couldn't breathe.

Gasping, he fought it off.

He heard them coming, their feet light and quick in the hall, which had no carpet. The door rattled. He heard Penny whisper, but she didn't open the door and scream. Something clicked, and they went away.

He waited, but they never came back. He hated the dark. The silky thing came down in his face again. The closet was too hot, and he couldn't stand the mothball smell. It was time to come out. He pushed at the door.

It wouldn't open. He knew then that Penny had locked it, and he didn't like her anymore. He pounded on it with both fists and yelled for Sharon to let him out, but nobody came. It wasn't fair. They were cruel, but he couldn't fight them. Not even after he got out. Because they were girls.

His tummy felt bad, and still the door wouldn't open. He yelled till he couldn't breathe, but nobody came. Nobody was fair. He lay on the floor. It rocked under him, and the dust made him sneeze—

He woke in the dark, still on the floor. Something heavy had fallen on his chest, and he felt too weak to throw it off. Still he couldn't breathe, and the silent dark was suffocating. He tried to yell again.

He couldn't yell because he had no voice. He couldn't see any walls, but he knew the place was bigger than the closet. A lot bigger. He wasn't breathing, but now he didn't need to breathe.

He was the Defender.

He remembered the seedship and Bannerjee's idiotic command and that strange space machine. Dimly, he wondered if he had been hauled somewhere inside it, but his belly still ached, and his brain wouldn't work. Without the umbilical or even the feeble energy he had somehow drawn from sunlight, he was powerless, dying.

And something—something was coming.

It crept at him silently out of the dark. At first, only a dark shadow-mass, but then he began to make out its shape. Something not much larger than he was, crawling on its belly. It moved like a cockroach, crawling and stopping, darting and stopping to watch him again.

It had no legs. No eyes that he could see. No jaws or insect antennae or anything else that he knew. It was low and wide and flat, with no projections anywhere, though it carried something on its back. Something disk shaped, flat as it was.

The disk was shining. Dim at first, it grew abruptly brighter. The increasing light let him see the place where he was. The floor was circular and huge, a good hundred meters across. The ceiling was nearly too high to see, but he found a bundle of thick cylinders like the trunks of close-spaced trees climbing toward it from the center of the floor. Everything was metal, dark as if with time, and he knew he must be inside that immense space machine.

The moving thing was metal, too, but gold colored, like the gold-filmed seedship and his own body. Darting and stopping, darting and stopping, it approached from the direction of the clustered tubes. His head hurt when he tried to understand it, but he knew it meant nothing good for him.

He wanted to fight the thing, but when he began groping for any weapon or possible strategy, he saw a wispy ghost of Megan's stricken face and heard a faint and soundless whisper. Radio, from the seedship? Or the voice of his own internal computer? Wondering, he knew no way to tell.

"Master Program to Defender. Mission is canceled. Data input reveals positive evidence of high technology on target planet. Control commands therefore forbid attempt to seed it. Repeat. Master Program to Defender. Mission is canceled. Beings of target planet are not to be attacked, on the surface or in space."

Despair crushed him, cruel as the weight on his chest. The rule was foolish. Even his name was if the program didn't allow him to defend the ship. Evolution had ordained the only real law, that every living thing must fight for the survival of itself and its kind. But he was not alive, not really, and Bannerjee's crazy edict was built into him. It had to be obeyed.

Yet he didn't want to die. Perhaps the rule had limits. He wasn't forbidden to escape from danger—if he could. Spurred by a surge of human desperation, he fought again at the thing on his chest. Again he found too little strength to remove it.

The flat yellow bug-shape had darted close. It stopped again as if to watch him. The thing it carried tipped on edge and swung one round face toward him, beaming brighter. Gratefully, he drank the radiation in. More than merely light, it warmed him, woke him wider, made him stronger.

Again he tugged and thrust. Still the disk held him flat, but not with gravity. His head and his struggling limbs had no weight. They were still in orbit, and the force was something strange to him—not magnetic, certainly, because he had a sense for magnetism.

He felt the disk-thing scanning him. A whole spectrum of probing radiation. Infrared, furnace-hot. Ultraviolet. Radar. Even gamma rays. Never meant to help him but still what he was starving for. Alive again with that new energy, he braced himself to cope.

What could the bug want from him?

If it was a defender of the planet, stationed here in orbit to challenge space invaders, it must have taken the seedship for an enemy. It had no way to know they hadn't come for conquest. If he could somehow explain the ship, perhaps it could yet be saved.

Those two great continents had looked empty enough, even to his telescopic vision. No visible cities, no patterns of roadways or farmland, no industrial smog, no hint of high technology. Somewhere, if only on an island, there might be room for the human seed to grow.

After all, his captors had clearly wanted him alive. If he could begin some intellectual contact, they might be persuaded to tolerate a small colony. The best of Earth's life and mind had come stored in the ship's computers. In due time, if the seed found root, such treasures might be bartered for added living space. Even, perhaps, for new science and culture.

He twisted himself to wave one hand, wondering if the bug would understand any gesture. As if in answer, the disk tipped farther toward him, its radiation changing to a quick-shifting pulse. He felt it throbbing out the seedship's own contact initiation signal, replayed precisely as the ship had sent it.

Intelligence! Quivering with elation, he listened to the soundless signal. A beep and a pause. Four beeps and a pause. Nine, sixteen, twenty-five, until his count of squares was 256. Then an empty box, sixteen pixels to the side. Simple patterns flashed inside it: triangle, square, trapezoid, a ragged circle. A bigger box, flickering with new detail. The signal came faster, faster, till he could make the pictures move.

The star, a brighter dot against the strange constellations he had seen. Its whole planetary system swelling away. The four gas giants with all their moons in orbit. This inner planet, moonless, tiny at first but growing to fill the frame. The ship's outline. His own picture, complete with the linking umbilical.

Perhaps—

Tomislav lay naked again with his head in the scanner, enduring the cold sensors on his eyes and his throat, feeling faint from the stuff in his brain and trying not to shiver. Shivering caused noise in the pickups, but so did sweat; Rablon said they had to keep him cold.

Waiting for Megan's voice in the headphones, he couldn't help a pang of guilt about his lust for her or escape a secret shame being so jealous about the way she smiled at Wardian and Rablon and even poor old Brink. He had been celibate too long.

While Olga died.

Back in La Jolla, yearning for him, grieving for all they had lost. Creaking feebly every morning when he called in that dreadful mockery of the singing voice he had loved so long, bravely saying she could wait for him to finish if he was really shaping seed to spread mankind across the stars. He knew how much she needed him.

He had promised to be there when she died. But he had promised his mind to Megan, promised all that Bannerjee required. He hated the chill and the stink and the sting of the needle and lying still so long, but the project did mean more than any single human being. If just one new world could be seeded with a better human breed—

The headphones began to click and squeak and howl, but not with any human voice. Images flickered in his head. Nothing he knew, they were stranger than Chinese ideograms or the structure of an unknown gene. Flashing, fading, they ran faster, faster, until he began to see pictures mingled with them. Symbols from math and chemistry, genetic structures that he knew, scrambled words. English. Greek and Latin roots, scientific German. The squeaks and howls became a clanging jangle, at last a voice.

"Attack Command to Unidentified." Loud and slow, cold as sledges on an anvil. "Transmit recognition code."

He knew no recognition code.

"Attack Command to Unidentified. State your place of origin."

His place of birth was Schenectady, while his father was still there with the GE labs, but that failed to satisfy the voice.

"Attack Command to Unidentified. Describe creation by Master Builders."

The Ibsen play, when Olga was in Little Theater.

"Attack Command to Unidentified. Establish submission to Total Control."

His parents had got out of Europe barely ahead of the Nazis. He knew no other Total Control.

"Attack Command to Unidentified. Establish purpose of flight to—"

The voice became a rattle of clicks, and he saw a bright star creeping across a pattern of constellations he had never seen.

"Attack command to Unidentified. Establish reasons for your arrival here."

He was here in the lab because Olga had let him stay, because he believed in the project and trusted Bannerjee and loved Megan next to Olga, but that wasn't what the voice demanded.

"Attack Command to Unidentified. Establish reasons for your own survival."

He had work to do. The seedships to launch. Olga to care for, so long as she needed him. The Biowand researches to complete. His benign viruses to perfect, to save others from Olga's hell.

"Attack Command to Unidentified—"

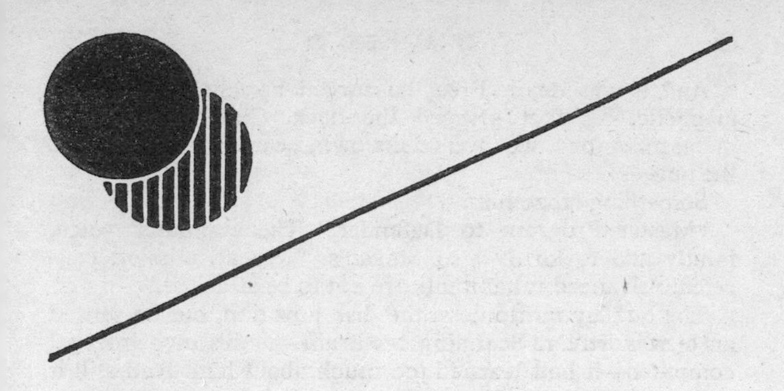

The bug meant to kill him.

The probing had stopped. That ruthless intrusion had left him battered and drained, but now his head was clear again, his brief elation gone. For the encounter had been no meeting of civilized minds, but rather a trial for his life on charges never stated.

Still he wasn't sure what the creature was or what it wanted, but he hadn't pleased it. He hadn't known the recognition code. He had failed to identify himself as a creation of the Master Builders, whatever they were. Attack Command had not invited him, and it didn't want him here.

Backing abruptly toward the clustered columns from which it must have come, the bug stopped again. The disk tipped to focus all its radiation on him. Savagely, it blazed.

A lethal blast if he had been anything alive.

But he was only half alive. Built of synthetic molecules designed to endure all the hazards of open space for a million or a hundred million years, his body was more than half metallic, and energy was his food.

Feasting on that concentrated power, he twitched and shrank, flailed his arms and let them float, hoping to seem to be dying. Relaxing, eyes staring blankly, he felt the bug coming nearer, felt a final radiation burst.

When that ceased, he snatched at the heavy metal oval that held him down. It clung fast. With both hands, he twisted, thrust, strained again. He felt vibration, felt the object heat and crack, saw smoke exploding.

And it was dead. Free, he surged upright. Once more magnetic, his feet gripped the deck. Clutching the hot metal mass for a weapon of his own, he swung to hurl it at the bug.

Something froze him.

"Master Program to Defender." The computer voice, faintly and forlornly also Megan's. "Repeat, mission canceled. Advanced inhabitants are not to be attacked."

The bug lay motionless, the disk now dim, but he sensed an alert hostility. Scanning his brain—or his own internal computer—it had learned too much about him. And still it meant to kill him. Knowing now that he was immune to radiation, it would look for something deadlier.

Trembling, he swung his missile higher. Why should he obey that insane injunction not to fight? With the ship and the mission in danger, he was the Defender. Trapped here, the umbilical broken, he was on his own. Surely, he would be allowed to defend himself—

"Master Program to Defender." A fleeting image of Megan's saddened face. "Repeat. Control command forbids approach to planet or hostile action against its beings." The silent voice must be his own internal computer speaking; the ship's radio couldn't reach him here inside these metal walls. "You will not attack."

He flinched from the mocking hints of Megan because he knew they were only accidental artifacts picked up by that imperfect scanner so long ago, on an Earth forever lost. Chance malfunctions now, hazards to his duty.

Defeated, he tossed his useless weapon to the floor. It struck without sound; if the craft had ever held an atmosphere, that must have leaked away long ago. Rebounding silently, the thing sailed weightlessly away. The bug darted farther back from him. The disk shone brighter for a moment, tipping to trace the thing he had thrown, then went out.

Blind in the sudden dark, he sprang aside and stood crouched and wary, waiting for the bug. Surely, his computer would let him guard himself. His feet caught a faint vibration, perhaps when the dead missile struck the wall, but there was no attack.

Slowly, his eyes adjusted to the gloom. He saw his own limbs glowing, deeply and eerily red, saw light on a tiny patch of floor around him. Puzzled for an instant, he knew it must be infrared. Still hot from that blazing assault, his body was radiating energy his adapting vision could now detect. When it cooled, he would be blind again.

Disabled, too, when his chance recharge was gone.

Beyond that tiny glow, darkness walled him in. He couldn't find the bug. Had it fled, perhaps to find a better weapon? Or was it lurking somewhere near, watching, waiting till he ran down again? He had no way to know.

He felt driven to action, to use his dwindling store of strength and time—but what was there to do? Standing trapped in the overwhelming dark around his narrow crimson cave, he was ignorant, unarmed, forbidden to fight—

Trembling, he knotted his fists.

"Defender to Master Program." Defiantly, he addressed his own computer. "At least I can move. I can try to learn where I am and what has captured me. So long as I don't try to harm anything."

"Master Program to Defender." He hated that quick inflexible voice, even knowing it came from somewhere in himself. Hated the meaningless echo of Megan. "Repeating control command. You will not attack. You will not resist. You will not interfere."

It had not forbidden him to move. Planless, empty-handed, watching for the bug, he struck out to find those clustered pillars. They loomed suddenly into his dim glow, not a dozen meters ahead. Most of them featureless pillars of some dull metal, but he found an oval door in the thickest, a vertical shaft inside. Wide enough for the bug, it yawned black.

He clutched the rim and thrust himself through to light it. A circular pit, not two meters across. Darkness filled it, above and below his faint glow. He hung there a moment, wary of the bug, but he saw no movement, felt no vibration.

Kicking off, he launched himself upward. Smooth metal walls flowed down around him. Another dark doorway. He caught the rim, pulled himself through. All he found was another vast and empty floor, stretching into soundless dark. Back in the pit, he pushed farther on.

A circle of pale light grew ahead until at last he came out into a cavernous space that extended all around him, filled with great, ghostly shapes that shone dimly blue.

Immense machines, all half transparent. Visible not with his faint glow but somehow with their dim shine.

In a moment, he understood. What he saw was gamma rays. The shapes were nuclear reactors, shining from old contamination. And lofty racks of fuel for them, burning dimly through massive shielding with the faint blaze of atomic decay. Black shadows beyond were enormous tanks that must have held mass for ionic engines.

He clung there, dazed. He had known the thing had to be an orbital spacecraft. Fission engines, these were still enough like the seedship's fusion engines to let him guess their function. And to tell him that the craft had been built for interstellar flight.

To other stars? Or had space invaders flown it here? From the unknown world of the Master Builders? Under Attack Command? Could it have been a bigger sort of seedship? Sent to plant its makers here? Shivering, he tried to imagine what kind of creatures they had been.

Nothing moved around him now. Nothing except the dancing atoms, and even their radiance was faint. These mighty engines had been cooling for ages he could only guess, certainly many thousand years. The invaders—if the great craft had really brought invasion—could be rulers of the planet now.

He dropped back into the pit, and his orientation spun. The engine room became the bottom of it. Giddy from the shift, he kicked off into the dark. Already his body-glow was fading, the darkness closing in, and he caromed clumsily off the dim wall.

His mind was dimming, too. A dark doorway slid into view, strange until he remembered that empty space and the one above it where he had first found himself. Cargo holds, he told himself, if this was a ship. Groggily, he wondered what they had carried.

Weapons, perhaps, for the conquest of the planet? Colonists to claim it? Tools to terraform it? Machines, supplies, libraries—everything to plant some alien race and culture as the builders of the seedship had hoped to plant humanity?

Perhaps. He saw no way to tell. His imagination began piling up nightmare things crouching beyond his dying body-glow. Shivering, he shrank back into the shaft and climbed until he saw light again.

Light stronger than his own. He gripped the rim of the door through which it came and lurched out of the shaft into another immense compartment, dimly lit from six high openings spaced around it. The central tube, with its cluster of surrounding columns, towered behind him into the dark.

Swaying unsteadily, the pull of his feet growing weaker, he stumbled across another vast floor and into the brightest opening. A metal tunnel, many meters long, it brought him into increasing light and at last outside the craft, to a dazzling view of open space and the sun. He clung to the lip, drinking in hot energy.

The tunnel opened into the bottom of a long metal canyon—one of the hollows he had seen from space. Berths for smaller spacecraft, yet themselves immense, perhaps 200 meters long. Landing craft, perhaps, brought to take the invaders down to the planet?

The canyon walls had once been bright, he thought, but they were scarred and stained red from long exposure to micrometeors and the solar wind. Above him and below were massive fittings that must have secured the landers.

If that was what they had been.

Looking for some more-certain evidence, he pulled himself back into the tunnel. The strong sunlight was food he hungered for, but he had no time now to let it feed him. Not until he could learn more and feel safer from the bug.

One by one, he followed the other tunnels. The next brought him back into life-renewing sunlight. Two opened on inky midnight and the Milky Way. The last let him see the planet's blazing crescent. Too sad to move, he let his eyes linger on it.

His vision adapted to let him see wreathing spirals of cloud and a greenish hint of land. With better luck, it might have grown the new human tree. But the seed of man had come too late. If their little ship had not been hit by that micrometeor, if they had arrived ahead of the invasion—

He pulled himself away, sick with defeat and his own predicament. The Defender had not been engineered for vain despair, but not for fighting, either. Even if they had landed first, he might still have been forbidden to battle the invaders. Certainly, the new human colony would have been ill prepared to meet attack from space.

Hating that bleak mood, he tried to shake it off. The Defender had been designed for action; emotion only got in the way. Even with any helpful action banned, he felt driven to move on. Clumsily reeling, he stumbled back into the central shaft, kicked himself upward.

Dull metal slid by him, and two black doorways. Another circle of light appeared and grew ahead. He emerged at last on another deck. Immense and circular, it reached beyond the range of his dim body-glow, all around him and high above.

Here at the top of the shaft, he thought, should be the control room. Looking for evidence of that, for astrogation gear or traces of the vanished crew, he found scores of dark metal masses standing motionless in rows along six narrow avenues running back into the gloom from a small clear space around the pit.

Odd-shaped objects taller than he was. Machines, perhaps, eternal as the seedship, designed maybe by the Master Builders on whatever far-off world they had ruled—designed to operate the craft for Attack Command? Carefully, making the most of his dwindling energy, he shuffled to inspect them.

Light flashed behind him.

Spinning to face it, he met the bug.

Most of those looming, boxlike masses were time-tarnished metal, nearly black, but one was warm enough to glow like Defender's own body, dully infrared. Taller than the rest, it stood far off, at the end of a shadowy alley. If the others were a robot crew, shut down now, he thought this one might be the commander, still in operation. The bug had come from somewhere behind it. Gliding silently and fast, the thing stopped in the middle of that gloomy avenue, twenty meters away.

His own heat-energy had cooled too long. Swinging groggily to meet the bug, he found himself floating off the deck and had to make a desperate stab with one magnetic toe to get back. Unarmed and bewildered, too far gone even to plan any action, he could only hang there, waiting.

The bug lay still, the disk on its golden carapace turning slowly bright enough to show the wall of a thick-ribbed dome that curved up beyond the red-glowing block. The great craft's nose arched high above him. Scanning it for any weapon the Master Program might let him use, for any hopeful chance, he found only ancient metal.

He saw the disk tipping toward him. The light of it focused to fix him with an unsteady beam. He yearned for another burst of its restoring radiation, but the swift-pulsed flicker stayed too faint to help him. A rattle of static. A soundless howl. A harsh, inhuman voice.

"Attack Command to Unidentified."

"Guest—" he tried to say. "Guest to Attack—"

"Attention, Unidentified. You establish no authority for

existence here. Attack Command requires your removal—"

"Removal not required!"

Trying to shout, he saw no hint that the bug received anything. It lay inert, looking as lifeless as a metal ingot. The flickering signal had ceased, but the gray-glowing face of the disk was still fixed upon him like a solitary eye, alertly hostile.

"Guest to Attack Command." He tried again. "We do not resist. Our own commands protect you. All we seek is to survive—"

He saw the second bug.

Darting from somewhere about that red-glowing tower, it stopped close behind the first. They looked almost identical, featureless, flat masses, but the second carried something else on its sleek yellow shell.

Something cylindrical, pointing at him.

He gathered his last energy and tried to sharpen his fading senses to study it. A dark hollow tube. A missile launcher—with a dark projectile already emerging! Desperately, he accelerated. Swaying aside, he reached fast enough but very gingerly to grasp it, let the momentum of its heavy little mass spin his body until its direction was reversed.

"Master Program to Defender!" The warning rang in his dimming mind, edged again with that mocking trace of Megan. "Advanced beings are not to be attacked—"

Obediently, as the missile left his fingers, he turned it slightly upward to let it miss the bugs. Before his vision went out, he saw that it would strike that red-glowing sentinel.

"Defender! You will not injure any being—"

The computer voice was fading, but its commands no longer mattered. All awareness dying, he was floating off the deck—

The blast had thrown him off the truck. He lay in foul mud, blood in his mouth, cold rain drumming on his back. A reek of spilled gasoline. Too near. He fought for breath, fought to drag himself farther, slid back into the muck.

A second soft explosion. A gentle roaring, louder than the rain. He heard the driver's strangled prayer to the mother of God, heard Prieto screaming. Poor devils, but nothing he can do. Howls and hoarse curses. Three quick shots. Then only the roar of the fire till the wet weeds on the bank above him began to hiss and crackle.

Heat increasing. The rank stink of the charred weeds and a bitter whiff of burning hair and flesh. Cold rain trickling. Salt sweat biting where the hide had been scraped off his hands and cheek. He needed to lie there longer, to get his breath and clear his throbbing head.

But the ammo—

Got to get further while I can. Head up and never mind the giddiness. Fight the muck and breathe the stink. Grab that bush. Claw up the bank. Slide back and try again—

A hard concussion. The ammo, too soon. Duck and run. Christ, my knee— Damn thing numb and then the crunching pain. No good for anything. Down in the mud again on hands and the other knee, dragging the leg, scrambling for cover in the jungle.

One royal hell of a fix for an old pro at the game, but I'm not done for. Yet. Not if I can make it back to the wreck of the chopper and work the radio—

He was floating—

Somewhere in the dark. In the hospital tent, he thought at first. Under ether, maybe; he felt no pain, not even in his knee. Butch and Mascarenas must have come back with the other chopper to pick him up. But where were all the jungle croaks and chirps and shrieks? Where was anybody? Trying to turn in the bed to see where he was, he found no bed. Only empty darkness all around him.

He was actually floating, his body turning slowly in the air—but here, of course, there was no air. He saw faint light and then the bugs drifting above him under the black-ribbed vault.

Killed?

Watching their slow tumble, he saw no hint of life or action. Two odd-shaped slabs of dull-gold metal, they had no visible limbs or organs of sense, no wheels or tracks or anything else projecting. Even the shining disk and the missile launcher were gone.

Helpless, disabled, and adrift in that frigid gloom, he clung to his dulled awareness and waited for some new attack. None came, and he wondered dimly why. If the great spacecraft had been left in orbit to defend the planet, why had it fought him so feebly? Perhaps, he thought, those missing landers had carried the crew away, leaving only the robots aboard. And, after thousands of years, perhaps they were running down.

His own run-down body kept very slowly spinning, like a tiny world in space. The two dead bugs went by again, like companion planets. The black vault climbed again above him, an ominous sky with a pale moon in it. The moon was the disk. Floating near him, it was turning to light the deck beneath. When his own rotation let him see it, he found the shaft through which he had come, the radiating alleys of identical block-shapes around it, the taller thing the deflected missile had hit now no longer glowing.

Dead!

"Master Program to Defender." That cold internal reprimand shattered his momentary triumph. "You are defective. You have malfunctioned. You have killed advanced inhabitants—"

"The missile was their own." Stubbornly, he defended his rebel self. "They fired it themselves, inside their own craft. They should have known it had to hit something."

"The being it struck was killed." The sternly brittle voice still held a hint of Megan, Megan sounding hurt. "A being of advanced intelligence."

"If it was a being—"

The nearer bug was swimming back into view. Not quite floating, it was falling, as he himself was, drawn gently down toward the starcraft's center of mass. He saw that it would pass close enough for his foot to reach it.

Nerved with a sudden hope, he twisted to find the drifting disk. It at least was still somehow alive, still luminous with energy he needed. Eagerly, he measured mass and distance and velocity. When the bug was near enough, he nudged it with one weak toe.

A feeble nudge, but enough to send him gently toward the disk. If not exactly toward it, maybe close enough. He waited, judged its motion, reached again. His fingers touched it, turned feebly magnetic, drew it to him.

Basking in its power, he wished it had been stronger—and wondered if his touch had turned it brighter. As that dead block-shape came closer, he swung the disk to find the spot where the missile had struck.

A jagged hole blown in the dark metal case. Coiling

cables beneath and thin shelves crowded with close-spaced rows of glittering crystals. Oddly shaped and strange enough, yet arrayed like Rablon's supercubes; he knew the shelves must be circuit boards.

"Defender to Ship!" Triumph surging high, he forgot that he was talking to himself. "The thing the missile hit was no live being. It's a computer. On all the craft, I've found no sign of life. No atmosphere, no quarters or stores for any living crew.

"Which means we could try a landing—"

"Master Program to Defender." Megan's sad image quivered and vanished in his mind, a ghost he would never escape. "Repeat: mission canceled. Encounter with advanced orbital craft is itself adequate evidence of highly evolved technology here."

"But it didn't evolve here. The nuclear drives—everything about the craft says it's interstellar. It brought invaders here from another star. Sent out by something its computers called the Master Builders, operating under what they called Attack Command."

"Master Program to Defender." He hated its merciless insistence. "You found empty housings where their landing craft were carried. Your report implies that they reached the planet. If high technology exists there now, from whatever origin, it is forbidden to us."

"We've scanned the planet," he protested. "We got no data indicating any sort of technology there. Nothing electronic. No visible signs of advanced intelligence. Perhaps the things that tried to land were robots, too. Maybe run down by now. Which means we aren't stopped yet—

"If I can get back where I belong!"

Hugged against his belly, the disk gave him a little life. He surveyed the deck as he fell closer, measured his way to the dark central pit. The shattered shell of the dead robot commander rose to meet him, and he thrust it aside with one bare foot.

Deflected, he fell back into the shaft. Its dark walls drifted slowly up until a gray gleam struck through an oval door and he pulled himself out into the cold twilight that filtered through the tunnels from those empty berths.

Carefully, he launched himself out of the tube through the gloom toward the brightest tunnel mouth. Here, near the center of mass, his body flew true. He came out at last into the bottom of the hollow where a long landing craft had lain.

Into healing sunlight.

Anchored to the meteor-scarred metal at the tunnel's lip, he drank it in. Slowly, the great craft rolled. The sun was gone too soon beyond the rim of the cavity, but it would be back. He watched the marching stars until the planet rose above the other rim.

Splendid and immense, now near the full, it looked close enough to touch. He traced the snaky rain-dazzle of wind-covergence around the equator, searched the blue-black zones of tropical ocean, found the cloud-piled archipelago and then the two great continents.

Red flecks of desert. White glints of ice. Wider green reaches half veiled with cloud. Senses keener now, vision turning telescopic, he swept the visible land again and still found no hint of intelligent engineering. Searching the energy spectrum, he picked up only the rustling static of lightning in the storms. No evidence, he thought, that any invaders had ever landed.

"Defender to Ship," he called into space. "Hostile action ended. No evidence of advanced life now existing here in orbit or on the planet. Mission can continue—"

"Ship to Defender." The answer came instantly, bright with Megan's gladness. Her smile flashed across his mind, so lovely that old agonies awoke to throb again. "Homing on your signal."

He clung where he was, waiting for the ship and its haunting ghost of the woman he had loved—that they had loved, all those ghosts that haunted him. The good sun returned. Drinking in its golden wine, he pushed those poignant pains aside.

Chance wisps of a world dead forever in the black abyss behind them, they would never really matter. Why should he care whether Don Brink had ever gone to war again or who had won Megan Drake? He was the Defender, with a new world ahead, a fallow field so far as he could tell, waiting for him to plant and tend the human seed.

THREE

MURDERED WORLD

He woke to the pull of unfamiliar gravity.

"Ship to Defender." Megan's image danced across his mind, as stunning as she had ever been, and the ship's brittle voice seemed to quicken with a hint of human joy. "We are down safe on Mansphere. Our mission can continue as soon as feedstocks are found. That will be your duty now."

Feedstocks—

Memories of stark emergency shocked him out of drowsiness. That earlier awakening, when he found the ship adrift in space, fusion fuel exhausted. To make it live again, he had burned the precious feedstocks they had brought for retranslation into human colonists for the new world. He must replace them now. If he failed—

"If you think this job is tough—"

Brink was following Tomislav out of the scanner lab into the blazing Albuquerque afternoon. The sessions always lasted too long. He hated the lab, with its persistent antiseptic stink and its sense of unending tension. They kept it too cold, and he hated the radioactive brew they pumped into his brain. It always left him feeling weak and bad, somehow not himself, drained of all vitality.

"Translating human genes and human culture into computer code—that's the easy part. We've got a hundred-million-dollar lab, teams of experts here and in several universities, months of time to cope with unexpected bugs. Years if we need them."

Tomislav was overweight, breathing hard because he had never become used to the mile of altitude, but still he walked too fast.

"The tough part will be the back translation, out of computer language back into live human genes. And processing those into the minds and ways of our new race. The whole endowment of science and art and ethics and everything else it will take to make them really human. Out of the ship's master computer, back into a civilization."

He wanted a drink, but alcohol would only make his reaction worse. His head was already stuffy, and the sunblaze hurt his eyes. He must be getting allergic to something in the radioactive mix.

"There won't be labs." Puffing, the big biologist turned at the curb to let him catch up. "Not on any planet where we can let a seedship land. No engineering teams to help. Nothing but the tiny ships themselves, down in environments sure to be strange, most of them hostile."

"With odds like that—" He shook his uneasy head. "Do we really have a chance?"

"Perhaps the only one mankind will ever have. So Ben Bannerjee says, and I think he's right. We've got to make the most of it."

Tomislav himself looked worn with work and strain, sad eyes red and blue pouches under them. On his way now to phone his dying wife.

"That why—why I'm here." Wearily, he wiped a sweaty shirt sleeve across his pale wet face. "When I ought to be back with Olga in La Jolla. I know the odds against any single seedship, but Megan hopes to launch a thousand. If they seem small for all they must accomplish, so do mustard seeds."

Still astonished at the thing he had become, he explored himself again and his dark birthcell. The narrow walls around him, something hard and slick, yet yielding slightly to his searching fingers. The throbbing umbilical that linked him to the ship and powered him from its compact reactor. His own half-metallic flesh, colder than the cord. And his empty crotch—

Touching that, he tried not to let it hurt. Tried to accept himself as only a Defender, engineered not for any life of his own, but just to serve the ship. That ought to be, would have to be enough.

The cell was tipped, so that he lay leaning on the wall. Searching, he found and struck the bulging opener. The wall cracked under him. Sliding through the thin-lipped slit, careful with the umbilical, he descended into symphonies of sensation.

Something softly brittle, crackling to his weight. Hot sunlight, white and blinding. Whispering windsongs. Medlies of unfamiliar odor—vividly perceived through all his golden skin even though he didn't breathe. Briefly overwhelmed, he closed his eyes, dimmed all his senses, until he could adjust himself to strangeness.

Mansphere!

A fallow field waiting for the human seed. Megan herself had named it a million years ago, but the rest of it was mystery, altogether new, its treasures and its hazards not yet known. Maybe still damaged, the ship's computer had at least got them here.

If he could find feedstocks now—

Adjusting to the storm of new sensation, he opened his eyes on man's new world. Green and black. Sun-fire blazing. He found his bare feet ankle deep in a lush carpet of vividly green fibrous stuff, a little like grass or moss. The little ship stood beside him, gold film blazing against the sun, his golden cord coiling up into his birthcell. Rockets and tail fins buried deep, it leaned precariously. He thought the landing must have been rough.

"Ship to Defender." Its synthetic voice wounded him again with that accidental trace of Megan's. "We confirm difficult landing due to clogged laser injector. Fusion engines damaged on impact, now inoperable and beyond repair. We compute various consequent hazards.

"The most immediate is flood."

He turned to look for that. A lake of breeze-ruffled green, the land lay level for several kilometers. Hills rose all around them, steep black slopes climbing to red-stained limestone palisades. He found no flowing water.

"Flood?"

"Ship cannot take off again to search for safer site. We compute indicated high probability of rain water trapped here in coming monsoon season, rising many meters deep.

Ship cannot survive immersion. Feedstocks must be replaced without delay."

"That may be difficult. What sort of stuff will do?"

It catalogued what they must have to build the new humanity.

"Volatile hydrocarbons or other carbon-rich liquids. Our supply tanks still contain the other essentials: phosphoric acid, compounds of sodium and potassium, solutions of trace elements. We can process nitrogen from the atmosphere, hydrogen and oxygen from water, calcium from stone. What we lack is carbon in usable form for the assembler. The chemistry is not critical. We can use alcohols, light vegetable oils, or petroleum derivatives."

"I'll search." And he added, "If we do find anything, we can probably salvage empty tanks and pumps and tubing from the propulsion system. To build processing equipment—"

Looking for hints of anything that might be processed, he turned to scan that wide green glade. Bright plumes were scattered across it: taller tufts of colored blades, orange, crimson, indigo. Flowers? Their colors evolved to draw insects—or evolutionary analogues of insects—to carry pollen? Wondering, he saw nothing crawling, nothing flying, nothing moving. The silence struck him. Except for a whisper of wind against the ship, he had heard no sound on Mansphere.

A dim alarm chilled him. Searching from space, scanning the energy spectrum, they had found no hint of intelligence. No evidence, in fact, of any life higher than plants. He recalled those robots in orbit and the riddle of their mighty craft.

An interstellar starship, its nuclear rockets so cold he knew they had not burned for many thousand years, the six landers gone from their berths. If the Master Builders had shuttled themselves down to the planet, where were they now?

Why had the ship observed nothing alive? Nothing higher than these strange plants. Was something here deadly? Deadly even to such sophisticated beings as the robot builders must have been and waiting now to kill the seedship and its human fruit.

He scanned the green plain again, and the high hills around it. The growth on the nearer slopes looked jungle thick and strangely black. Above, the dark-red iron stains in the limestone cliffs had the color of long-dried blood.

Turning uneasily back toward the ship, he shivered in spite of himself. It looked far too puny for its ambitious destiny. Half its gold skin had burned black in the heat of their descent, and a black wound yawned where his crudely welded patch had been torn away. Mankind's best chance to live again, it looked achingly forlorn.

"Ship to Defender." A fleeting glimpse of Megan's face, lean lined and lovely. Green eyes wide and dark and empty, sick with foreboding. She was staring at him, shaking her head, as the image shivered and vanished. "Report possible feedstock sources observed."

"Defender—"

Dejection checked his answer, but he tried to shake it off. In spite of such chance hints and glimpses, the ship wasn't Megan. Like all his own longings and alarms, the bits of her in the computer were only accidental errors in the scanner pickup.

"Defender to Ship." He tried again. "No possible feedstock source observed within range of power cord."

Shivering with dread, he picked up a golden coil of the umbilical in both golden hands. Nearly as thick as his thumb, stiffly pliant, hot now from the sun and pulsing with the energies that were his life.

"Then you must search farther."

"Before I can leave the ship, I must improvise another power source."

A moment of delay, then the cold computer voice.

"Impossible. No resources available, without the use of feedstocks, to fabricate any alternative power source."

"Without power—"

"You can use sunlight."

"That is inadequate—"

A flash of scaring pain. The golden cord dropped off his belly, whipped away across the green, vanished back into that dark slit from which he had been born. His vision dimmed. Mansphere faded like a dream. Its burning sun and pungent scents and breath-soft wind gone in an instant.

Blackness crushed him down.

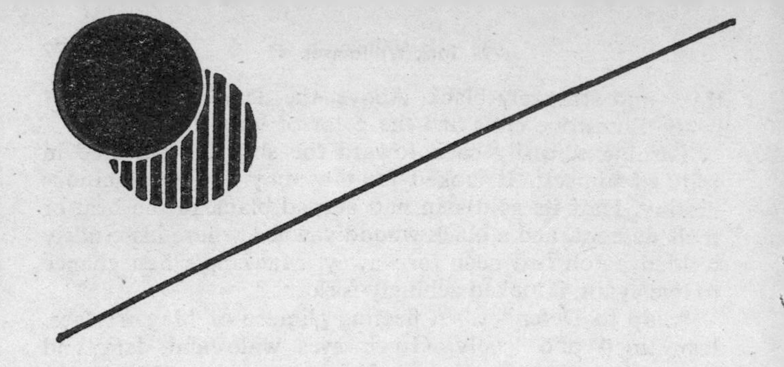

Sirens screeching faintly, somewhere far away. The ambulance gently swaying. Megan beside him, holding his hand, tender as his mother long ago. Cradled in her care, he didn't have to worry over the drugs in his brain or the seedship project or anything at all—

Somebody moaning and hard heels clicking. The thin, chemical hospital odors. Bright light glaring. His own sweat, clammily cold. His head still drumming but now clear again. He lay on a hard, narrow bed, oxygen tubes in his nose.

"Dr. Ulver?" Megan's voice, and he saw her by the bed. "Okay now?"

Too damn much respect, but he didn't say so.

"Okay." His throat felt dry and sore. "Where am I?"

"The Lovelace clinic. You passed out in the scanner."

"Sorry—"

"We're the ones to be sorry." She was leaning nearer. He liked her wry smile and her lean-hewn features and the hint of scent she wore. "Seems you have an allergy to something in Tomislav's brain transfusion. Sent you into shock."

"Can he try something else?"

"Better not. The specialists here say the next reaction could hit you harder."

"If he can—if he wants to try a different mix—I'm willing."

"Galen—" She made him happy, breathing his name. "Galen, I can't let you risk your life."

Her hand caught his again, cool and strong and caring.

"I don't mind—mind the risk." His voice was weak, and

he tried to clear his scratchy throat. "Let me—let me tell you why."

"Just rest. I'll be back, but now you'll need to sleep."

"Please!" He clung to her hand. "I need to keep on trying. If you'll let me tell you why—"

"If you must—" Her fingers returned the pressure of his own. "If you're strong enough—"

Gulping at the dryness, he tried to gather himself.

"I was a sickly kid."

His voice came too faint, but she was bending closer, nodding.

"Born on a Blue Ridge farm where things were pretty primitive. Polio before I was five. On crutches for years. A burden on my parents—for more than just the polio. Too much, I guess, for my father. He went north to look for a better job, and we never heard from him again. Mother worked to keep me. Sewing, painting china, typing reports for my uncle—he was an engineer, a sort of maverick freelance engineer. She did anything—"

He had to pause for breath and strength.

"Too much, I guess. Kept me too close. Taught me at home till high school. She used to read aloud, and I learned to live in books. Never many friends—for a lot of reasons. None very close, though my uncle was exciting to me when he came with something new to type. I learned about science from him. Science and space.

"Space—that got to be all I lived for. I built model rockets and my own telescope. Went through Georgia Tech. That with a lift from my uncle after mother died. Somehow got to be a specialist in nuclear propulsion. Early enough to work on Orion with Taylor and Dyson. A wonderful time. We were almost off to Mars—or thought we were."

A little ruefully, he tried to smile at Megan.

"But of course—" He was husky from the oxygen, and she raised his head to let him sip a little water. "Of course the funding stopped. The world got paranoid about anything atomic. Most of the others went back to something else, but I kept on. Dreaming about a new angle on fusion propulsion I couldn't sell to anybody else. Doing math and drawing plans and making models when I couldn't get support.

"My life." He sighed, not entirely sad about it. "The only life I'd ever learned to live. Or ever really wanted, though sometimes I wished I'd been closer to more people.

I never married or even came near. Even now, I guess I'm still a loner.

"But—"

He couldn't even try to say what he felt for her. The only woman he had ever known who really shared the dream of a fusion engine. Not that it could matter. He was an old man now. Too old for her or anything except this last alluring hope she had rekindled in him.

"That's the reason why," he whispered. "Why I love—love the project. My chance at space, when I thought the last chance was gone. So please tell Tomislav I want him to try another mix for the brain infusion. No matter if there is a risk. That is, if you need me—"

"We do." Her green eyes and smile were medicine he needed. "Of course we do, if the doctors agree you're really able. Nobody else really understands your ideas for the fusion engine or even thinks it could work."

She leaned quickly closer, and he felt her cool lips touch his forehead—

Waking unwillingly to the burning at his belly and the hard duties of the Defender, he knew Tomislav must have tried another mix. Otherwise, that moment with Megan couldn't have reached the computer.

He lay sprawled face down, the sun hot on his back. Adjusted to it now, his skin was drinking up its energy. Not so much as the umbilical had fed him but at least enough to let him move. He swayed to his feet.

"Ship to Defender." He hated the brittle voice, with its mocking trace of Megan. "Report your plans for securing vital feedstocks."

Plodding back toward the ship, he reviewed all he knew about Mansphere. Surveying it from orbit. Deciding to try the north continent because it seemed to offer the best resources. Selecting this humid southeastern peneplain, here just above the delta of a mighty river that sprang from the glaciers on the great central massif. With an unknown world to search, he had no plan.

"Need is most urgent. Utmost haste imperative. Report possible sources."

Haste? The word was a savage jab. On only sun power, he couldn't move fast or bring feedstocks back even if he found them. Unless—

Could he use the disk? Wondering, wondering even what

the disk-thing could be, he stopped to shake his head. Searchlight? Weapon? Power battery? He neither understood nor trusted it. After it fell into his hands on the orbital starcraft, it had served him well enough. But before that, still controlled by the alien robot, it had tried hard to kill him.

"Ship to Defender. You will take the disk."

He knelt to open the access door. The alien device lay where he had stowed it. A bit more than a quarter meter across, not half that thick. One face was black when he opened the door, the rest dull gold. As if in response to his touch, the black face lit.

The disk was magnetic. When he slid it to his naked back, his own magnetic grasp could hold it there. In a moment, he felt the radiation from its glowing face against him. Far less than the umbilical had fed him, yet stronger than the sunlight. Perhaps it would serve again.

"Defender to Ship." He put out his hand to lean against the dark-scarred hull. "I'll look for seeping petroleum or any sort of vegetable stuff we can ferment into alcohol—if yeasts exist here, or analogues of yeast, to ferment anything. Lacking data for any firm plan, I mean to work inland, keeping near the river. If I find feedstocks, I may need to float them back—"

"You've got to find them, Don." The voice suddenly almost Megan's, tremulous with her emotion, calling him by Don Brink's name. "Soon!"

When he reached the jungle, it was dead. A wall of cruel black thorns, tens of meters tall. Its leaves had fallen. A thick black mat, spongy now with rot, they stank with a strange reek he hated. His whole body sensed something deadly in them.

Quivering with revulsion, he stopped to study one lone unfallen leaf that clung among the thorns. Thick and tough and leathery, ribbed with dark-red veins, rimmed with fishhook spikes. He saw no likeness to anything Terran, but neither to the live growth behind him.

He found no fruit, nothing that looked fermentable. Something in the spiny leaf stung like poison. Flinging it aside, he pushed into the brittle tangle. The driving sun, combined with the disk-thing's radiation, had fed him strength enough for his tramp out of the level swale, but the going grew harder now.

Even though few leaves were left, the close-woven bayonets and barbs cut off too much of the sun, and they dragged too hard against his ebbing strength. The slope had grown too steep, and the slimy leaves slid treacherously underfoot. The pain in his navel grew sharper again, a craving for the power he had lost.

Mansphere spun faster than old Earth, and night caught him still battling the tricky slope and the dead, unending jungle. The planet had no moon, and total darkness fell. Mind and senses slowed, he had to stop until his eyes adjusted to infrared.

That lit an eerie blood-red glow on the jungle blades and the boulders fallen from the cliffs above and even the rotting leaves. Guided by it, he toiled on until he came to the cliffs themselves. They halted him again, their ruddy glow too dim to help him climb them, and he had to wait for sunlight.

Waiting, sunk into a groggy half sleep, he groped again for those stray shards of the men he had been: Tomislav and Rablon, Ulver and Wardian and Brink. Genetic engineer, computer designer, rocket builder, astronaut, mercenary soldier. All gathered by Megan for expertise to be recorded in the seedships' computers, all held by what they felt for her.

His fingers had strayed toward the ache in his empty crotch. He snatched them away, trying to recall what he was. A yearning half thing made of those mismatched bits, he hungered for wholeness. Most of all, he longed for Megan—hungered for her with the yearning of all those men inside him.

They all had wanted for her, and she had given them all the same warm affection, with no favorite that he knew. Unless—

Ben Bannerjee!

Recalling how long she had known him, the tone of her voice when she spoke of Ben, the look in her eyes when she saw him, the tenderness of her touch on that twisted, child-sized shoulder, he wondered if Ben had been her real love. Not that it could matter now. She and all her men were a million years behind, only random accidental echoes in his brain.

The sun rose. Life rekindled and senses sharpened, he found a water-carved slash where he could climb the cliffs.

On a high ledge, he stopped to look back for the seedship. Far below him now, shrunk with distance, the level swale was a shining emerald set in black. He couldn't see the ship.

"Defender calling."

"Ship to Defender." The answer came instantly. "Awaiting report."

Guided now by the signal, his telescopic vision picked up the ship. Absurdly small and futile, leaning crazily. A single tiny seed fallen into alien soil, where it couldn't hope to grow. After a moment, he shrugged and spoke again.

"Reporting no success. No indications of seeping petroleum or other geological organics. Nothing discovered fit for fermentation. No clues for farther search."

"Ship to Defender." The merest trace of Megan. "Search must continue."

The Defender had not been meant to despair. He went on. Beyond the high rim, he found another dry black tangle floored with malodorous rotting leaves. It was eerily still, dead as the one behind, showing no more promise of any feedstock source. Too brittle for him to climb, the jungle blocked his view of everything ahead and cut off half his energy.

The human snippets in him might have turned back or simply stopped, but he was more machine than human. The machine plowed on. Crashing through the jungle when it could, turning to try another way when it was blocked, stopping when it must to store power from the shadowed sun or the disk on its back.

Time passed. The sun climbed and sank again. Dusk was closing in before he stumbled into a long, oddly rectangular clearing. Decaying leaves and broken stone piled the floor, but he came to a narrow strip where running water had washed it bare.

Stone, oddly smooth and white and flat. Bending, he found seams in it, oddly narrow, oddly straight. An ancient pavement! He explored it. The broken stones were fallen masonry, he found, when he brushed aside the rotting leaves to inspect them. Five tall white pillars towered above the jungle at one end of it. Remnants of a shattered wall rose at the other, a graceful arch surviving, and parts of a high curve that must have framed a vast oval window.

Mansphere had been alive, with mind and art and high technology, before the black thorns grew.

His vigor fading with the daylight, he staggered through that shattered arch into an infrared shadowland. Crimson javelins stabbed from the clotting dark, and he blundered into mountains of broken masonry he was too weak to climb.

The toppled fragments puzzled him with their hints of tragic history. Bright as stained glass, so long as the waning light could show him any color, they were mostly white but sometimes black or sapphire blue or marble veined, shaped of something hard and dense as diamond. Many still showed clean curves and planes, tantalizing clues to what the ruins must once have been, but some had flowed into shapeless glassiness, perhaps from fire. His magnetic sense grown sharper in the dark, he felt metal beneath the rubble and the reeking leaves. Masses of crumbling rust that must have been machines, flattened blobs that had flowed to savage heat. This had been a city, a magnificent metropolis, murdered long ago.

Stumbling on through ever-denser dusk, he came upon a huge unbroken dome swelling out of the debris. It was the pedestal for a tapered column topped with a dismembered statue that was eerily aglow with its own ruby incandescence.

Shivering, he stopped to stare at the mutilated figure. Though head and arms were missing, the nude legs and torso looked almost human. Almost a woman's, but a little too thin for its soaring height, the whole anatomy delicately refined. She had been beautiful; her tall perfection pierced him like a blade.

Her humanity perplexed him.

"What sort of thing will I be fighting?"

A stray moment of a million years ago, abruptly alive in his mind. A planning session in Megan's office. They sat beside the glittering plastic-spiked stellarium, whose points of flashing lights were stars they hoped to seed.

"Not you, Don." Her fine eyes seemed quizzically ironic. "Remember, we're picking up only a small part of you."

"Whatever—whatever you have to fight—" Tomislav was flushed and wheezy, Albuquerque too high for his emphysema, and he had to pause for breath. "It won't be anything human."

"Or civilized," Megan said. "We won't invade civilized worlds. Since we talked to Ben, Rablon's rewriting the Defender program to make sure you don't try that."

He loved her even when she scolded him.

"Whatever you meet—" Tomislav annoyed him, always lecturing at him as if he were a dim-witted freshman football star. "Civilized or savage, the odds are enormous that no creature you meet will resemble us. In our evolution, we've made too many crazy turns for anything else to follow them all.

"I doubt you'll encounter anything as ferocious as you are."

He shrugged and grinned at Megan. An inspired creator, in love with all life, Tomislav would never forgive his own delight in the old game of mortal combat or even admit that the seedships might fall where they would need Brink's fighting know-how.

Her feelings for him were kinder and more complex—

Recalling that long-lost instant, the Defender grinned again, wondering wryly how the mostly silent bits of Tomislav still alive in him would feel about this murdered human or semihuman world. Was it proof that evolution here had retraced the human track? Terrible evidence, too, that some alien evolutionary cycle had created predators more ferocious than mankind—

Another notion startled him.

Could this dead race have been as fully human as the

glowing statue seemed? Sprung from another one of Megan's seedships, planted here a geologic age ago, while their own was still disabled and adrift in space? The statue's seeming strangeness due perhaps to genetic alterations Tomislav had engineered into the seed or to long evolution since or simply to the divergent conventions of a different art?

The shattered figure couldn't say. Wondering what sort of ferocity had come to kill the city—maybe all of Mansphere—he shivered to a chill of human dread. Was the killer still alive, waiting to blight whatever fruit their new seed might bear?

Heavy with weariness and shock, dull for want of power, he sat down on a red-burning stone—a tapered cylinder thicker than his body, perhaps one of the missing arms. Groggily, he wondered what that lethal agency could have been?

Something sudden, he imagined, overwhelming the planet by surprise. The sort of mutant universal virus Tomislav had taken such pains not to create? An asteroid falling? War without a winner—

Attack Command?

The robot watchers he had fought and stopped out in orbit darted back again to haunt him. The six landers missing from those empty housings on the starship—had alien raiders descended in them to devastate the unwarned planet?

Likely enough, that left haunting questions. Where were the invaders now? Long centuries must have passed since the city died, maybe millennia. The starship's nuclear rocket had been cooling for many thousand years. Were the invaders also dead? Wiped out, perhaps, by some last desperate strike from doomed Defenders?

What sort of thing could have been so ferocious?

His locker stank when he opened the door to get the A papers he was taking home to show his mother. Everything was off the hook and the little shelf, all piled together in the bottom. His sweater had a cold, clammy feel when he picked it up. It was dripping wet, and the stink was piss.

It made him feel sick and weak and awful, but he didn't throw up. He shut the door and stood with his back to it, cold and shaking, watching the other kids running past him down the hall. Most of them didn't look at him, but three big boys stopped for a minute, snickering and grinning at him.

When they were gone, he went back to his home room. Miss Konick was still there, writing something in her grade book. Her bag was on the desk, and he knew she didn't like to be delayed, but she shut the book to see what he wanted. He couldn't say the word to her, but he told her somebody had wet on the things in his locker.

"I'm sorry, Marty." He wondered if she really was. "Do you know who did it?"

He didn't know who, and he didn't know why. He decided not to tell her about the boys that snickered because he didn't really know they were the ones.

"I'll report the incident to Mr. Clough, but I don't know what he can do." He knew she was impatient to go wherever she went, but she sat looking hard at him so long he began to wish he hadn't bothered her. "Listen, Marty." Her bony face twitched at last into a worried scowl. "I'm afraid there's a reason things like this keep happening to you."

"Please—" It was hard to breathe. "I haven't done—done anything—"

"Not exactly." Her lips set harder, and her stern eyes kept sweeping him till he was almost afraid to look at her. "But still there's something somebody should tell you. I know these tricks are cruel, but in a way you do ask for them."

Choked up, trying not to cry, he could only shake his head.

"You're smart, Marty. You read a lot and know a lot, and you love to show off in class. You ought to realize that the other kids don't like that because they think you're putting them down. I know you're upset now, but think about it, Marty. You might be smarter not to act so smart."

He couldn't stop the stinging tears.

"You may go." She reached for the grade book. "But think about it."

The long hall was empty now. He dumped everything out of his locker into the waste basket and scrubbed it out with paper towels from the boys' room and washed his hands with soap. The lock was broken, and he left the door open. Walking home, shivering without his sweater, he tried to think about it.

How was he to blame? He sobbed and shook his head, hating Miss Konick because she said he was. Hating Mr. Clough and those three boys and everybody at Jefferson Central because nobody really liked him.

If he couldn't even answer questions when the teachers asked—

Sitting straighter on that great broken arm, he dragged himself groggily back to Mansphere. The planet's murder had been a crueler thing. Its people could not have been to blame. Not unless they had made their world so rich and fine and beautiful that some alien creatures envied them.

Anyhow, it was time to call the ship.

"Defender reporting." He paused to listen. "Defender to Ship."

Nothing.

"Defender!" He used all the power he could gather from the disk till the effort left him drained. "Defender calling to report discovery of extinct native culture, perhaps a human culture. No possible feedstock source so far found. No indication of useful feedstocks existing anywhere."

Nothing, still.

"Answer!" Human panic had begun to edge his voice. "Answer if you can—"

All energy spent, he sank back against the shattered arm. There would never be an answer, it struck him, not until he was closer to the ship, because it was below the cliffs he had climbed, out of radio range. The seedship had been designed to cope with every predictable problem, but this wasted world could not have been predicted. The ship's hull was not an efficient antenna; neither was his body. He was all alone—

"Support Unit Alpha Ten." The near voice jolted him. The swift, inhuman rhythm of the disk, when the robots had used it out in orbit to answer his initial contact signal. "To Unit Defender. Reporting information. Volatile hydrocarbons do exist here."

Dazed, he tried to gather himself.

"Where? Where are any hydrocarbons?"

"Volatile liquid hydrocarbons exist at Attack Base Alpha Prime."

"What—" He was trembling with emotion the Defender didn't need. "What is Attack Base Alpha Prime?"

"Information. Attack Base Alpha Prime is command complex established by Attack Command as main support center for operations here—" Static clattered in his head. "Here on planet designated Mansphere in your incomplete vocabulary."

"Is anything—is Attack Command still alive?"

"Negative. Attack Command is not alive."

"What killed it?"

"Information: Attack Command includes no living personnel."

"So it was manned by robots? Like those I met on the starship?"

"Affirmative."

"Is it still operational?"

"Negative. Operations suspended when local resistance ceased."

"When?"

"Attack Command suspended operations here—" His head buzzed again. "Date in Mansphere time: nine thousand seven hundred eighty-nine orbital periods past. Data lacking for conversion to Terran time."

He had data for that. Farther out than Earth had been, farther from a hotter star, Mansphere had a longer year. Converted, the time since the planet's death would be just over three hundred Terran centuries. Hardly a heartbeat, perhaps, against all the ages since Megan launched the seedships but still an enormity of time that woke him to an eerie instant of human emotion.

The unchanging deathly stillness. The red-blazing spears and daggers all around him, growing fainter as they cooled. The monumental columns of the ruin behind him, still defiant of fate and fire and time. The mighty arm on which he sat. The tragic beauty of that mutilated nude towering through the thorns.

Frozen in that moment of awe and terror, he shrugged to break himself free. Human emotion could only hamper his service to the ship.

"The hydrocarbon feedstocks at Base Alpha Prime? Are they available to us?"

No response, until he began to wonder why.

"Hydrocarbons of type designated feedstocks exist at Base Alpha Prime." The disk spoke at last. From out of sight behind him, out of reach, from beyond any human understanding. Its swift stacatto revealed no feeling. Of course not, he told his troubled human selves. Merely another machine, even less alive than he was, it had no feeling to be revealed. "Availability undetermined."

"Where is the base?"

"Information. Support Unit Alpha Ten to Unit Defender. Location of Attack Base Alpha Prime—" A clatter in his head; the disk's translation program turning data into words he knew. "Distance: one thousand seven hundred sixty kilometers. Direction: north, seven point one three degrees west of local meridian. Altitude: two thousand four hundred eighty-one meters—"

"Can you guide me there?"

"We can update distance and direction."

"Show me the way." He swayed to his feet. "We're going to determine that availability."

That night, he didn't get far. As the jungle cooled, the red fog thickened so that he couldn't see the rubble barriers until he blundered against them. Every time he asked the disk, it told him very promptly whether he was facing Base Alpha Prime but very little else. When he wanted more facts about the base or Attack Command or the Master Builders, it reported data restriction or translation failure or, more often, made no response at all.

To the human in him, the dimming crimson gloom became a shadow of hopeless dispair. The alien base was too far away: 1,700 kilometers would be a thousand miles and more. The trek to reach it would take him too long. Without the umbilical, he lacked strength to carry enough feedstocks back to the ship even if he found them. Evading so many questions, the disk had come to seem a very doubtful ally.

Yet the machine part of him kept running on to the limit of its power. Reviving when the sun rose, he climbed a rubble mound and tried again to call the ship. Again he got no answer. Pushing on alone, he came into a wide avenue paved so well the thorns had failed to conquer it entirely. He followed it north, tramping all day through amazing ruins he had no time to study. Night stopped him in the boulder-fields around a raggedly circular lake. A crater, he thought, where a missile from space must have fallen.

Two days out of that haunted necropolis, the land began to lift. The dead jungle thinned enough to make climbing easier. Three days more and he left its last brittle sticks behind him, at the rim of a high, seemingly endless park-like plain, still alive and softly green.

Strangely enough, its growth looked more like the lichens and low shrubs of summer on the arctic tundra than the lusher stuff in the swale where the ship had come down, and its vacant expanse woke a stray recollection of the Kenya highlands, beyond the Great Rift Valley. A momentary bit of Don Brink, who had been sent there by agents of a man he never saw to kill a gang of elephant poachers and bring back the ivory in their camp.

Meaningless to the machine in him, that fleeting memory left his human side wrenched and aching. The green vastness needed grazing things, impala or buffalo or cattle. But it was dead. No game trails or wheeling wings or voice of anything at all. Feeling wearily forlorn, he wondered whether the ship could ever really return it to life.

A world without elephants would be a sad place. One without impala and cheetahs. Or mockingbirds and bumblebees and dogs. Maybe even cats and mice—Don Brink had despised cats, but Rablon had loved them and women who resembled them, and cats would want mice.

Perhaps, with all the genetic-engineering know-how Tomislav had programmed into the master computer, animals might be recreated. If the disk did not betray him, if he could actually find enough of the right feedstocks at the base, if he could get them to the ship with time enough before the monsoon floods drowned everything—

If—too much hung upon it.

The axis of Mansphere was tipped nearly forty degrees. Enough to make its seasonal changes extreme. Every day stretched longer as they progressed farther north. The going easier, the Defender was many kilometers closer to his goal every time he asked the distance. Even at night, driven only by the disk, he was able to plod a few kilometers more.

Every day the land climbed higher. The tundralike cover thinned and changed at last to desert: bare red rock cut with dry arroyos and only sparsely tufted with thick-leafed things evolved to conserve every drop of the rare rainfall.

A noon came when he cast no shadow. A long day that let him make many kilometers, yet its very length alarmed him. Time had run too fast. The monsoon storms must already be marching off the ocean across the continent behind him. The flood waters would rise too soon around the ship, and the sun would too soon retreat south again, leaving him to the disk's uncertain mercy.

One cool dawn, he discovered a new shape above the fading infrared of the north horizon. An enormous moon rising, he thought for a moment—but Mansphere had no moon.

"You observe Base Alpha Prime," the disk informed him. "Distance one hundred nineteen kilometers."

Its shining wonder chilled him with dismay. A huge silver dome looming high enough to catch the sun while the desert lay still dark around him. The alien citadel, built thirty thousand years ago by the killers of the planet.

Had they all been robots?

When he asked the disk, the swift drumbeat of its inhuman voice informed him only that no data were available. All the endless day, he watched that immense bright shape swell slowly as it climbed from the shimmer of heat on tufted scrub and naked stone until by sunset he could see dark ribs arching up across its mirror-brilliant fabric. A structure many hundred meters tall, city sized.

The human in him tried to imagine what he might find inside. The secret of the planet's death, perhaps the awful weapons used to kill it? The feedstocks he needed—or ancient traps still set for anything alive?

Eyes lifted to its riddles, he failed to see the brink. Other perceptions checked him: a sense of the sudden decrease of surface density ahead and a muffled thunder from far away and far below, felt with all his skin.

An unexpected chasm, so vast it struck him giddy. Shaken, he dropped to hands and knees to peer across the jagged edge. Bare stone fell sheer for thousands of meters to rocky shelves and broken pinnacles and a dark inner gorge already clotted with dusk.

His eyes adapted to find the river that had cut it, a narrow-seeming silver ribbon. That far-off roaring was water falling into clouds of shining spray. He recalled the gorge from space and this mighty river. Born of the glaciers around the great caldera that had built the continent, it sliced down across this plateau to the southeastern ocean where the monsoon was rising.

He saw no way across.

"Defender to Unit Ten." He collected himself to challenge the disk. "Why didn't you warn about this barrier?"

"Data not requested."

"How can we get across it to the base?"

"Data restricted."

"We've got to get into that dome."

Unexpectedly, something had turned it talkative. "Information: admission to Base Alpha Prime forbidden except to Master Builders."

"The things that built the robots?"

"Affirmative."

"Are they here?"

"Negative. Attack Command was launched to prepare the planet for them. The planet has been prepared. We await their coming."

"You've been waiting for thirty thousand years?"

"Information: computed by the revolutions of this planet, the delay is less than twenty thousand years."

"You still expect them?"

"Attack Command will wait until they come."

"Then I've got a surprise for you." Even to him, the words were startling. Don Brink's more than the Defender's. "Things change as ages pass. Living things evolve, even the Master Builders. That is why you did not recognize me. I am a Master Builder. I have come with new orders that now control Attack Command."

The disk dimmed its radiation. Without its power, he swayed to his knees.

"If you command Attack Command—" Its swift rhythm became hesitant and faint. "You will repeat recognition signal."

"Recognition signal is restricted. It is reserved for direct communication to Attack Command alone."

"Information: Attack Command now inactive. Access forbidden. You cannot reach Attack Command—"

"I will—"

It cut him off. He fell through red gloom, almost into the pit.

Palm Springs in scorching July.

Up at dawn, he had found his own breakfast and hiked out beyond Tramway Road, explaining to skeptical city cops and private guards along the way that he was a house guest of Victor Vane. The whole sky was burning before he got back, but he had learned to love desert heat, and the air-conditioned house felt clammily cold when Vane's silently efficient Filipino let him in.

"Hullo, Brink." Puffy eyed and rusty voiced, Vane beckoned him into the kitchen. "Our chance to talk, with the women still in bed." Wearing a dirty bathrobe, Vane looked sallow and broken, years too old to fit his movie image. "We played poker last week, and I've heard how good you are at your special calling. I'm hiring you to win a poker pot."

"Listen, Mr. Vane. I do play poker, but never professionally. Just to kill time while I'm waiting for the right sort of job at the right sort of pay—"

"I'll pay." Vane was mixing himself a Bloody Mary. His hands shook. "And if it's danger you need to make the job feel right—"

"I don't cheat, if that's what you mean."

"Your opponents will do the cheating. If you're sharp enough to catch them at it, you'll see." Vane shuffled to sit at the bar. "I'll outline the job—"

"First, I want a drink."

Vane was offering the bottles, but he wanted cold water. He got it at the sink.

"Call me an idiot," Vane was muttering. "But I've been robbed. Playing poker for stakes I couldn't afford on a yacht out of Long Beach. With a con man, it turns out. A slick bastard who claims to be a Saudi prince with oil billions to burn—I finally got smart enough to hire a private agency to find out what he really is."

"So? Why do you need me?"

"Listen, Don. I—"

He stopped to gulp the rest of his drink. The glass clattered when he set it on the bar. He sat for a moment merely staring, ravaged face twitching, a mute appeal in his bloodshot eyes.

"Sorry." With a pained grimace, he jerked himself straighter. "Things have gone bad, Don. I was on the ragged edge before I met that thug. Fool enough to think I might win enough to pull me out. Now—"

He sloshed vodka into his glass and tossed it off straight.

"The last chance I've got—if you'll help me grab it." Vane shivered as if he felt the clammy cold. "A scam of my own." His bleary eyes turned anxious. "If you'll lend your able hand—"

"Scam?"

"Listen, Don, before you say no. Here's the scheme. I'll introduce you as a playboy banker out from my own home town. Your dear old dad has just passed away. You've come into the money, and you want action. I've got together eighty thousand dollars—not mine, Don, and about the last I can borrow. Twenty for your advance, if that's enough, and sixty to show. They don't know how totally broke I am, and we let on you're into millions.

"The crook will likely have a couple of honest suckers at the table, along with his shills, conning you all along—with my money. I've watched you, Don. You can beat the rat, and you're sharp enough to catch him if he tries to cheat. Play it right and you can take his gang for a million-dollar pot."

"If he's what you say—"

"He will cheat. Or try to if he's losing." Vane drew a ragged breath. "That's when you might need to fight."

"I don't like that sort of fight—"

"You can beat him, Don. At the cards or however. I'm betting—betting everything." Vane looked at the vodka bottle as if he needed it. "I know the odds look a little grim, but from what people say, it's the sort of sting you can carry off."

"People talk too much."

"Quick money, Don." His voice fell, hoarsely pleading. "Whatever you win—and get away with—we split between us. Even. Could be half a million apiece. Maybe more if we're lucky." His lax lips twitched. "They took that much from me."

"How do we get off the yacht?"

"I've got a speedboat. Luis will be out in that, waiting to dart in and pick us up when we flash a signal." Trembling, he leaned across the bar. "Will you—"

"I don't like it, Vic." He squinted into Vane's disappointed eyes. "Too much like the script for one of the B films you used to make when I was a kid. I've got a code, and I'm not crazy. No matter what you hear people say.

"But—"

He had good uses for a sure twenty thousand. Even for his share of that speculative pot. Besides, that sagging, wasted face kept stabbing him with ironic recollections of the clean-featured screen hero Victor Vane once had been. The magnificent image he had taken for his boyhood guide.

"You'll go?"

"A chancy thing." A little sadly, he scowled at Vane. "But perhaps it might be done. With air-tight planning. If we can trust Luis—"

Half awake in the still-crimson dawn, he groped for recollection of the game on the yacht. Nothing came except the drowsy certainty that Don Brink had lived to play his own hard games again. Revived a little farther as daylight increased, he tried to stand and sprawled again beside that red abyss.

The disk was gone.

Too weak to move without the disk, he lay drinking up the first cold sunlight and groping for ploys against Attack Command. A grimmer opponent, he thought, than Don Brink had ever hired himself to fight. The stakes were big enough: mankind's rebirth. His opponents, alien robots. The rules unknown.

Were bluffs allowed?

Probably not; the disk had not seemed naive. Its disappearance left him wondering why it had ever aided him. Simply to use him for a vehicle to bring it to the robot base? And left him now because he could carry it no farther?

He saw no certain answers.

When he could, he rose to look across the brink. The mirrored dome stared back, a blind, enormous metal eye, mocking him with secrets too remote for him to guess, with the promise of all he wanted and power to kill the human dream.

The only move he knew was to reach and challenge it. Yet its very nearness tantalized him—the intervening gulf slashed four kilometers deep, its giddy walls too steep to climb, the white water roaring down the inner gorge still another barrier.

Alive with the climbing sun, he plodded north along the rim, west and north again, searching for a crossing. Higher toward the main massif, as he recalled from orbit, the great river hadn't cut so deep. Perhaps, somewhere up above the falls—

Perhaps—

He tried not to dwell upon all the hazardous uncertainties around him here or the monsoon floods already creeping from the coast to drown the seedship. He had nearer tasks enough, to pick his minimum-energy path across the rock-ribbed desert, to avoid the stone that might turn or the brush that might trip him, to drink all he could of the sun.

That giant eye followed even when the twists of the rim made him turn his back upon it, bright and blind, never farther, never nearer. Once, yielding to hopeless human emotion, he shook a golden fist into its alien gaze. Never even winking, it stared him down. Machine again, he toiled on.

The sun itself turned foeman. Nearing the zenith, it bathed too little of his absorptive skin. Reeling groggily through the blazing noon, he almost went over another unexpected precipice.

The lip of a branching gorge, slicing south across the desert as far as he could see. Too small to show up from space, it looked appalling now. He was swaying on the rim, scanning its sudden cliffs and tricky talus slopes, looking for any possible path, when he saw the flyer.

A high, dark mote with a thin red tail, it came from toward that glaring silver eye. His own eyes turning telescopic, he watched it drop to wheel a kilometer above him. Its design puzzled him. A trimly tapered shape the color of weathered aluminum, with stubby airfoils that looked too small to control it. The crimson tail was heat from a pulsing jet that seemed inadequate to lift it.

"Master Builder to aircraft above." With less hope than sheer desperation, he hailed it. "If you receive me, please acknowledge."

It did not acknowledge.

"Master Builder to aircraft. Message to Base Alpha Prime. Top priority, instant transmission required. We have arrived to complete our ancient plan for this planet. We require full control of the invasion base and all other facilities on the planet or in orbit, effective now. To that end, we hereby demand immediate identification of all existing units of Attack Command.

"Aircraft will now transmit recognition signal."

Circling very slowly in the brassy sky, it transmitted no signal.

"Master Builder to Attack Command. We require two metric tons of volatile liquid hydrocarbon feedstocks supplied at once to the rocket vehicle in which we landed. We have information that such feedstocks are available at Base Alpha Prime. You will indicate plans for instant compliance."

It indicated nothing.

"Master Builder to aircraft. Information for emergency transmission to Attack Command. Subject: consequences of failure to supply required feedstocks and facilities for rapid transportation. Attack Command will be disabled, as we disabled orbital starship."

Still no sign.

He shook his fist and staggered south. His human hopes began to lift as the westing sun added a little to his energy. Again and again, he stopped to search the gorge until at last he found a chimney that with luck might take him down to a sloping ledge that looked like a path to the faraway floor. The other wall still frowned forbiddingly, but the machine in him was not dismayed.

He scrambled over the rim and into the chimney. It proved difficult, its weathered walls crumbling unexpectedly. He was too feeble and too clumsy. Deadly shadow crept into the lower gorge and climbed too fast to meet him. A wisp of cloud drifted into the narrowed sky. Perhaps a finger of the far monsoon.

Sudden, paralyzing dark—

Somebody banging at the door. Men shouting at his mother. Cops with guns rushing at him—then backing away, crouching to look for somebody else.

"Rablon?" He wasn't what they had expected. "You're Martin Rablon? How old are you?"

"Fourteen, sir."

"If you're really Rablon—" The cop stopped to scowl at him and his computer. "I'm Lieutenant Karst. We have a search warrant for these premises. A warrant for the arrest of one Martin Rablon. You have a right not to talk till you see your lawyer—"

He could hear his mother, still downstairs, asking quavery questions.

"Sir—" He was getting up, but the cop waved him back

into his chair. "Please, would you tell me what you think I've done?"

"If you're actually Rablon, you'll soon be telling the judge."

The other cops were all over his room. Pawing through the tools and parts on his work table. Dumping his computer magazines off the homemade shelves. Dragging everything out of his closet. Even rolling up the bed to look under the mattress.

"If you're looking for dope—"

"That thing?" Karst pointed the gun at his desk. "That's a computer?"

"Yes, sir." Still frightened, he was proud of the computer. "I guess it does look like junk. Mostly built out of salvage parts, still on breadboards. But I've got it working—"

"What's it for?"

"Games mostly. Mom lets me hook it to the TV."

"Games?" Karst bent to squint at the flickery little CRT. "That's a game?"

"Part of one, sir. A subroutine in a program I'm doing for a new space adventure—"

"By God, Harry!" The other cops had dumped his wastebasket on the floor, and one was waving a handful of fanfold paper. "Here's where he hid it."

Karst snatched the crumpled paper and scowled at him again and rushed downstairs to use the phone. He heard his mother, shrill with fear. She came back with Karst.

"—serious charges," he was telling her. "But now I think the bank may want to modify some of them. We'll go there first."

Security guards at the bank marched him into a glittery office with Mr. Preston's name on the long, clean desk. There were chairs, but nobody offered them. Three bankers came to sit scowling across the desk. He knew Mr. Preston's fat bulldog face and little rimless glasses from the TV commercials.

"Mrs. Rablon." Mr. Preston waved the fanfold sheets and growled at his mother. "Do you know what these are?"

White and trembling, she shook her head.

"These are bank records." He was loud and angry. "Our most confidential records. The names and account numbers and current balances of our largest depositors. Complete with all their secret computer passwords. Information that enables the thief—the holder, to transfer any amount of money to his own accounts anywhere in the world and then tell the computers to erase every trace of his own connection with the crime. It was only a freak of luck—a malfunction, in fact, in one of our computers—that led to our detection of the culprit."

Red jowls quivering, he stopped to glare.

"How did your son obtain them?

She looked at him.

"I just phoned," he told Mr. Preston. "With my computer hooked to the phone."

"Phoned?" Mr. Preston was turning redder. "You expect us to think you got free access to God knows how many millions—actually billions? Just by telephone?"

"Yes, sir."

"Who've you got with you, working this scam?"

"No—nobody, sir."

"Martin?" The youngest banker was quieter, suddenly almost friendly. "Would you tell us how you did it?"

"With my computer, sir."

"And aid, I imagine, from confederates in the bank?"

"No, sir. All I needed was a way to let my computer program talk to yours. I used the numbers on my mother's cash and credit cards, and the punched cards about the penalties, when she was overdrawn."

"You wanted to get the penalties back?"

"No, sir. That wouldn't be honest."

"You didn't take anything?" The younger man had begun to look relieved. "Anything at all?"

"No sir. Just to test the program, I did tell it to take one cent from each of the twenty biggest odd-numbered accounts and credit one cent to each of the biggest even-numbered accounts. But I didn't take a cent. The next day, I had the program put the pennies back where they had belonged."

"You—" Mr. Preston was a mad bulldog trying to bark and strangle on a bone. "You—"

"I—I'm sorry, sir, if that made trouble. Just twenty pennies, out of all those billions, and the totals still the same. I didn't think anybody would ever notice."

"You—you whelp—" Mr. Preston stabbed a shaking finger at him. "We'll lock you up—lock you up for life—"

"Martin, we have to notice pennies." He thought the

younger banker was trying not to smile. "You drove our accountants crazy. Now I think I see what you've been doing. Will you tell us why?"

Shrinking from the red fury trembling on that bulldog face, he had to gulp before he could speak, even to the friendly man. "Sir, I saw Preston on TV. Promising everybody that your new electronic banking system was absolutely safe because your security codes couldn't be broken. I wanted to see if what he said was true."

"The impudent—" Mr. Preston shook and wheezed and sputtered. "Impudent—"

The other banker stopped him, pulling at his sleeve and murmuring at his ear. He growled and glared and finally stalked out of the room. The friendly man came around the desk to where they stood.

"Martin, our experts have always told us our system was secure. I guess they'll be surprised when they hear what you've done." Wanting to smile, he grew serious again. "A serious violation of the law, but I'm pretty sure Mr. Preston will agree for the bank to drop our charges. That is, if you'll promise not to meddle again."

"I—I promise, sir."

"Mrs. Rablon, you have an unusual son. Are you sending him to college?"

"I've always hoped to."

"I believe the bank can arrange a scholarship if he'll do some work for us." His smile had broken through. "Martin, I imagine our computer people will be setting up a new security system. I think we'll want you to help us tell how safe it is—"

Waking slowly to a dull crimson glare, he thought at first that he was still fourteen, living with his mother in the shabby old house in Winnetka. Wondering if Mr. Preston had set the house on fire, he tried to call his mother, but he had no voice, not even strength enough to lift his throbbing head.

But his eyes were open. He saw the tall cliffs, glowing faintly infrared, and knew then that he still lay sprawled where he had fallen, on a steep gravel slope below that crumbling chimney. He wasn't Martin Rablon any longer, but stranger memories haunted him.

Machine-shapes dancing, too quick and too queer for him to see them sharply. Computer machine-language rattling in his head, too fast for him to understand. Mr. Preston's security codes and secret account numbers and computer passwords, mixed up somehow with identification signals and control programs set up by the Master Builders to direct Attack Command.

His head ached. He couldn't remember anything. Not clearly. Yet somehow he felt a lot better about everything. Because now he wouldn't have to get across the canyon and steal feedstocks and try to get them back to the ship before the monsoons came.

Relaxed, he went back to sleep.

Golden sunlight woke him, now with strength enough to stand. Somehow not surprised, he found the flyer waiting on the ledge beside him. The same trim jet-powered craft that had come out of the base to follow him. Somehow he knew enough to fly it now, though most of its mechanism was still as enigmatic as the disk itself.

The mass inverter that loaded ordinary water into a reversed gravity well to make a gravitic mirror—that didn't fit the physics he knew, though he thought it might explain the motion of the disk. Other items he understood. The laser injectors that drove the fusion power unit, the airfoils and the flight control system, the tiny jet engines that burned hydrocarbon fuel—old Galen Ulver, working with the craftsmen of some other world, might have been the design engineer.

He wasn't certain whether the disk had actually been bluffed, yet he saw no other reason for it to leave him the flyer and its fuel. Five metric tons of volatile liquid hydrocarbons, more than the seedship could use for translation back into human tissue, the weight precisely compensated by five tons of lift from that perplexing mirror effect. All he had to do was spill enough of the uninverted water ballast to match his own weight and the flyer would be afloat. With the monsoon rains only just begun, he could be back in time.

Score one more, he thought, for Rablon and Brink and all Megan's team, even little Ben Bannerjee, in their desperate game to keep mankind alive. Shivering a little, remembering the scanner's chill when you had to lie naked in it and the giddy sickness you always got from Tomislav's isotopic mix trickling out of the needle into your brain, he climbed into the cockpit.

FOUR

GENETIC MAL-FUNCTION

He flew fast and high, in haste to return to the seedship before the sun set. A long flight, 2,000 kilometers across cragged canyons and rust-red desert and monsoon storms, but his joy of victory made it brief.

"Defender to Ship." A hundred kilometers out, he tried to share his elation. "Defender reporting."

He paused to wait for its answer, the human in him yearning for the human ghost trapped in the ship's computer memory, for any glimpse of Megan Drake's lean loveliness or the hints of her voice that often warmed its swift, synthetic speech.

No reply. Apprehension stabbed him. Had the monsoon come too soon? Had water already seeped inside the wounded hull, drowning the fragile computer and killing that beloved ghost?

"Defender to Ship." Undismayed, the machine in him tried again. "Reporting acquisition of aircraft fueled with hydrocarbons chemically similar to lost feedstocks. Analysis shows them fully adequate as carbon source for retranslation into organic tissue. Ship's mission can now continue."

Megan's image alive in his mind, the human in him wanted to say more. Wanted her to share the toil and strain of his grueling desert trek and the human triumph of his return. Wanted her gratitude and admiration now. But the computer in him always overruled such impulses, which, after all, were only minor chance malfunctions.

He said no more. Listening again, he heard no response.

The range, no doubt, was still too great, his feeble signals too completely muffled by the airframe around him. Gliding down now toward the sun-gilded towers of monsoon cumulus, he imaged the landing site.

The cliff-rimmed cup, the scowling scarps of black thorn jungle, the level swale below them. He dived through a bright cloud-wall into gloomy chaos. Convection battered him, too savage for his little skill. Sun power cut off, his golden frame sagged against the controls like an unplugged machine. Awareness flickered and with it all his eager human shards of memory and feeling, dimmed like candles in the wind.

He lost the ship's location.

Yet he clung to himself, striving to make the most of his diminished energy. Adjusting, limiting every motion, he fought though a wild updraft and dived again, down out of the dense cloud-roof that lay upon the cliffs. In clear air, he searched the rain-hazed hollow.

Already flooding. A mud-red torrent foamed down from the canyon above it, and a broad yellow lake was rising from below. Rising fast, toward where he had left the ship, its dead rockets buried in the swamp, the battered hull leaning crazily. He couldn't find it.

The human seed—

He reeled with human panic, but the machine in him was still efficient. His eyes went telescopic to scan the landing point again. Soon he found the toy-sized craft. It had fallen over since he left, and it lay too near that sudden yellow sea.

"Defender to Ship." Overwhelmed by the absurd futility of all their toil and pain, he felt a shock at his own computer's crisp, unfeeling precision. "Aboard aircraft coming in to land."

"Which Defender?"

Too long delayed, that brittle crackle held no hint of Megan, and the question dazed the human shards inside him.

"There is only one Defender."

Another endless instant, then the same swift, inhuman twang.

"Correction: you are Defender One. Information: when you failed to report or return from search for replacement feedstocks, we programed the production of two additional service units. That effort has overloaded all facilities, depleting emergency feedstocks carried for Defender reproduction, but Defender Two has been safely born. Successful birth of Defender Three not yet certain—"

"I didn't—didn't know this was possible—" He felt faint and shivery with more human emotion than he could handle. "Where is Defender Two?"

"Two has flown to the south coast to obtain replacement carbon-rich feedstocks for the retranslators. It has reported the discovery of native plants yielding high-grade oils that will fit our needs—"

"I have feedstocks aboard. The jet fuel—"

"We do not require them." The metallic jangle cut him off. "Defender Two has reported analysis of oils now in stock or transit. They answer all requirements, and we are already adapting assembler programs to utilize them."

"Have we time—"

Stunned, he had almost forgotten the flyer. Caught in a sudden squall, it pitched and veered, swept toward the cliffs that rimmed the upper canyon. He fought to save it, feeling too feeble and slow at the controls.

"Flood problem resolved." The toneless staccato came from far away. "Defender Two has lightened seedship by removal of useless fusion engines and other equipment now unneeded, sealing hull with welded waste metal. We can be floated now to a secure location above high water, where translator supplies are being stored."

In command again, the machine in him wheeled the little craft safely away from the mist-hidden cliffs and glided down through gray skirts of rain. Dropping the intake hose to suck up ballast water, he landed near the ship.

Back safe—but his human elation had been shattered. Clambering heavily out of the cockpit, he stood swaying giddily, ankle deep in weeds and mud. His skin tingled to the manifold odors of Mansphere: the rankness of the drowning weeds, the swamp's dank reek, a faint foul taint of the dead thorn jungle, washed down on the floods. Mixed with stranger scents, hints of ominous enigma. His dimmed perceptions were overloaded.

"Defender—Defender One to Ship." Even his own computer signal had become uncertain. "Reporting for duty."

"No duty now required." The answer staggered him

again. "Defenders Two and Three will be more efficient units, redesigned for service under conditions prevailing here. We compute no present need for service from Defender One."

"I exist—"

Voice and strength and mind were fading with the light until all he knew was the stunning jolt of loss and a merciless craving for energy.

"I exist to serve—"

"No service needed."

"There will be need—"

"Information for Defender One." The ship's computer cut him off. "Change of service status, active to standby, effective now, duration indefinite."

"But, please—"

"Ship to Defender One. Production of Unit Three requires all available capacities. Communication terminated."

Drained of everything, he stumbled to the seedship and fell across his birthcell in its narrow nose. The slit was closed. Scrabbling along the narrow seam, he found the bulge of the opener, hammered on it with a feeble fist.

"Ship to Defender One." The quick synthetic voice rang cold as the driving rain. "Information: production chamber is now occupied by third service unit, which is not yet ready to emerge. Umbilical unavailable to you."

He slid down into the mud—

He saw Crowler walking ahead of him off the plane and hailed him inside the terminal.

"Judge!" Once a county judge, Crowler still enjoyed the title. "Wait up! I didn't see you."

"Marty!" Crowler came grinning back to meet him and gripped his hand too hard. "I got on at Atlanta. First class, of course."

"A coincidence." He had never really liked Crowler, but he tried to smile. "I've been on a consultation trip to work with your engineers up in New Hampshire, but I wasn't expecting to see you back here."

"You whiz kids!" Crowler's grin widened, more tolerant than deferential. "I'm just a country lawyer. Your gene synthesizer—" He shrugged its wonder away. "Just a black box to me."

"A steady-flow multistage process." Defensively, he

began describing it as they walked toward the baggage claim area. "Completely automated. We meter the purified feedstocks through computer-regulated jets into a controlled flow of biocatalytic silicones. That first stage assembles sugars and phosphates and bases to form mononucleotides. The genetic codes are read in through a laser system that links the nucleotides into longer and longer chains, in stage after stage, till we get the famous double helix of DNA. We can install any natural gene we have in computer memory, or any new one you care to invent—"

"My own genes will do me." Crowler hadn't really listened. A football quarterback, still athletic, he was half contemptuous of anything academic. "The legal end is all I want to know about. I've come down to meet with the university regents. Just to make sure they don't intend to claim an interest in your patents."

"No problem. You wrote the waiver clauses into my employment contract."

"We don't take chances. I'm here to make certain you're sitting in the catbird seat." Too genially, Crowler clapped his shoulder. "Never worry, Marty. GEECO's going to make a fortune for you."

"Jayna would love that."

"I imagine she would." Crowler's overhearty voice had fallen oddly. "I'm renting a car, by the way, if you want a ride to the campus."

"Thanks, but Jayna's driving out to meet me." He found himself adding, almost against his will, "She'd love to see you. Maybe we can meet for dinner?"

She liked Crowler. The big lawyer had been here at Kingsmill half a dozen times this semester, first persuading him that it wouldn't be unethical to divert his computer science into commercial genetic engineering, then negotiating all the contracts. A cofounder of GEECO, rich with Texas oil, Crowler had taken them both to a game at the Astrodome and a weekend party at his Houston mansion, a rather wild affair that she had enjoyed somewhat too well.

He felt relieved when Crowler shook his head.

"Wish we could. But I've got to make an early-evening flight. To join friends for a South Sea cruise."

Crowler's luggage came off first. Expensive new-smelling leather in brown canvas covers. It was sitting outside a phone booth when he carried his own battered bag to the exit ramp to look for Jayna's maroon convertible. She wasn't there. He waited ten minutes and decided to call the house.

The leather luggage was still outside Crowler's booth when Marty dialed from the next one. The line was busy. Still busy, half a dozen times. He was outside the terminal, waiting for a taxi, when Crowler overtook him.

"Stood you up?" Crowler looked amused. "Let me drive you home."

He accepted. Crowler drove silently, preoccupied. Marty sat thinking uneasily of Jayna. Caught between academic demands and the press of his work for GEECO, he had been neglecting her, but now he could make it up. Money to redo the house and buy the Mercedes she wanted. Time for travel after commencement. To Japan, maybe, with a chance for him to meet the top computer people there.

He found her standing in the bedroom, staring at a gold-framed portrait. Their wedding picture—his heart paused when he saw what it was. Just out of the shower, she was rosily glowing and fragrant in a filmy robe. A tide of lust swept him toward her.

"Hold it, Marty. We're all through."

Gliding aside to evade his hungry arms, she sailed the picture at the wall. Glass jangled. She gestured at the bed, and he saw her cosmetic case and travel bag still open where she had packed them. He stood blinking at her, suddenly too weak and sick to speak.

"I didn't expect you to take it so hard." She shrugged, inspecting him with an air of almost casual detachment. "Bob's picking me up after his session with the regents. We're flying out to Fiji in the morning to join some of his Texas friends." Animation warmed her well-kept, smooth-tanned features. "They've got a yacht."

"Jay—Jayna—" His voice broke hoarsely. "Why—"

"I suppose you don't know why."

She paused to nod, frowning at him more critically.

"Because you've never understood me, Marty. Or anybody, really. Except your damned computers. I guess you think I ought to be sorry for you because you think you're hurt. But honestly, I'm not."

Her flash of hard resentment shocked him.

"I know you like to screw me. That's what you'll mostly

miss. Why you look so sorry for yourself. But the fact is, you never knew or cared for what you had."

Eyes defiant, she flung the gauzy robe open to show him all the pink perfection he would never have again. Feeling cold and almost nauseated, he stood staring at her hard red nipples till his throat ached and tears began to blind him. Because it simply wasn't true. He still loved her as he always had, more than he had ever loved anyone, in the only way he could—

He came painfully awake, lying face down in matted weeds and icy muck with rain drumming on his back. Martin Rablon no longer, he thought for a moment he was Don Brink again, sprawled in the muddy ditch where he had fallen beside the burning ammo truck in that Colombian jungle. He thought he had to get farther away before the mortar shells began exploding, but he felt too weak to move.

Able at last to lift his head, he found the seedship's patched and battered hull beside him in the mud. It looked too forlorn for its great mission—not that he had to care. The new Defenders would be assuming all his duties, and it didn't matter who he was.

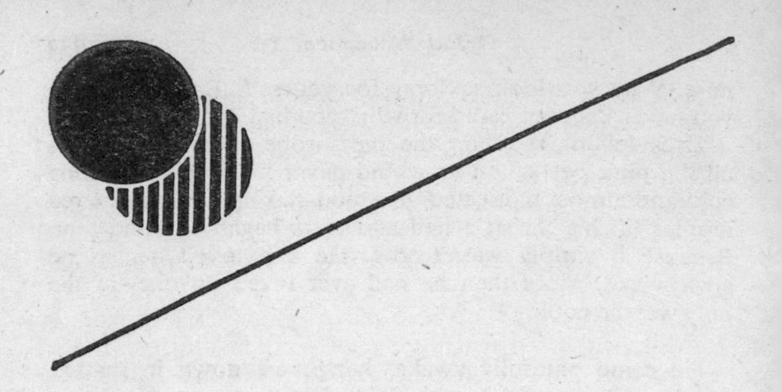

He found no heart to speak to the ship, and it didn't speak to him. Feeble in the monsoon gloom even after full day came, he had to scratch and claw at the worn hull to pull himself erect. Beyond it, he saw a little pile of rusting metal. The ruined Ulver engines Defender Two had discarded, with their laser gear and pumps and pipes and cables.

Junk.

Swaying weakly in the rain, he shook his head and turned away. For that was what he was. Standby status, duration indefinite. Because the ship no longer needed him. The machine in him dead, the human side still sick with Rablon's dazed desolation.

But he found the flyer when he turned. Still his to use unless the ship required it. Its lean gray lines revived human hope, human wonder and imagination. If he wasn't wanted here, it could carry him to explore more of Mansphere, to grapple again with the planet's unsolved riddles.

In time, perhaps, what he found might earn him active status. For Defenders could be needed even after the new Adam and the new Eve came naked from the machine. Mansphere would be no Eden. Instead, it was more the cursed ground outside, gone to thorns and thistles. Literal thorns in the jungle. The curse just as real, and deadlier. The robots he had met Satanic enough, conquerors of the planet once and waiting now for the coming of their builders and masters.

He had bluffed the robot once. Or had he? Leaving the

flyer for him, with fuel enough to serve as the feedstock he had been demanding, they had stopped far short of recognizing him as one of their Master Builders. What now? Would they allow the new human colony to live? Or act to wipe it out as ruthlessly as they must have exterminated the race whose relics he had found? What if the actual Master Builders really did arrive, thirty thousand years delayed?

Any answers he could discover might still benefit the mission. At that thought, the machine inside him moved again, and his battered human spirit lifted. Alive once more, he had to think of energy. His eyes returned to that rusting junk.

To unused bits of power cable. Not so thick as his lost umbilical but maybe thick enough. Splashing through the muck, he gathered the scraps he could find. Perhaps thirty meters altogether. He stumbled with them back into the cockpit, out of the rain.

Slow and clumsy in the gloom, he spliced and welded them into a single cord and shaped a terminal to fit the scar that was his navel. Recalling things he hadn't known he knew, learned perhaps while he had lain in unconscious contact with the alien disk-thing, he opened a hatch in the deck to wire himself to the flyer's generator.

The shock knocked him out.

For a moment, he was Don Brink. A green kid again, his first time in the ring, billed as the Mystery Mauler in that stinking little Tijuana arena. Set up for a knockout before he ever learned how to fight, he saw Bitterman's shills making bets they would never pay on him to win, setting up the suckers to be taken. Half blind with the blood in his eyes, he reeled through four savage rounds before he got the killer punch—

In another moment, or what seemed like one, his body-machine had adjusted itself to the unfamiliar current. He hauled himself off the deck, feeling good again. When he looked out of the cockpit, even the sky seemed brighter. In fact, it was. The rain had stopped while he was out. He saw blue sky and a shaft of golden sun.

"Defender calling!"

Megan's voice, more human than he had ever hoped to hear it.

"Defender Two to Ship. Returning with oil nuts from

the south coast. Will drop them at the upriver production site."

If the ship replied, he didn't hear. Looking in the direction of the signal, he found a bright diamond flake flying down that shaft of sunlight. His eyes went telescopic, and he saw her.

Megan, winged!

Flowerlike, the first gorgeous bloom of the manseed here. Nude and beautiful, her perfect body brightly metallic. The wings looked perilously fragile, but they were lovely. Long and trimly tapered, golden veined, shimmering in the sunlight with a flow of flashing color, their mechanism not entirely clear, though he could see that her own hands and feet controlled them, fitting into grips and stirrups.

The oil nuts were slick brown egg-shapes the size of coconuts, carried in a net on her back. Though they must have made a heavy load, she was gliding easily, the rainbow wings hardly moving. He followed her up the flooding river, lost her behind a jutting cliff.

He sat watching, dazed by all he hadn't known and wounded with an unwilling envy, until he saw her soaring back out of that cloud-shadowed canyon into dazzling sun. Gliding low above the yellow foam of the rapids, she tipped the brilliant wings to pause and hover for an instant over the ship before she lit on its tapered nose.

Megan! Transformed into a golden goddess, crystal winged. Not thirty meters from him. Quivering, only half believing, he watched her step from the stirrups, watched the wings fold and roll themselves into a trim double backpack.

She stood looking at his flyer with a bewitching frown of wonder. Overwhelmed with feeling, he could only stare back at her, tangled scraps of memory whirling through his mind. Broken moments of eagerness and aching pain, when Brink and Rablon and the rest had loved or lusted for her a million years ago.

None of them had ever seen her naked, not that he knew, or so utterly lovely. This gilded vision showed him all of Megan as she must have been, full breasted and complete. The lean, high-cheeked features and all her flowing grace. Even the golden eyes held a glint of Megan's green.

They found him.

"Don!" Megan's voice, grown even more musical, startled and delighted, calling him by Don Brink's name. "A dream I never hoped to see—"

She jumped toward him off the ship. Scrambling out of the flyer, he splashed through the muck to meet her. She was in his arms. Alive—more alive than he was. Bare, hot and passionate against him, her searching mouth to his.

"I've been so lonely, Don. So terribly alone—" Luminous with joy, she drew back to look at him. " 'Guess now who holds thee?' " Softly quoting the lines, she shivered. " 'Not Death, but Love.' "

Thirstily, desperately, she crushed him back against her, but then she must have sensed his agony. "Don?" Her rapture sank into a sea of terror. "What's wrong, Don?"

Cold and quivering, he pushed her back to let her see his naked crotch.

"Oh—Oh, no!" Her body grew rigid against him. "I'm so sorry for you, Don. So terribly sorry."

He felt her shaking as if with human sobs.

"What—What happened to you?"

"Nothing—" His own voice broke. "Except—except that I'm a Defender. Designed to guard and serve the mission. Not for sex."

"So—so am I—" Her trembling whisper sank, but she shook her head in hot denial. "But I remember when I was Megan—a lot of her got into the computer, the same way so much of Don got into you. Her love for you—and all the terror and the pain she was trying to escape with the seedship project.

"Oh, Don—"

She clung hard against him, velvet and agony, till he moved to ease the clumsy coil of his power cord between them.

"A horrible joke." A bitter little laugh. "Fate has played such dreadful jokes on both of us. When I woke up here in Eden, remembering how we loved each other—how emptily—how we died without each other a million years ago, I thought of Emily Dickinson."

Her voice fell again, whispering: " 'Because I could not stop for Death, He kindly stopped for me; the carriage held but just ourselves and Immortality—' "

She shivered in his arms. Aching for her, for both of them, he wanted to console her.

"We're still Defenders." His own voice seemed unsteady. "With our work—our work still to do. That's what we were made for. The way we feel—feel about each other—it's all an accident."

"A dreadful, dreadful accident."

A lead-colored cloud-roof had rolled back across the cliffs. In a sudden gust, cold raindrops pelted them. He nodded at the flyer. Wordless, she climbed ahead of him into the cockpit. At last, with less emotion, they talked again.

" 'There must be guests in Eden—all the rooms are full.' " Her tawny-green eyes resting sadly on him, she seemed to be remembering. "Egan loved poetry—I guess I never told you. We used to read it aloud. Sad, romantic stuff about love and death. We wrote poems to each other. Mine were pretty bad, but some of his were wonderful. I wanted him to publish them, but he said they were just for me."

Her eyes caressed his face.

" 'How do I love thee?' " she murmured. " 'Let me count the ways.' " She reached as if to touch him, but her hand fell back lifeless against her shining thigh. "I never forgot you, Don," she whispered wistfully. "The way you were the day I found you in Acapulco. Your knobby thornwood cane. Your knee still in that awful cast. You looked old. Old as Uncle Luther when he died. Sick as poor little Ben. And you were so terribly down—I could tell by the look in your eyes and the shave you needed.

"But I loved you, Don. I've always loved you, from that very day."

Her hand caught his. Golden, warmer and stronger, maybe tapered a little more gracefully than he remembered Megan's, yet tremulous with entirely human feeling.

"I don't quite know why. Because I knew what you were—"

"A professional killer." He grinned at her wryly. "Once you called me that."

"Soldier." Her hair was fine golden wire, very short, worn in Megan's way. Gently reproving, she shook her head in a way it wrenched him to recall. "I hated killing—or thought I did. Hated most of the causes you said you'd fought for. But I couldn't help admiring you when I got to know you. The cool way you looked at everything, ready to battle anybody. And—and all you are. Somehow you woke feelings I didn't know I had—"

"You woke a lot of feelings in me." Ruefully, he squeezed her hand. "Not that I could put them into poetry. Or that you ever let me do much about them."

"I know." Somberly, she smiled. "I watched you change, Don. The moment we met, that dreadful scowl turned to a grin. You looked brave again and twenty years younger. I knew what you wanted before you ever hinted. Because I wanted it, too."

"You always put me off."

"You thought I was a fool." Her face tight with pain, she glanced down at his sexless nakedness and very quickly away. "Now I know I was. But then—" Her fingers gripped harder. "I couldn't help what I was—the part of me that didn't get into the computer."

"The part—the part that put us here." He tried to smooth his voice. "So I guess we ought to be grateful. Wardian used to say it was your misdirected or maybe redirected sex drive that kept driving you to get the seed-ships engineered and built and launched." He added, "We all talked about it, because I think we all wanted you."

Frowning thoughtfully, she nodded.

"The notion would have shocked me then. But I knew—and I suffered for you, Don. Suffered for myself. For all I couldn't help." Her arm slid gently around him, and she seemed to sigh. "I'd grown up—grown up wounded. Egan went to shrinks and wanted me to. He said we'd been too close just because we had nobody else. I don't know. I did miss him dreadfully when he was killed. Until I found the project and the six—"

"Six?"

"The men with me." She leaned to scan his face. "With me in you." The gold-green eyes turned sad. "And poor, poor Ben. Ben Bannerjee. Gone because we couldn't pick him up. Never well enough for the scanner, but he—" He felt her tremble. "He's alive in us still. If we gave the mind, Ben gave the soul."

She was silent for a time, staring through the gray rain-veils at the cliffs that rimmed the restless lake.

"I loved him, Don. And all the rest of you. Even Marty

Rablon. An egotist. Brilliant with computers but never able to show how much he cared for anybody. Marty needed me."

A wistful smile touched her face.

"And Galen. Poor old Galen Ulver. Could have been my grandfather. Dying, really, when I found him because his dream of space was dead. He loved me—most of all for reviving the dream. Enough to keep him enduring those scanner isotopes in his brain."

The smile gone, she frowned into the rain.

"Ivan was harder to reach because he cared more for the project than for any of us. Obsessed, of course, with guilt for his wife and staying with us as a sort of atonement. Creating life for this new world because he couldn't save it there.

"Hard to love, but my heart ached for him."

He waited for her to go on, but she sat silent, staring at the silt-yellowed flood climbing toward the ship.

" 'So there was a Deluge,' " she murmured, " 'and swept the World away.' "

"That's most of us," he prompted her. "But what about Wardian?"

"Captain Mack?" Her eyes widened, startled. "I don't see Captain Mack in you."

"I don't recall much of him."

"I might—might have loved Mack Wardian." She looked off into the storm. "A lot of women did. Because he was the image of any girl's hero. Lean and handsome in that yellow jumpsuit, born with wit and social grace Marty never learned. He shared what I felt for Emily, at least enough to quote her once.

> I taste a liquor never brewed
> From tankards scooped in pearl.
> Not all the Frankfort berries
> Yield such an alcohol."

Her voice turned wistful.

"Yet he never let me close. I never quite knew why because he was always charming to me and loyal to the project—he sacrificed as much as anybody to get us into space."

A moody pause.

"Not that any of it matters now." Her voice seemed forlorn and far away. "Not with all of them—all of us—dead so terribly long ago. Just thinking of them now—" She shivered. "It makes me so dreadfully sad. Sadder than I ever was, even back with Egan.

"Not very cheering." He moved a little from her on the seat, easing the awkward pull of his umbilical and trying to break himself out of her gloom. "But they were all troubled people trapped on an unhappy world, spending their lives—the best of their lives—to give mankind this new chance. We're here to finish what they started. With help, I hope, from another Defender when it's born—"

"Defender Three isn't an it." Cheered more than he expected, she was smiling at the rust-washed seedship. "We've already been in touch. Three is nearly grown, and mostly Captain Mack."

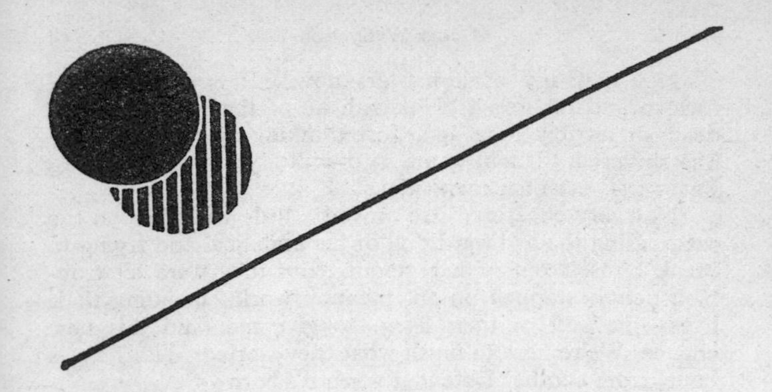

Megan's office in the Albuquerque lab.

"We've established the technology." Rablon, as usual, too masterful. "Automatic gene transcription into computer code. Automatic retranslation, out of that and back into new human beings, on planets where the seeds take root. What we need from you is know-how to help us get them sowed."

Marty Rablon. Tall and lean and sallow skinned, with black-rimmed glasses and too much black hair. A genius, no doubt, but unduly arrogant about it and generally hard for him to take.

"A fabulous project if you can pull it off."

He turned to Megan. She was easier to look at and the reason he was here. Fresh and young and lovely, as intense as Rablon about the project but fetchingly modest about her own brains and beauty, maybe unaware of how desperately she tempted him. Probably a virgin and off limits to him.

"We've come a long way, captain." Warming to her eager smile, he wondered for a moment if she might lead him to break the code. "But now we need you terribly."

"There are other astronauts."

"We've checked them out, and we always come back to you."

He frowned uneasily at Rablon. "You want to transcribe my mind?"

"Impossible," Rablon rapped, as if that had been an idiot question. "All we want is a computer transcription of your space skills. For all those wild press reports, we can't read minds. The scanner works indirectly, through computer analysis of the input from half a hundred channels—everything from brain waves and unconscious muscle tensions to isotopic radiation modified by synaptic biochemistry."

Wardian looked again at Megan. "How long does all this take?"

"Too long." Rablon spoke for her too promptly. "Several weeks to get the computer pickups tuned to the individual brain. Sometimes longer, because the process isn't perfect. Months more to analyze and edit what we need and filter out what we don't." Resting on Megan, his owlish eyes seemed possessive. "Dr. Drake was our first victim; she has spent a day or so of every week in the scanner for nearly two years."

"A long ordeal." She looked both apologetic and enchanting. "Minds are tricky to transcribe, and the scanner isn't altogether automatic. We'll need you here at least a few months."

"I'm sorry." Seeing the hurt on her revealing face, he hated to say it. "But I simply don't have that kind of time."

"If it's money, Raven Foundation has it."

"It isn't." To ease her disappointment, he had to say more. "I'm an astronomer-astronaut. Half my life, I lived for space. NASA gave me just one mission. One wonderful month in the orbital observatory. No funds in sight for anything more. I resigned to fly for Delta.

"Now I'm going after what looks like a better chance."

"Better?" Rablon seemed indignant. "Think about it, Wardian. What we offer you is a kind of immortality. Time enough for you—a selected part of you—to reach the stars."

"The thing I mean to do will more likely kill me." With a shrug for Rablon, he turned back to Megan. "You've heard of the Solar Sail? We hope to sail it out to Mars. Nothing official yet, but we're setting up an informal group. People from Nasa and the European Space Agency and even the Japanese. A six-year flight, out and there and back. The whole thing chancy, with long odds we never do get back. A ten-person crew, with landing craft and equipment for a surface station. I'm in line to be the senior scientist—if I quit Delta now and work full time with our planning group.

"With that coming up, the best I can do is wish you luck."

"Stay over, captain." Her urgency touched him. "At least tonight. We'll put you up here at the lab. Dr. Tomislav's flying in this afternoon. Talk to him and let Marty show you how the scanner works."

He agreed. Only partly because the concept of the seedship had taken hold of his imagination. Her own unconscious allure was stronger.

The scanner looked like a ten-million-dollar torture chamber when he saw it, and Rablon's brags about it turned him further off, but he did want to meet Tomislav, a Nobel prize winner for his epochal advances in genetic engineering. An aging man, overweight and haggard, breathless when he got to the lab.

Megan took them all to a Mexican restaurant for dinner. The *chile rellenos* were too hot for his taste, and Rablon lectured too long on the software interfaces between DNA and his micromolecular memory cubes. He was glad when Tomislav said he had to phone his wife and get some sleep.

Back at the lab, he and Megan sat a long time in her car. She talked about her twin brother, who had conceived the project, she said, to redeem his brief and tragic life. About the crippled Indian genius and her own Uncle Luther, who had been captured by the dream and passed it on to her.

Her light lilac scent seemed stronger in the car, and he felt half drunk with her unsuspected physical allure. Yet he didn't try to touch her. His code forgotten, he found his first respect for her mind and her ideals merging into something he had never felt for any woman. A passion so close to worship that he felt unworthy of her.

Lying a long time awake in the bare guest room, he reconsidered the style and the aim of his life and his plans for that possible Martian adventure. Set against the daring grandeur of the seedship project and his new adoration for her, that uncertain chance to die on Mars began to matter no more than his flying or his hang gliding or the casual sex the code had allowed him.

Next morning, he told her he was ready for the scanner.

* * *

She wanted to know where he had been.

"The ship said you left to look for feedstocks. Right after it landed. You never came back. That's why Three and I had to be programed."

Out in the rain, he hadn't noticed her odor, but now it filled the flyer's narrow cockpit. A fragrance new to him, though he thought it held a hint of Megan's lilac scent. Its exotic hothouse power was suddenly overwhelming. His whole body tingling to it, he felt a blaze of hopeless lust.

Sick and quivering with the agony of that, shrinking from her excruciating loveliness, he collected himself to tell what he had found on that long trek north. The ruined city seemed to astonish her.

"A human city?" Her green-gold eyes went wide. "How can that be?"

"Perhaps our seedship is the second one to get here."

"If so—" Even her frown was tormenting witchery. "What killed it?"

"Attack Command, the robot disk-thing told me."

"Robots? Here on Mansphere?"

"As I piece things together, they exterminated everything alive on the planet. They've been waiting all the ages since for whatever sent them."

The ship had told her about their encounter with the great orbital starcraft and its robot crew, but she seemed dazed by what he said.

"I've flown thousands of kilometers." She shook her head, reluctant to believe him. "Up the river. Down it to the coast. To the offshore islands where I found the oil nuts. I haven't seen any ruins. Or met any robots."

"You wouldn't expect many relics left. Geologic change must have buried nearly everything. The ruins I found, and the statue, were of some diamondlike synthetic stuff. Even it was mostly shattered, maybe by missiles from space. I found the crater."

Silent for a moment, she seemed convinced.

"Could that be why—why I never saw anything alive? Nothing even like insects." She bent toward him, shivering. "Do you think the robots killed everything?"

"I wish I knew."

"That will be our next duty now." She sat straighter, her voice grown firmer. "To find out if the robots are still a danger. To defend the ship against them if they are. We must learn what they did. What weapons they used—no missiles I can imagine would kill a whole planet and leave it habitable."

"I was thinking that." He shook his head, deadened again by bleak depression. "But the ship doesn't need me now, not since it programed new defenders to replace me."

"It will," she promised him. "When we report the situation. But it can't talk now. It's too busy with Three."

"I hope—hope it finds some duty for me." His voice quivered. "Though I don't know how to deal with the robots. I fought them on the starship, and I played a sort of game against the disk. To what I guess is a draw. But still I don't understand them."

"How'd you get the aircraft?"

"I claimed to be a Master Builder. One of the creatures the robots have been waiting for."

"And it believed you?"

"You never know. It never told me much. I think it tried to drain my brain while I was out, but it was gone when I woke. It did leave the flyer for me to find. Maybe just buying time to study us. Even if they do believe—"

He tried to look aside, to break the ache of her loveliness.

"They must still be watching us. Maybe from their orbital craft if they've been able to repair it. More likely using other agencies we don't know about. They'll learn too soon that I was lying. Whatever we decide to do—maybe raid their base—I think we ought to do it now."

"Not now." He couldn't look away. "Not till we have Three."

Eagerness alight in her gold-green eyes, she peered through the rain-haze to the lake and the tiny machine that had been their womb.

"He'll be here soon. Unless—"

Frowning, she turned again to him. For a moment, she was wholly Megan, with the same frown lines he recalled from times of trouble with the project.

"We're never quite—quite what we were programed to be." Even her tremulous whisper was Megan's. "Because of all the genetic malfunctions caused when that micrometer hit the master computer. The ship is afraid of a difficult birth."

Something startled her. Silent, listening, she shivered in distress and turned from him to climb out of the flyer.

"Megan? Is something wrong?"

When she didn't answer, he knew the ship must have called her on their private channel. He watched her splash out to it and scramble to its nose. Perching there, her back to the driving rain, she spread her crystal wings to shield the birthcell.

The narrow hull lay flat, rust-red now where the gold was gone. Yellow waves were already breaking around it, and the cliffs above them echoed the roar of falling water. The water was rising fast.

Watching her, he felt heart-wrenching pity. In spite of her gold-filmed body, her vivid wings, and her computer-generated brain, she was still terribly human, nakedly vulnerable.

"Megan? Can I help?"

She ignored him.

Her circuits were all busy, he supposed, with the problems of the ship and the dangers to Defender Three. He ached to aid her, but Defender One was no longer required. Sitting helpless in the cockpit, he could only watch her battle with the beating rain.

The day dragged forever, with no word from her.

He saw her wings sagging, saw their rainbow colors darkening into drab brown and gray. Her energy came, he knew, from the light the wings absorbed. Open wide to the sun, they worked superbly, but in the battering wind she couldn't spread them far. He called twice again, offering to let her have his own power cable, but she gave no sign that she received him.

Dusk fell, and the moonless dark. Seen by infrared, she became a crimson ghost huddled under the monsoon squalls. Dim crimson glints danced on the black waves around her. Her wings were lifeless now, plastered flat against the hull, and still the new Defender remained unborn.

Another night of endless waiting.

He sat by Olga's bed or stood beside her or sometimes paced the hospital room. The night before, he had injected her with his synthetic virus. He meant it to be benign; he had engineered it to repair her rare genetic defect. A secret, desperate medical experiment, made without informing her doctors because there had been no time for any normal testing and because she herself had begged him to try it.

It nearly killed her. The emergency staff called Schrad and Brickman back from their homes to bring her through the crisis. He felt certain from their faces that they knew what he had done, but they made no accusations. Restrained, he supposed, by their respect for him and by helpless sympathy. They knew she was terminal.

Her condition, late that second night, had finally stabilized. Reeling with fatigue, he stayed on with her, though Schrad wanted to put him to bed under sedation. Watching her, hoping for some delayed positive effect, he remembered how vibrantly alive she once had been.

Once Miss Schenectady.

They met at Union in freshman biology. Half smitten himself, the instructor introduced her to the class. Tall and straight, radiantly alive. She stood up, smiling and winking at some friend in the class but then blushing shyly, and he adored her instantly.

Hopelessly. Conscious of his accent and his ethnic origins and his lack of social aptitude, he could only envy the dapper instructor who somehow knew her. Yet, by an incredible lucky break, they were assigned to work together in the lab, dissecting a cat.

It made her sick. He couldn't help laughing when she upchucked into the sink. Furious and beautiful, she slapped at his face and grabbed her books and ran out of the lab. Afterward, amazingly, she forgave him. He did the dissecting, she kept the notes, and they lived together after the second semester of their senior year.

Now—when he saw the terrible flatness under the blanket, heard the slow, raw rasp of her unconscious breathing, saw her balding skeletal head with the oxygen tubes in the nostrils and the fixed rictus of pain on her shriveled, unconscious face—

The recollections were unendurable.

He stalked the empty corridors and came back to look at her again and yet again. No change. Never any change. He knew at last there never would be. Because the genetic damage already done could not be reversed. Even at the best, his virus could only prolong her agony. His work had come too late.

Too late for Olga, anyhow—

The infrared was fading into gray daylight before Defender Three was born. The rain had stopped, but the rapids still boomed down the canyon behind him, and the ship was half afloat in the muddy lake. Megan crept back from its nose, dragging her lifeless wings, and he saw the birth-slit gaping partly open, still crimson with the vital warmth she had been protecting.

The new Defender was a strange helpless-seeming thing at first, pale wings crushed close around its twitching limbs. He saw golden hands thrusting, grasping, parting the thin wing-tissues. Saw the golden head lifting—

Wardian!

Blinking into the light, cocking his head to listen to the thunder of the rapids, raising a wavering hand to shade his eyes, peering out across the lake to the black thorn jungle, finding the flyer on the shore and waving cheerily at him.

She had told him Three would be mostly Mack Wardian, yet he shivered at the likeness. All gold toned, but the arrogant nose was the same, the clean-featured athletic distinction, the eagerly appealing smile when he found Megan. The eyes, even, were flecked with Wardian's blue.

The sun rose clear. Feebly at first, clumsily wavering, the wings spread to drink its light. They stiffened swiftly, opened wider. Life began to flush them. Pale pastels brightened into patterned panes of sapphire and emerald and ruby framed between the darker ribs.

Aching with an unwilling envy, he watched the new Defender step from the birthcell to stand on the rusting hull. A golden god, diamond winged. The wings shifted, giving him a frontal view. Anguish stabbed him. Three was fully male, as magnificently male as the original human Wardian must have been.

Megan's wings had brightened, too, their drabness become rainbow wonder. She raised them high, shook the water off, tipped them to the sun. Perched now on the tail of the ship, she was a splendid human bird, golden glowing, luminous with joy.

She must have spoken to Wardian on some shielded channel, for the new Defender swung suddenly to find her. Shivering with electric delight, the two came very slowly together on the waist of the ship. He watched them kiss, hesitantly, gently, then lock hard together. He saw the umbilical come away from Wardian's belly and retract into the birthcell. The dark slit closed. And still they clung together, fused with a desperate fervor the programers could never have planned.

Clung forever, moving only to follow the sun with high-swept wings. Watching from the cockpit, he tried not to hate them, tried to remind himself that all their feelings, even his own savage bitterness as much as their burning passion, were only accidental hazards to their duty as Defenders. But the machine in him had been turned off, discarded. Wholly human, he felt wholly hopeless, abandoned and alone.

He tried to tell himself that he ought to share their joy. Though they might never know, he had made them what they were. If he had not replaced those damaged memory cubes in the ship's computer, Wardian would no doubt be as sexless as he was. Maybe Megan, too. The irony of that was a blade twisting in him, because he could not repair himself.

Could the ship reprogram him? Hopeful for an instant, he shook his head at the notion. If he asked, the ship's computer would merely remind him that sex was not included in the duties of a Defender. It would probably add that the making of Two and Three had used up those special feedstocks brought all the way from ancient Earth.

The new Defenders took a long time recharging, but at last they slipped apart to soar one by one off the ship and drop near him on the shore. The shimmering wings folded, rolled against their backs. Hand in hand, they walked toward the flyer.

Relieved, he slid out to meet them.

"Hullo, Brink." The golden man stepped ahead, speaking with Wardian's pleasantly precise and faintly British accent, smiling with Wardian's casual confidence. "Megan has been telling me about your adventure in search of replacement feedstocks."

Trying to seem happier than he was, he gripped the powerful half-metallic hand.

"You captured this machine?" Wardian swung with a grin of admiration to inspect it. "A novel sort of lift? I'm keen to look it over. You know, old boy, we Defenders have got a gorgeous mission here."

"I didn't know—" Flinching a little from Wardian's fleeting glance at his patched-together umbilical and his naked loins, he couldn't help recalling his own standby status. "I didn't know—didn't know about you and Megan."

"I believe the oil nuts she found will meet our needs." Wardian reached back to catch her hand and draw her to his side. "Though our best congratulations are certainly due you. Considering—"

Wardian caught himself but went on at once, his fluid tones grown too hearty.

"You did it, Don! A remarkable victory. Considering all your handicaps, it's no surprise that you had to leave so many things undone."

"At least—" Seeking escape from Megan's quivering pity, he turned to the lake and the half-drowned hull. "At least we have the feedstocks now. The mission can go on."

"In time." Wardian nodded. "Though actual production will have to wait. Megan has the ship sealed and trimmed to float. As soon as the flood crests, we can tow it up the canyon. Megan tells me she has cached a good supply of oil nuts there, on a bench where we can haul the ship above high water."

"Can I—" Urgency wrung him. "Will I be needed?"

"I hope you are." He felt Megan's anxiety for him. "I'll try to find a place for you.

"Don't sweat it, Don." Wardian dismissed his concern

almost casually. "We'll do whatever we can. But we've got more urgent problems calling for us now. The same ones that seemed to baffle you—not that we blame you for giving up what was impossible for you."

He swayed where he stood, feeling faintly ill but trying not to show it.

"Our first priority has to be learning what killed the planet. No point in producing people if they can't survive here."

He had to nod.

"Beyond that, we've got to check out your reports on those alien robots. We need to know a lot more about their origins and their history and the military base you say you saw. Specifically, we've got to verify that they actually accept us as their creators."

"They left the flyer for me," he said. "That's all I know."

"We'll soon learn more." Wardian smiled into the clearing sky. "Time to take off. For a look at the city you found and a search for whatever killed it. We hope to get back before the ship's afloat. You'll be standing by, of course, though, in case of something unexpected."

Megan came on to him after Wardian turned away. Her golden arms gathered him against her nude, unendurable splendor, and the hint of lilac in her scent was tearing agony.

"I'm sorry, Don." He knew the words were just for him. "So dreadfully sorry, because you know how terribly—terribly I loved you. 'Weaned from life and torn away in the morning of your day.' " She kissed him, pulled away, and drew him back again, quivering against him. "But you see—"

She turned in his arms, looking after Wardian. Bright head high, facing the lake, he had spread splendid wings. A forward leap and he lifted off the muddy beach.

"Chin up, old boy!" he shouted as he climbed. "Defenders don't despair!"

Clinging to Megan for one last bitter instant, he had to let her go. Her green-gold eyes were fixed on Wardian, as if she had forgotten him, and he heard her murmur, " 'Of all the souls that stand create, I have selected one.' "

Sadly, fixed in unwilling wonder, he followed them into the sky. Wardian seemed uncertain at first, and Megan hovered near, but soon they both were climbing strongly. Beyond the black-rimmed lake, where the wind struck the high red cliffs, they caught an updraft that let them soar into the sun.

They dwindled until his eyes went telescopic. He could see their eager faces then and sense their rapture. High and free, they danced together. Spinning, diving, darting close enough to kiss, whirling through games of pursuit and escape until she let Wardian capture her.

Dead inside, he looked away when they mated.

His father was a mining engineer, orginally British but a naturalized American. They lived in Montana the winter he was fourteen because his father was making a new survey for Canadians who wanted to reopen the old Silver Belle. Miss Krimkin was his teacher in the three-room Bell Butte school. She was blonde and beautiful, and he adored her.

Today was an icy February Friday, with a bitter north wind gusting down the canyon past the empty town, and he was afraid he would never see her again. His father had finished the survey, and they were leaving for Denver tomorrow.

He missed the bus on purpose after school and hiked three miles in the snow, down to Mercer's Mercantile. He had eleven dollars, with the ten from selling his skis, and he spent it all for a Valentine chocolate box.

The numbing dusk was thick before he got back. He was afraid Miss Krimkin would be gone, but her Chevy was still parked against the snowdrift outside the building. He saw Mr. Wranker's pickup over by the gym; he was the principal and the coach, and he liked to work out after school. Everybody else was gone.

Trembling and breathless, his heart pounding hard, he slipped into the old brick building. In spite of the cold, his hands were sweaty on the paper bag, and he didn't know what he could say to tell her how he felt. He stopped in the hall outside her room, afraid of what she would think.

But tomorrow—tomorrow would be too late.

He pushed inside. The air seemed oven hot, sharp with the sulphur smell of coal in the red-hot stove and rich with her exciting perfume. Two Coke bottles and a whiskey flask stood on her desk with the grade books and her bag, but her chair was empty. He heard her make a sort of gasping cry before he found her. She was lying on the floor by the upset coal scuttle, with Mr. Wranker half on top of her.

Staggered, he shrank back into the hall. He had always liked Mr. Wranker, who had given him his old skis when the first snows came and taught him how to use them, but now he felt numb, stunned by what he saw. He wondered for a moment if Mr. Wranker had raped her, though he didn't know much about rape. Then he heard them both giggling.

For what seemed a long time, he felt too weak and queasy to move or even think. At first, he couldn't understand. Then, looking back at the bottles on the desk, he remembered something his father told him when he wanted to know about his mother.

"Never trust a woman." His father's pale eyes had an odd, far-off look, and his voice seemed sad. "I guess you'll have to love 'em. They'll all make suckers of us, every bloody one, till they've got us where it hurts the most, and then they crucify us."

Suddenly, now, he felt terribly sorry for his father. Now he understood the way they lived, with no real home, and he knew this was a lesson he would not forget. When he heard Miss Krimkin shriek with ecstasy, he pulled the door very carefully shut behind him and tiptoed back down the hall.

Outside, he threw the chocolates into the snow.

When he brought himself to look again for Wardian and Megan, they were gone beyond the cliffs. Gone on to learn how Mansphere had been murdered—and no doubt to make skyborne love again. He watched all day, but they did not return. Before sunset, the monsoon clouds rolled in again, and blustery squalls swept back across the lake.

"Defender One. Defender One to Ship."

He hardly dared expect an answer because he had been thrown away, but he was afraid for the ship. The muddy waves were higher now, washing against the hull, now and then breaking over it. He wondered if it would really float.

He received no answer.

"Defender One to Ship." Desperate, he tried again. "Do you have contact with Two and Three?"

"Ship to Defender One." Its brittle, synthetic voice spoke at last, now without that haunting trace of Megan. "Contact with Defenders Two and Three lost when they flew beyond radio range. We are standing by on all channels. We anticipate their early return."

"Can I—can I serve? At least till they return?"

"You remain on standby status. No service now required."

The gray dusk faded into infrared. All night the rain drummed on the flyer and raked the dark lake. The ship lay deep in it now, flickering dimly crimson through the waves that broke across it. All night he watched it from the flyer, listening to the unending thunder of water in the canyon, longing for something he could do.

"Defender One to Ship." He called again at dawn. "Do you have contact?"

"No contact."

"I'm taking off," he said. "To attempt radio contact with Two and Three. Climbing out of the valley into line-of-sight range of a wide area. My signal should reach far beyond the ruins they planned to explore."

"Ship to One. Confirming reassignment to active status. Contact with lost Defenders rated urgent. You will attempt to reach them."

Active status!

Human delight blazed for an instant, like a skyrocket exploding inside him, but his mechanical half had no time for joy. Already busy, it was moving to dump ballast for the flight. He took off across the flood water, which now spread south and east in a vast brown sheet until it spilled through a gap in an oddly straight, far-off hill. The hill, it struck him, must once have been a dam, built to hold a great artificial lake now filled by long millennia of silt.

Wheeling away from a squall, he turned back into the canyon. Just inside its cliffs, he found the shelving bench where Megan had planned to take the ship. A broad ledge, still half a dozen meters above the lake level, sparsely overgrown with something green. Searching with his telescopic vision, he found her preparations unexpectedly complete, with tons of oil nuts neatly stacked against the cliff. A small machine stood beside them: a simple press, neatly built, ready to extract oil for the ship.

Stuff for translation into the new mankind—if the new Defenders got back in time to rescue the ship and finish its ancient mission. He soared over yellow foam and booming chaos, climbing into the clouds and out again at last, into the sun's hot dazzle.

East and south as far as his vision reached, the floor of cloud lay luminous and level. North and west, all along the rim of the high plateau, the cumulus towers were blue ice and white fire, with that shattered city lost somewhere beneath them and the dead thorn jungle and all the riddles of Mansphere.

"Defender One calling!" Though the flyer's frame interfered, he tried to beam his signal toward those hidden ruins. "Calling Two and Three. Urgent. Please acknowledge."

Listening, he heard nothing.

"Don Brink." The human cry escaped his computer controls. "Calling Megan! Calling Captain Mack! Answer if you can!"

Again he tried, still again, until he feared there would never be an answer.

"Don to Megan—"

"Ship to Defender One." The faint robotic voice cut him off. "You will return at once. Ship afloat and in danger. Defender service now required."

Service now required!

He couldn't help a thrill of human satisfaction, though it came with a pang of human guilt, and it left him still anxious for the new Defenders. They were lost, their fate unguessable, and he felt unworthy to replace them. Lacking their wings, their special adaptations, he was ill prepared for anything. Yet—and in spite of himself he shivered with elation—he was no longer junk; the mission was again his to defend.

The ship was gone when he reached the lakeshore, but he was able to follow its signal to where it drifted like a sodden log, already half a kilometer closer to that narrow spillway. Hovering gingerly over the ship, he nudged it with the flyers' landing skids, rotating it to find the rusted fittings where the auxiliary drive-mass droptanks had been attached to help it lift from Earth-orbit to solar escape velocity before they were jettisoned.

He reeled out the ballast hose and took on water enough to settle the flyer very gently on the unstable hull. Scrambling down, he used loops of his umbilical to lash the seedship's fittings to the aircraft's skids. When the rain paused, he drew power through the umbilical to weld them fast. Back in the cockpit, he towed the ship out of the current, toward the head of the lake.

Gray rain was sweeping in by then, but he didn't really care. The machine in him was running again, with a programed function to perform, and he was not unhappy. Hauling the ship out of the water would have to wait until the flood had crested, but good feedstocks were ready for the translators now and there would be time enough to process them into mankind for Mansphere.

Almost happy now, he remembered a fiesta. Blazing sun and blaring bands and the overpowering cologne of the general who had hired him. Adrift in a golden haze of captured Cutty Sark, he was riding in an armored limousine with the reeking general and half a dozen tipsily giggling *señoritas*, following a captured *Izquierdista* tank from the captured presidential palace to the cathedral, where a captured Marxist bishop was waiting to bless the counterrevolution. Crowds were cheering *El Bolivar Nuevo,* who was the general, and *el commandante Breenki*—

A million years ago.

FIVE

HUMAN HARVEST

He waited to aid the first man's birth.

The deluge had ebbed, and the seedship stood where he had hauled it from the water. He had found driftwood to build a rough stair that climbed the scarred hull to a little platform outside the birthcell in its narrow nose.

Standing there, he heard the first muffled thumps inside, saw the dark slit crack. It spread slowly wider. The odors of birth poured out, strong and strange. The sunlight struck pink human flesh, uncertainly stirring.

He tried to help, but a black-haired fist struck his hand away. Groping blindly at first for the rim of the spreading slit, the new man leaned to peer out. Fully mature and fully male, eyes narrowed against the light, squinting sharply at him.

"Welcome," the Defender whispered. "Welcome to Mansphere—if you understand me?"

"I am Egan Drake. Who—" A rusty squeak, yet somehow half familiar. "Who are you?"

Egan Drake!

The name triggered an avalanche of shattered recollection from a million years ago, broken moments of human purpose and human pain. He yearned again for Megan Drake, that older Egan's sister, longed even for her tantalizing ghost, caught in the computer until it emerged in the gem-winged splendor of Defender Two. Hope thrilled through him that another Megan might be born. Hope instantly erased because she wouldn't be for him.

Swept by that tide of mixed emotion, his own computer

mind was nearly overwhelmed. Swaying on the little platform, clutching the rail, he leaned to look again into the newborn man's wet, bewildered face.

In the green-flecked eyes, he saw a hint of Megan that wrenched him again with aches of love and loss he thought he had forgotten. The stubborn chin was a haunting riddle until the hoarse rasp of that once-familiar voice recalled it from Don Brink's mirror.

"Who are you?"

"The Defender." Engineered for human smiles, for contact by sound as well as radio, he tried to ease the man's half-hostile puzzlement. "Defender One. I am to assist you."

Unsteady at first, the man emerged. Naked but burdened with a heavy backpack that looked like pliant brown leather. Blood from his navel was clotted and drying on his black-haired belly. Still gripping the birthcell's lip, he frowned around him warily.

At the soaring cliffs and the great waterfall roaring over them. At the wet red silt the flood had left on all the slopes toward the mud-yellow lake that still filled the lower canyon. At the little gravitic flyer sitting anchored to a higher ledge. His nose wrinkled at the reeking drift the flood had left, rotting stuff washed down from the thorn jungle upriver.

"Where—" The man's troubled eyes came back to him. "What is this place?"

"You can speak," he said. "Don't you remember?"

"Remember?" The man frowned and shook his head. His hair fell long, black and wet and glistening. "Remember what?"

"What we are."

"Words—I do get words." The man nodded uncertainly, staring off into the mist that billowed from below the waterfall. "A voice—a woman's voice—saying I would wake up in Eden." He goggled at the Defender. "Is this place Eden?"

"Not yet," he said. "It can be a garden. Or whatever you make it. We're on a planet named Mansphere. It will be your home. Your children's home. A new home for mankind."

"I—I have no children."

"I hope you will have."

"How I—" The man squinted again into the dark birth-cell and swung back to challenge him. "I don't remember much. Nothing I can understand. I want to know what you are and how we got here."

"That's the seedship." He gestured at the scarred hull behind them. "Launched from old Earth, when men were in trouble there. Carrying human genes and human culture in computer code and designed to transplant mankind to any planet it might reach. Damaged by a micrometeor in space and adrift a million years. But down safe at last, the retranslators working."

"Manseed—" the man whispered. "I was—told about it." He turned to frown at the flyer. "But that—what's that thing?"

"An aircraft. Jet propelled, with lift from a gravity mirror."

"Gravity mirror?" A blank headshake. "What's that?"

"An effect created by using fusion power to invert the mass of common water. I don't quite know how."

"Where—" The man blinked. "It is not from old Earth."

"Something unexpected. We found robots here. They conquered the planet thirty thousand Terran years ago. Waiting since at their base for the creatures that built them. I got the machine from them. When I told them I was one of their builders."

"So they are friends?"

"Robots." He shook his head. "Still pretty much a mystery."

"Then we're in danger?"

"Could be." He shrugged. "They know where we landed, but that site has been flooded. I moved us with the flier. If they come looking for us, they may decide we drowned. Perhaps they'll never look."

"So—" The man squinted over the high red cliffs into the empty sky. "What can we do?"

"Keep under cover. Carry on the plan to colonize Mansphere. All we can do." He shrugged again. "The plan begins with you. The first man here."

Grinning, groping for the elation the occasion seemed to call for, he reached to clap the man's muscular shoulder. "If this were Eden, you would be Adam."

"My name is Egan." The man shrank from his reaching

hand, eyes slitted to the sun and watchfully mistrustful. "I think you were first."

"I'm not a man."

Shivering a little under that coldly searching stare, he spread his golden hands, dropped them to touch the clumsy cable he had rigged to his navel.

"I'm an—an artifact." The word was hard to say. "More machine than human. Born of the ship the way you were but still really part of it. Call me its crew. Designed to maintain it and defend its mission."

"Defender? Defender?" Muttering that, the man scowled at his golden form, with a stabbing glance at the empty bareness where genitals might have been. "I begin to remember what the woman said you Defenders would be."

The curly black beard was still shining wet, strong with the reek of birth. Beneath it, the broad pink face turned grimmer.

"Better than I am. Taller and stronger. Live statues of shining gold. Some of you winged. With senses and powers no man ever had. You never need to sleep or rest or even eat."

"Because we're more than half machines." Trying to disarm the man, he spoke about his nature and his limits. "I'm running now on electric power. It comes through this." He touched the umbilical. "From this battery pack I borrowed out of the flyer. Without it, I'd stop."

"You might stop." A sardonic accusation. "I'd starve."

"You can grow food—"

"Or die." The man's fists knotted. "Unless I sweat to grow food out of the mud. The woman's voice told me that."

"Surprised?" Mildly, he appealed to reason. "Human beings have to eat. They always had to eat. From all I recall, you'll enjoy it. You'll find seed in your pack and food to last till you get your first harvest. Later, the ship can make other things you'll need. The pack itself should come apart to make garments for you now."

"Mud!" The man scowled down at the silt the deluge had left. "Stinking mud."

"Soil. Rich enough—we've analyzed it. The seed you have has been edited to thrive in it. Later, after your fellow human beings have all been born, the translators can be reprogramed to produce other types of Terran life. Cattle for milk and meat. Horses you can ride or harness—"

"Muck!" The angry outburst cut him off. "I was made to sweat in the muck. You were made a god. Why? Tell me why wasn't I—"

Old Town in Albuquerque.

They were eating that night at El Comanchero, down on San Filipe. Proposing the excursion, he had hoped to be alone with Megan, but Rablon somehow got himself and Wardian included. She was hard to get alone.

"She exerts a force-field to hold us." Wardian was wryly philosophical about her. "Like electrons around a nucleus. Or planets around a star. A bit rough on all of us when we get too selfish but good for the project. It's the tension that keeps us united and drives us ahead."

All except Rablon had margaritas. He ordered Scotch on the rocks—a prime antidote, he declared, to scanner sickness. One was not enough. The third let his ego show.

"Gods! We're creating gods."

"Please, Marty." Wardian touched his arm to warn him. "We aren't going public yet."

"They will be gods." Rablon's owlish scowl swept the tables around them as if to challenge any listener to doubt his miracles. "They have to be if we expect them to safeguard the seedships and create the seedling races. If we didn't make them supermen, they wouldn't have a chance."

He was Don Brink, still the new recruit, dazzled by Megan herself and the audacity of her dream but not yet at home with Rablon's computer jargon and Ulver's fusion physics and Tomislav's promised wonders of genetic engineering.

"You're talking about the—" He had to grope for the phrase. "I guess you would call them the children of the seedship?"

"Not so, Brink." Rablon frowned as if offended by his ignorance. "The children of the seed will be human as I am. Born into a strange and maybe unfriendly environment, they'll need help to get established. We're engineering the Defenders to provide that help."

"Thanks." Uncomfortably, he shrugged. "I didn't know."

"The Defenders are designed to be superiour because they have to be superior." He wondered if Rablon saw himself that way. "They'll require no food or air, and they'll be immune to nearly everything. Sensitive to a wide radiation spectrum and able to operate on nearly any source of energy. Electric power, sunlight, even gamma radiation. Winged, if they need wings. We're loading alternative programs to let the master computer adapt them to cope with whatever hazards they happen to meet on the target worlds."

"If you can do all that—" He looked hard at Rablon, resenting his long black hair and his reedy stridence and his intellectual arrogance. "What are you doing for the human beings they'll be defending?"

"All we can. They'll be better men than you are."

Better than Rablon? Wanting to ask, he swallowed the question. Megan was too clearly fond of him, too willing to forgive him everything. If he sometimes drank too much, that was because his wife had lately left him. If his talk sometimes got obnoxious, his genius was still essential to the project.

"Better than homo sap. Not just clones, because we can pick and modify the best genes there are. Filter out the defects, at least those we can isolate. Improve intelligence and vigor and longevity. Limit animal aggressiveness, though we can't eliminate it. Not altogether. Even Tomislav admits we'll have to keep enough for self-defense."

Rablon sat silent for a moment, scowling at him through black-rimmed glasses.

"He's afraid of you, Brink. Afraid we'll have too many of our future people following in your peculiar footsteps."

Though Rablon probably didn't care, Tomislav had never forgiven Brink his career as a fighter for hire or even quite forgiven Megan for insisting that the Defenders might require a bit of his ability. When Brink looked at her now, her quick smile heartened him. Intense yet aloof, she seemed aware of all of them, fond of each one, but her devotion to the project always came first.

Trying hard to tolerate Rablon because of all he felt for her, Brink couldn't help another challenge. "Have you imagined how they'll feel? The children of the ship, when they meet the Defenders? When they find they're only human, knowing we could have made them godlike."

"But we can't." Rablon was always too elaborately patient about such points. "For a number of quite sufficient reasons. First of all, the Defenders will be sterile."

"I don't see why. If you know how to grow them—"

"Inside the seedship." The careful tone and the cold little smile put him down, as if he had been a backward child. "By retranslation from computer code into half-organic units. They'll emerge full grown from the production chamber—as the first humans will. The humans will be complete; we can record existing genes for the human reproductive system, pretty much as we find them. But, given the state of our technology and the risk of damage to the seed in space, it's impractical as well as unnecessary to risk attempting to design functional reproductive systems for the Defenders."

"Eunuch gods?" Watching Megan and watching them, Wardian had seemed discreetly amused at their clash, and he was trying to moderate it now. "Do you suppose they'll be happy?"

"Happy?" Rablon shrugged. "We're engineering them as special service units. Programed to perform emergency functions, not to enjoy human emotion."

The waitress had come to offer another round of drinks. Wardian shook his head to check her, with a sharp glance at Rablon, and turned understandingly to him.

"Don, there're other reasons, too, why the people we plant will have to be human. Making Defenders will take special elements—the ship can carry feedstocks enough for only two or three. Human beings are made of more abundant stuff. Elements we ought to find anywhere.

"And we hope the race will keep on evolving, adapting to each new environment, which means we must provide the best gene pool we can. The retranslators will be programed for at least forty individuals. Coming one by one off a production line inside the ship, a few weeks apart.

"As I understand our plans—"

Urbanely modest, the tall astronaut looked at Rablon to wait for confirmation.

"Twenty couples." Rablon nodded, staring after the waitress as if he wanted to call her back. "With a wide range of genes designed to provide an adequate evolutionary base."

The owlish scowl returned to him.

"Get it, Brink? The Defenders couldn't evolve. Even if

we could somehow make them fertile, they'd find themselves trapped in a genetic dead end. Their gene pool too small and too highly specialized."

"I can't argue with any of that." He found a wry relief in Megan's sympathetic glance. "But still, if I were one of those new humans, waking up on some new world to find that I might have been a sort of god—

"I wouldn't be terribly happy about it."

He wanted to help the man make tools.

"You've done your thing." Without much grace, the man waved him away. "I'll do my own, beginning now."

Born with knowledge and skills, the man searched for flints and flaked them into blades. Hewing driftwood, he made a wooden hoe and dug furrows for his seed. To irrigate his garden, he cut a narrow ditch from the pools that gathered spray below the waterfall. Though the monsoon season had ended, easterly winds still brought afternoon rain. When the first shower came, the man ignored it, working stolidly at the ditch until the Defender ran down to offer shelter in the flyer cockpit.

"Thanks, Defender." Stubborn faced, the man waved him back. "But the rules are what you made them a million years ago. The games's mine to play."

He stooped again to his hoe. At last, however, with the icy drops pelting harder, he left his work and scrambled up the cliff into a shallow cave the river had cut in some past age. After the rain, with his ditch overflowing, he leveled the cave's clay floor and carried rocks to begin a mud-plastered wall.

Pink at first, blistered and peeling, the man grew brown. Grew lean, eking out the scant rations from his backpack. Grew visibly harder, toiling through long days to keep his garden weeded, to extend and bank his ditches, to complete his shelter wall.

Through those first few hard days, working with wary eyes on the sky, he repeatedly asked the Defender for more information about the robots. About the great dead starship that had brought them. About the disk-shaped thing—weapon, power source, signal device, itself robotic—that had guided the Defender so near the robots' ancient surface base, only to abandon him before he could enter.

"Where is this base?"

"North," he said. "Two thousand kilometers across a desert plateau. Then on beyond a canyon I couldn't cross."

"A long way off." A thoughtful scowl. "If they found us, what would they do?"

"Nothing, maybe. The disk-thing never told us much. We brought it with us off their starship. Knows a lot about us. Knows may be the wrong word—the thing's a computer, loaded with control codes we've never broken.

"The robots did give me the flyer—with jet fuel in it we could have used for feedstock. That's all. Really all we know. I guess it's possible they caught or maybe even killed our other Defenders. But we haven't detected any search for us."

"You think we're safe?"

"I try to hope so, but they're still a riddle. If they didn't accept me for one of their makers when I said I was, why did they give me the flyer? If they did accept me, why don't they give us more?"

In his own turn, the Defender stared past the rust-colored cliffs and out across the draining lake, toward the alien base.

"No way to know." Baffled, he shook his head. "If they've been waiting thirty thousand years, I guess they're willing to wait forever." He nodded at the birthcell. "We're waiting, too, for your first companion."

"A woman?" The man grinned with the most emotion he had showed. "For me?"

"That's the plan. If the two of you agree." He shrugged to cover a pang of envy. "If you don't there'll be others. The ship is to bear forty of you. Thirty days apart."

"I'll be ready." The man frowned at the ship, calculating. "Call me when her birth is near."

Getting ready, the man cut armloads of the grasslike stuff that grew higher on the bench, to make a bed. He brought the first food from his young garden: succulent lemon-colored stalks that he tried with evident relish and a few early tomato-red fruits. He gathered driftwood for fuel and sweated over a flint-carved fire-drill till blue smoke rose.

The Defender built a fire of his own, to burn limestone for calcium the processors required for human bone. He pressed more oil from the nuts Defender Two had gathered before she was lost, hydrocarbon feedstock for retranslation into human tissue.

All the last night, he waited on that narrow platform outside the birthcell. Though the busy computer told him nothing, a glowing spot of infrared showed the kindling life within. Slight vibrations revealed its movement. Still he waited, till the night's dim crimson faded slowly into dawn.

"Defender—" Coming down from the cave, the man paused to hail him. "Is it time?"

"Today. Later today."

"Call me. I want to be there."

Whistling, hoe on his shoulder, the man strode on. The mood was happy, the notes clear and true, a medley of tunes Wardian and Tomislav and the others had known and loved on the vanished Earth. A cheering sign, the Defender thought; the children of the ship would soon be more than Stone Age savages.

The lips of the birthcell were something other than ordinary metal, perhaps half organic, their gold film worn and scarred but free of rust. He felt their increasing warmth. Heard the thumps inside. A black crack split them, and he shouted for the man.

The man dropped his hoe and hurried toward the ship but stopped on the way to fill both hands with red-ripe fruit. The slit widened faster than before. The birthscents poured out, powerful and strange—though the Defender caught a haunting trace of Megan's lilac.

The woman's hand came out, and her pink wet arm, grasping blindly. He caught the hand, warm and small and strong. It closed on his. The pliant lips spread wider. Clinging to steady herself, she came out into his arms.

Megan, bare. Except for the brown backpack—

For a single giddy instant, he was Don Brink again. Beside that motel pool, with the slick-haired manager escorting Megan to the table where he sat, bad leg propped up and aching from the guerrilla metal in his knee. Megan, his first dazzling glimpse.

Recollections wrenched him.

Her easy-striding vigor and the pleasant way she filled her trim business suit. Her dark hair glinting red in the sun. Her quick hand clasp when the manager introduced them. Her luminous smile, half shy, gravely perceptive, incredibly warming with the eager interest in him dawning in her eyes. The heady breath of lilac—

His instant lust came back.

His burning perception of her ripely tempting readiness and his instant sense of latent passion in her, kindling his own hot urge to wake it.

Lust and instant pain.

Because he was too old for her, wounded and malarial, his life used up—

"Megan—" Trembling, he whispered her name. "Megan—"

Because this newborn beauty was Megan Drake, here on Mansphere, alive again. The leanly vivid features, the red-gold gleam of her dark dripping hair, and the bright-green glint of her eyes, now impishly daring. Yet he saw her quick headshake.

"I was meant to be Megan." The richly vibrant voice that he recalled, another wounding echo. "But if this place is Eden, my name will be Eve."

With summer ending, the dawn had been chill. He saw her shiver, shrinking from the wind. Her damp arms wrapped him, and she snuggled to his warmth. Nude and breathless and odorous with lilac and all the overwhelming scents of her birth. He felt her nipples hardening, felt the sticky blood oozing hot from her navel.

"Eve—please!" He pushed at her wet flesh, too feebly. "We aren't for each other. If you are Eve, you must wait for your Adam—"

Her parted lips had found his mouth.

"You'll be my Adam. Because you're Don. Dear Don Brink!" Still clinging, she drew back a little to smile into his face. "Even golden, I still know you. Even here in Eden. God in Eden!"

Eyes closing, she pulled him passionately back.

"I always loved you, Don." She trembled, straining against him. "Loved you terribly. From when I first saw you at the place in Mexico. Though I know the old Megan never could tell you—"

"Defender—" He felt the man's calloused fingers on his arm, heard the breathless accusation rasping at his ear. "You—you were to call me!"

The man had dropped the fruit he had brought for her. Bursting on the platform, it spattered blood-red juice. Muddy handed, the man was pale and breathing hard. His narrowed eyes swept them both, glazing with fury.

"I didn't—didn't expect her so soon." The Defender pulled her clinging arms away and swung her toward the man. "This is Egan," he told her. "Egan Drake." His voice quivered with emotion a Defender shouldn't feel, but he tried to grin at her. "If you are Eve, he's to be your Adam."

Green eyes wide, she recoiled from the man.

"He isn't Egan." She shook her head, cringing. "Egan was my brother." She swayed back against the Defender. "I don't like him, Don." Her voice quavered higher. "I never will."

He looked uneasily across her naked shoulder into the man's savage anger.

"I—I'm sorry." His voice broke awkwardly. "But I did call when birth began. I never meant this—"

"Don't lie! I believe what I see."

She twisted her head to glare at the man.

"You—you get away!" Her lips had curled, and her tight voice lashed through half-shut teeth. "Stay away. Better stay away, because I—I hate you. I always will. Stinking animal! Slobbering to rape me. Panting to drag me into your stinking cave. To make me your slave, grubbing in your stinking mud. I won't do it."

Sobs began to shake her.

"I never—never will."

Without meaning to, the Defender found himself stroking her goose-pimpled flesh.

"Bad luck." He shook his head at the man, trying to seem more sympathetic than he felt. "We'd planned for things to go better. Next time, I'm sure they will. But I hope you can forgive her—"

"Her? Or you?"

"Both, I guess," he muttered. "Though I never meant—"

"I can see what you meant."

"Remember—remember what we are." He saw the man's fists knotting. "Remember why we're here—to replant the human race. If Eve is not for you, or you for her, others will be born—"

Not listening, the man plunged at them, fists wildly flailing. Stepping aside, the Defender swung the woman out of danger. A muddy foot slipped in the spattered fruit. The driftwood railing splintered. The man toppled off the platform.

"Don't—" the woman sobbed. "Don't let him have me."

He slid out of her arms and ran down the stair. The man had fallen half a dozen meters. Clutching at the posts beneath the stair, he was dragging himself painfully erect, mud smeared and bloody nosed. Red fists clenched again, he glared up at the woman.

"Stay safe!" his harsh jeer rasped. "With your precious tin god. At least you know he'll never rape you."

Spitting mud at the Defender, he blundered blindly toward his cave.

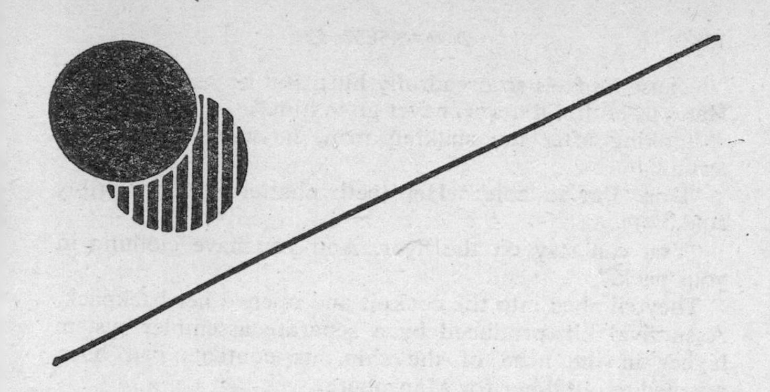

"Egan, wait!" he shouted after the man. "Listen to reason. We can't wreck the plan. Not after so many have given so much. Remember, other women will be born—"

The man stalked on.

"Let him go."

With a helpless shrug, he turned back to Eve. She had followed him down the stair, and he felt her shivering arms slide around him.

"I'm sorry, Don," she was whispering at his ear. "Terribly, terribly sorry! Because I know what we were meant to be. Parents of the new mankind. I know I was meant for him—but I just can't! Because I love you so—so dreadfully!"

"Megan—" That ancient name came out in spite of him, and he turned to her sadly, shaking his head. "You can't love me—"

"But I do—"

"You can't love a—a *thing*." His voice quivered and caught. "That's all I am. A unit of the ship, though I do have bits of people in me. But if you think I'm human—"

He pulled a little back and turned himself to let her see the umbilical cable and his naked sexlessness.

"You see what I am. Why I can't love anybody."

"Don—" A gasp of pain, but she did not recoil. "I'm sorry for you. So awfully, awfully sorry! For you but not for me. I don't care. You're still the one I love."

Trembling, she clung tighter.

"I'm sorry, too, for him." She stared after the man.

"Because he feels so dreadfully hurt. But he hates me now. Hates us both. I'll never, never go to him."

Looking after the stalking man, he could only shrug again.

"Don, I'm so cold." Her teeth chattered. "So terribly cold."

"You can stay on the flyer. And you have clothing in your pack."

They climbed into the cockpit and opened her backpack. A survival kit, produced by a separate assembler system higher in the nose of the ship, its contents had been adapted to outfit her for Mansphere.

A two-piece jumpsuit of soft leathery stuff. Light but sturdy-looking gloves and boots. A waterproof cloak, wide enough to be a blanket. Helping her dress, he ached inside because the trim tan suit made her more than ever Megan. One greenish eye closed slightly, in a way of Megan's, as she frowned at a bag of little varicolored bricks.

"Food," he said. "Mostly concentrated proteins, to keep you alive till you can grow your own. These must be the seed." Another parcel, smaller. "Different kinds than Egan had. Engineered to suit the changing season—cooler weather, and dryer, with winter coming soon. Some of them for fiber you can make into warmer clothing."

The frown had bitten deeper, and he saw her troubled headshake.

"You'll need it," he said. "Mansphere has a longer year than Earth. With its axis tipped forty degrees, the winter will be hard—"

"Oh, Don!" He saw her tears. "I wish—I wish I were like you. So I could stay alive and we could be together. Together always! Without such terrific problems." Her desperate fingers caught his hand and clung. "We could be so wonderfully happy—"

"But you—you're human." His voice quivered. "I'm not. We can't change what we are." He drew her gently to him. "You'll be happy," he told her. "Happier than I can ever be. Because you are human—"

"I don't want to be."

"But you are." Pulling away, he tried to be firm. "You must make some sort of peace with Egan—"

"I—I can't! Because he has my brother's name. Because I

hate him. And I'm afraid. I won't let him drag me into his cave."

"Maybe you should sleep here in the flyer," he agreed. "But you and he will need each other. For winter, he'll need seeds from your pack. Need your help to cultivate them and store food for winter. You'll be hungry unless he shares what he's growing now.

"We must talk to him."

When she agreed, they left the flyer together. Another Megan Drake, slim and quick in the trim jumpsuit, pink skinned and tempting to him, her lilac scent still faintly clinging. Seeming younger than she had been in those poignant shards of recollection, she walked silently, gripping his fingers, trembling with dread.

"I'm starving!" she decided suddenly, perhaps to delay the encounter. "Thirsty, too."

"Egan wouldn't like us raiding his garden. But here's water enough."

They had come to the ditch. She frowned at him and then at the flowing water but dropped at last to drink.

"So you think it's so wonderful, being human?" With a grimace of indignation, she brushed crumbs of soil off her hands. "Having to crawl in the mud like some animal just to stay alive?"

"I wish I were human." Sadly, he glanced down at himself and back at her. "If I could change places with Egan—"

They crossed the ditch and climbed to the cave. The man's birthscent lingered around it, staled now to a thin, sour reek. They stopped outside the crude rock wall, Megan huddled uneasily against him.

"Egan!" he called. "Let's talk."

No response. She was tugging at his arm, silently imploring him to leave, before the man stumbled from his cave. Still smeared with mud and blood from his fall off the platform, he looked shrunken, sick.

"Get out." His voice was raspy. "I've had too much—too much of both of you."

"Listen—however you feel, you and Eve need each other. She can sleep in the flyer, but to stay alive you'll have to share. Seed. Work. Food—"

"I'll make out." He stooped for a rock. "As for the bitch—keep her out of my garden!"

The rock flew at Eve. The Defender stepped before her to catch it harmlessly.

"Egan, please!" He tossed the stone aside. "Remember what the project is. A million-year effort. Maybe the last chance mankind will ever have. Anywhere. We can't just waste it—"

"We're a long time too late for that." The man grinned bleakly through his red-clotted mask. "It was wasted back on Earth, when the scanner picked up too much of what mankind used to be. Or maybe out in space, when the micrometeor hit the ship's computer and garbled all the programs. Too many malfunctions. We're none of us what we should have been. Not even you."

A sardonic snort.

"And you call yourself Defender!"

Reeling from the impact of that, he had to nod.

"True," he muttered. "True. I know we aren't perfect. Neither were our makers. They meant for us to build a better world than theirs. And still we can try—try to be what we should have been. To do what we were made for—"

"Defend her if you can!" The ironic rasp cut him off. "But you aren't conning me. Any fool can see you were put together wrong—any fool except the bitch. Keep her if you want her. I don't need her or you."

"The ship does," the Defender said. "Remember, there are others coming."

"They'll need better robots." The man squinted shrewdly through his matted beard. "Those others can't be as crazy—as malfunctional as you are. I wonder if I couldn't get in touch—"

"Don't! Don't try that—"

"Take your bitch!" The man scrabbled for more stones to throw. "Get away!"

"Let's go!" Eve tugged at his arm. "He's the malfunctioning one."

She shrank behind him.

"Sleep on it," he begged the man. "Think things over."

"Here's what I think."

They retreated from a volley of hard-thrown stones. The ship was calling before they reached it. It had closed the birthcell, and now it required more feedstocks.

"We aren't stopped yet." He tried to grin into the woman's pinched, despairing face. "The ship's still alive. Thirty days from now, another man should be born. I hope—" His voice caught. "I hope he'll be saner."

"Oh, Don—" She blinked forlornly at him. "Don't you see—"

Sobbing, shaking her head, she ran ahead of him toward the flyer.

His kiln had cooled, so he opened it to refill the ship's lime bin. He pressed oil nuts and filtered more oil into the hydrocarbon tanks. When he looked again for Eve, he found her on the muddy slope below the ditch the man had dug, bent over a driftwood stick she was using for a hoe, scraping out another garden. She straightened to wave at him with one muddy hand, two fingers spread in a *V* that sent a tiny shudder of recollection through him.

Dusk fell, daylight fading into crimson infrared. He saw Eve limping back to the flyer, but he worked on. The ship required water. When it had lime enough and oil enough, he borrowed the flyer's ballast hose, running it from the intake pumps down to the ditch.

The retranslators and assemblers going again, he made a blade for Eve's wooden hoe from a scrap of metal that had been the inspection plate over the limestone bin. For most of the night, he worked to prepare and plant the garden Eve had begun.

Before dawn, his strength ran out, his battery charge exhausted. Plodding heavily back to the flyer, he slid off the backpack, set it to recharging, and hooked himself to the longer umbilical he had run to the flyer's generator.

Eve was uneasily asleep when he climbed into the cockpit. Megan still, younger and sadder than the Megan he recalled, hands blistered from the rough driftwood stick, dusty hair trailing across her childlike, tear-stained face. He heard her sob—and his power went off.

Blacked out, he crumpled to the deck.

"Don—" Her frightened gasp came faintly though the sudden dark. "What's wrong?"

He couldn't speak, couldn't move, but he felt the flyer tilt. A red shadow in his fading vision, she floated above him and on to the cockpit door. It swung open. As the flyer tipped farther, he saw the dim-glowing ground, dropping fast beneath them. Heard water splashing and a shout of savage elation. He found the man, warmer and brighter than the ground, standing where the flyer had been, staring after them. One hand still clutching a loose anchor cable, the other clenched into a muddy fist.

Chilled, the Defender understood.

While he was at work, while Eve slept, the man had crept up to loosen the anchor cables, waited in hiding to unhook his power cord and drain the ballast tanks. In the grasp of the gravity mirror, they were falling into the sky.

For a moment, he wasn't much alarmed. The flyer had been engineered for safety. He saw the emergency lever flashing red. A pull on it would vent the lift tanks and restore their balance. He tried to point, tried to shout.

His numb hand refused to move. He found no voice. Yet somehow Eve understood. He saw her hauling at the lever, but still they floated upward. He knew then that the man had somehow disabled the emergency system. They were already many meters high, flying off the planet.

He would probably survive. In space, the sun would soon revive him enough to let him recouple his umbilical to the generator. He could repair the controls, vent mass-inverted water to balance the lost ballast, restart the rocket engines, probably find his way back.

But Eve—

Rising from the planet's night side, they would be above the atmosphere before they met the sun.

Sick with helpless pity, he saw her faint red shape in motion again. She pulled him to the tilted door. Clinging desperately, she jumped with him. They spun down toward the canyon floor. A blood-red glow, it had sunk too far. He found the ship, diminished to a shining toy. The doll-sized man staring up at them, shaking a furious fist. He ached inside. They were too high.

Too high for her—

A fine fall Friday—and Megan alone!

The lab was shut down for the weekend, with Rablon away to read a paper at some computer symposium, Wardian and Ulver in conference with the Solar Sail engineers who still hoped to launch their flight to Mars, and Tomislav back in La Jolla at his wife's bedside.

He bought cold cuts and French bread and two bottles of a mild Chablis he thought she would like. She filled the picnic basket and drove them out through Tijeras Canyon and north off the interstate toward the Sandia summit. The cedar-scented air grew cooler. Happy with her, he liked her slight lilac scent and her skill at the wheel and just being with her.

Still ambivalent about his profession, she wanted to know about Kenya and the animals he hadn't even wanted to hunt and the poachers he had been hired to fight.

"You enjoyed that?" Her greenish eyes flashed keenly at him. "Killing men to defend the elephants?"

"A game—the game I love." He nodded. "The poachers had been warned to quit. Got their own message back, for us to go to hell. Armed like commandos and trying hard to get us first." In spite of himself, he grinned at her uneasy fascination. "The elephants can't hold out forever, but at least I gave a few of them a breather."

With a wry half smile, she drove on silently.

"Egan," he prompted her at last. "Your twin. You've never told me much about him."

"I've never told anybody. Not even Ben Bannerjee." Her

voice had fallen oddly, and she kept her eyes on the road. "But if you really—really like me, I suppose you ought to know."

"Like?" he whispered. "The word is love."

"If it is—" Her eyes seemed broodingly unhappy when she glanced at him. "It may change when you know."

She had turned off the crest highway into a narrower, less-used road that climbed through taller timber toward the crest. Turning again, she stopped outside a wide gate of welded iron pipe, secured with a chain and a rusty padlock. She gave him a key.

He had left his cane behind. Trying to seem younger than he was and not to show the twinges in his knee, he hurried to open the creaking gate and wave her through. The forest road beyond was overgrown with brush. It climbed again, until suddenly they were on the mile-high rim, with cliffs falling sheer to the smoggy city and the endless strip of river-watered green winding down the arid valley and the brown mesas rolling off beyond it toward remote blue ranges that bit into the bluer, unpolluted sky.

"Big!" he whispered. "Big as the Kenya highlands."

She stopped a dozen meters from the brink. The wind across it was cold, and they sat for a time in the car. Except for the wind, he heard no sound. Here above everything, sharing a feeling that all human concerns were overwhelmed by that awesome natural immensity, he felt nearer her than he had ever been. Turning at last to face her, he waited to learn why they were here.

"You asked about Egan." Solemn eyed, she paused to study him before she went on. "This land was his. He wanted to build a telescope here. Really!"

She had seen his astonishment.

"I think I told you he had big ideas—most of them a little crazy. We were barely twenty-one the year he bought it with his share of our mother's estate. He'd been a brilliant student in several fields before Ben steered him into astronomy—Ben worried about him as much as I did. He was eager about it at first because he had this idea for a new sort of telescope.

"An obsession. It haunted him for years, though Ben told him it would probably never work. A multiple instrument. Two dozen scopes, in fact, spaced along a Y like the radio dishes in the Very Large Array down out of Socorro.

Each one only moderately large but all of them focused on electronic image intensifiers, feeding into a computer that would combine them. He hoped to get the definition of a mirror three kilometers across. Able to see the planets of stars hundreds of light-years off."

"Why wouldn't it work?"

"Perhaps it would." Her voice seemed sadly wistful. "Though Ben was seldom wrong. Egan never got far enough to run any tests. Actually, this wasn't a good location. Maybe high enough but too much night glare from Albuquerque. There were financial problems and scientific problems. All too much for him."

She sighed.

"He always got some new enthusiasm before he finished what he started. That fall, it was the wife of a tenor at the Santa Fe opera. He threw up everything to go off with her to Mexico. She—and finally her attorneys—got what was left of his legacy. So he had no funds for the telescope."

He saw the pinch of old pain on her face.

"It was two years later he died, climbing another mountain he'd been warned about. The seedship project was his last big idea. The biggest. Everybody but Ben thought it was the craziest." A painful little smile touched her face and vanished. "Egan left the land to me. With a letter in his bank box saying how much he loved me and begging me to forget—"

Her voice caught, and he waited for her to go on.

"I never sold the land because it's all I have of Egan." She turned to look back into the tall evergreens. "We saw it first the year we were sixteen, long before he owned it. He was still into anthropology then, and we were dividing the summer between Uncle Luther's ranch and an Anasazi dig.

"I loved it. The sky and the wind and the sun. The long hot days in the pit, sifting dust. Even the sweat and the bugs, because I'd got caught up in the mystery and the tragedy of the Anasazi. Egan worked beside me. Never saying much, but I knew he was terribly unhappy. He had been sad for years, though he wouldn't tell my why."

She was staring away again, at the remote horizon and the empty sky, as if only half aware of him.

"We'd grown up too close—maybe I told you." Her glance seemed almost apologetic when it came back to him. "Because we had no family. Not except Uncle Luther, and we hardly ever saw him. Money enough from the estate but nobody except each other. One day at the dig, I'd asked again what was wrong.

"He said he'd tell me. On the Sandia crest. When the dig was over, we rented a car in Albuquerque, and he drove us up here—mountains had always obsessed him. This road hadn't been opened. We left the car back down the slope and hiked up through the timber.

"He wouldn't talk, even when we got here. Instead, he dared me to climb with him out on that rock." She pointed. "I was terrified, but I did follow him nearly to the top. He stood there a long time, staring out across the Rio Grande and down the cliffs. He was white and trembling. I saw he was ready—ready to jump."

Her pale lips quivered.

"He said he would if I tried to stop him. Standing there, shivering in the wind, he began to talk. Our lives were a tragedy, he said, because we were in love. He had to kill himself because he wanted me so much. Because I was his sister.

"He said he had to jump because it was the only way, and he wanted me to jump with him. I was crying by then. Terribly frightened. Terribly—torn. I told him he could—could take me if that would make him happy.

"Of course he wouldn't."

She looked back into his face with a bitter little smile.

"He loved me, Don," she whispered. "Really loved me. And of course he knew the thing would kill me. I tried to say—tried to say that didn't matter. He must have been brooding a long time about it. He said we could never live together except in hiding, afraid of everybody. That was why he said we had to die.

"He said we both had to die. But then, when we talked about it, he couldn't—couldn't kill me. He told me I could find another life because I had no guilt. But still he said he had to jump. I was crying, but I kept begging till finally he climbed back off the rock. For my sake, he said. He was crying, too, all the way back to the car, and I had to drive us back to town.

"And I—and I—"

She stopped, shuddering as if the chill of the wind had got into her.

"Thanks, Meg," he whispered. "Thanks for telling me."

"I had to." Her cold fingers caught his hand. "Because it's why—why I'm like I am. Why Egan conceived the seedship project and why it means so much to me. Escape, out of that terrible cloud. Atonement for everything we couldn't help. If you can understand—"

Her eyes were on his face, imploring, and tears shone in them when he nodded slowly, aching for her.

"I'm glad if you do." She clung harder to his hand. "Because you have a right to know if you do really care. I loved him, Don. As much, I guess, as he loved me. Though I hadn't—hadn't known—"

Again she shivered.

"It left a wound that never really healed. Maybe I should have seen a shrink, though they'd never helped him. I guess I blamed myself for loving him too much. The pain comes back. It hurts even now. When I ought to love—want to love anybody else."

Their fingers clung, but he found no words to say.

"After that," she said, "we kept apart. Went to different colleges—I used to think he changed from anthropology to astronomy just to get out of the past. He'd begun his own love affairs, which all ended so miserably. Most of what I knew about him came from Ben. I think it always hurt him terribly to see me. He said he was afraid—afraid he couldn't stand it."

"So long, Defender." A glowing red ghost and the man's mocking voice. "I'm pulling out tonight."

The crimson figure swam slowly into focus, leaning on a stick and bent beneath a heavy pack.

"Leaving you to keep on defending whatever monsters happen to hatch, and I hope you love 'em all. Till I get back." A raspy chuckle. "Because I'll be back. With a better lot of robots to take charge here—"

"Listen!" he tried to shout. "You'll never—"

The man would never live to cross those 2,000 kilometers of jungle and mountain and desert to reach the robot base. Not without a guide and more supplies than he could carry. Certainly not before savage winter fell.

But the Defender had no energy to speak or even to move his eyes when the red shadow-shape slid out of his vision. The stick whistled down to slash his face, whistled down again. He heard the grunts of effort, the sobs of frustration, the plod of boots, departing. The slashes merely stung, but he had to lie where he had fallen, half buried in the mud, till crimson gloom brightened into daylight, strong enough to let him rise.

The man was gone. The flyer, too. But the ship stood unharmed, faintly radiant with the warmth of its busy processors. Eve lay near him, half nude and already cold. Red mud clogged her mouth and eyes and nostrils. The man had rolled her over to rip off her cloak.

The Defender stood a long time over her, swept into a maelstrom of bitter recollection. Shattered fragments whirled in to drown him in pain. Lacerating moments with all the men inside him. Glimpses of the Megan they all yearned for. Imperfect people, all of them secretly defeated, existing at the brink of desperation, toiling for the project because its promise of some better human future was all they had to live for.

If this had to be the end—

It must not be. Fighting that tide of overwhelming desolation, he reeled away from the grave to call the ship.

"Defender One. Emergency report."

With no answer because it must have been busy with the retranslators, he had to try again and still again before he received its brittle signal.

"Ship to Defender One. Be brief."

"Our first creations—" He checked himself to shift into the code it spoke. "Defender One reporting loss of initial human units. Female unit dead. Killed by male unit, who attempted to release gravitic flyer into space with female and me aboard. Male unit has departed, stating intention to contact alien robots."

It stood silent so long he thought its circuits had returned to the processors.

"Ship to Defender One," it rapped abruptly. "Urgent assignment. You will pursue male unit. Capture it if possible. Return it for rebriefing on our mission here. If capture is impossible, you will destroy it. Further contact with alien robots must be prevented, regardless of risk."

"Assignment unnecessary," he protested. "Male unit rated severely malfunctional. Its contact with alien base rated impossible. Its survival away from here rated impossible. Advise cancellation of assignment."

"Ship to Defender One. You will undertake assignment."

"Defender One to Ship." Voice slowed with human dismay, he tried again. "Assignment extremely hazardous to me. Gravitic flyer lost. Battery pack exhausted, and recharge power no longer available. Winter season approaching fast, severely limiting solar power.

"I request—request reconsideration of assignment, with permission to remain here and supply feedstocks—"

"Feedstocks now adequate." The sharp synthetic signal cut him off. "Your service here no longer required. Defective human unit rated gravest risk to mission now identified. Acting to remove it, you are rated expendable.

"Assignment stands."

He dug Eve's grave down toward the river from the gardens and buried her sadly there, the only marker her driftwood hoe. On the trail at last, he crisscrossed the north canyon, toward the alien base, but found no sign the man had gone that way. Casting downriver, he picked up a vanishing trace of that sour birthscent, clinging to bare granite ledges that held no footprints.

Farther down, where the man had been less cautious or in greater haste, the trail grew clearer. The sweat-rank odor, often stronger. Occasional bootprints in patches of drying silt. Pungent whiffs of sap crushed from new green stuff grown since the water ebbed.

The monsoon lake still filled the canyon mouth where the ship had first touched down. Still draining fast, the flood water had left a broad rim of wet red mud below the jungle wall. The tall thorn thickets, dry and dead when the seedship came, had become a green-clawed barrier he knew the man could never penetrate.

The last deep footprints led him down to the lake and into a trap. Following too far, he sank to his hips in foul ooze. Outmatched, he felt, by a very shrewd player. A wave of gray futility washed over him. What hurt was not his own hard predicament so much as this dismal final failure of the whole seedship project. After all the ages, all the toil and pain, Eve and her Adam had been born far too human, no better than their imperfect creators. He himself had blundered miserably in his duty as Defender. Forlornly searching, he found neither redemption for himself nor future for the project.

But the machine in him ran on, unconcerned with human regrets. Floundering in the muck, he fought his way back to firmer ground. That battle exhausted him, and he had to lie a long time in the sun, recharging. Sunset found him not yet halfway to the ridge across the foot of the lake, a barrier so long and straight he thought it had to be artificial.

Power failing as the red dusk fell, he dragged himself a few meters into the jungle fringe and lay there waiting for daylight, groping for shards of his shattered hope. However malfunctional, the fugitive was stronger, quicker, maybe more cunning, an unpredictable madman. But, so the Defender tried to tell himself, he knew the planet better. Only half organic, needing no food, his body was almost immortal. Disabled in the dark, he could always go on again when the sun came back. In the end, with luck enough, he might yet somehow win this last grim game.

Not by capture, for the man would never surrender. But he would get hungry. He would get cold. Even with Eve's stolen cloak, he wasn't clad for the planet's winter, already too near to let him reach the robot base in time for any chance at shelter there.

Caught or not, the man would surely die.

His own problem, as the Defender tried to see it, was simply to witness the death or obtain proof of it. Failing that, unable to report his task carried out, he would be driven on to search forever, regardless of human logic or human despair.

Slowly, to his own surprise, he began to experience a bleak happiness. Glowing dimly crimson, the thorn-bladed jungle and the sullen river became a fantastic fairyland. His body dead till day came back, his brain—at least its human bit—still found elation in the chase. Toward morning, an early cold front blew in, with a rough north wind and chilling drizzle, but he endured it cheerfully, knowing how much more it must hurt his foe.

Once, for a moment, he was Don Brink again, back on the trail of elephant poachers trailing the herd toward the cloudy crown of Kilimanjaro. He lay where he had dropped in the wadi behind an anthill when the sniper opened fire from the baobob tree.

His few people were outnumbered, outgunned, trapped in a well-planned ambush. Pinned down, without water, with insects already crawling on him, yet he felt totally alive, his heart thumping with the tension of the game. The three behind him were men to trust, all down safe and now well positioned for defense. From the click of a pebble, he knew that Ahmed had moved to cover the brushy swale below, where the main poacher force would be waiting to attack. McCaine was on the other flank, and Jomo had dropped back down the wadi to guard the rear. He was pretty certain his first shot had winged the sniper.

After dark—

The ridge at the foot of the lake took him another day to reach, and its dense jungle overgrowth delayed him again. When at last he reached the farther face, it was an awesome precipice, falling a full 300 meters into the lower gorge. Bare, seamless stuff, azure-blue and diamond hard, it had been a dam before the robots came to kill the planet, and the lake still drained through the old spillway, roaring into the lower gorge.

Below the gorge, the land was nearly level, an alluvial plain that reached to the sea. Wider there and slower, the river wandered south and east in long loops that ran against ever-taller jungle walls, no banks left for passage. The man's fading scent led the Defender to a rift of driftwood on a sandbar where a broken stone maul and tracks in the mud revealed the building of a raft, nailed together with ironlike thorns.

Slowed by lingering clouds, the Defender spent three more days hammering his own raft together. Many more, drifting and poling toward the delta. From there, the man had turned north up the coast, confined to the beaches between the ocean and the jungle, leaving an epic written in flaked flints and dead campfires, in the clean bones and shells of things caught in the sea.

With unexpected craft and skill, the man kept ahead and tried to hide his trail. He had climbed points of rock again and again to look behind him. Once, where a granite bluff pinched the beach, he left another trap: a deep pit roofed with flimsy sticks and hidden under clean-swept sand. The clinging scent warned the Defender just in time. Safely past, he found the lookout where the man had been watching, waiting to return and bury him.

Tracing out that silent saga as they pushed up the coast to meet advancing winter, he found contempt changing into pity, pity into admiration. Alone and friendless, ill supplied and haphazardly clad, hunted across a hostile continent, the man survived.

Madman no longer, he had begun to show Don Brink's ways of thinking, Don Brink's competence, Brink's hardy resolution. He, the Defender, wondered if Tomislav had somehow got more of Brink's genes into the computer than he ever intended to allow.

Day by day, the retreating sun rose later, and the winds blew colder. Day by day, his own slow body become a greater burden. Day by grueling day, pondering every clue, he grew more and more convinced that the man shared his own bleak relish for the game.

A time came when the jungle wall was gone, replaced by sheer cliffs half a kilometer high. Dark volcanic rock from the towering mother cone at the center of the continent. Below them, wild winter seas roared across the reefs to crash against narrow boulder-strewn beaches.

At a last camp site in a half-sheltered cove, the man had left one more record, in dead fires and broken stone and the bones of sea-like things he had hunted for furs to wear and the flesh he had smoked on driftwood racks.

The trail, when he found it, led him up the cliffs. A difficult path, narrow and hazardous enough, itself a puzzle because it was sometimes cut beneath overhanging ledges where natural erosion could hardly have formed it. Reeling to the top against a bitter wind, he stumbled across another riddle. A long level rectangle, reaching far across the headland, glowing in the red dusk with a golden luminescence of its own. An ancient landing strip, he thought, still waiting for craft that never came.

Inland, almost too cold to glow in the Defender's infrared vision, the stark plateau showed no trace of any life. He recalled its look from space, brick red and barren in summer, climbing unbroken to the great canyon that sliced 3,000 kilometers across it from the central massif to the sea.

He lay that night on the edge of the strip, which seemed

warmer than the snow. In the gray daylight, he picked up the epic again, spelled across the scanty snow in marks of wooden runners and drops of frozen blood.

The sun was now far south, the days brief and bitter, his body fighting motion. Yet he had caught the heady scent of victory. With the sea behind, with no new source of food or fuel anywhere, with the robot base still far away, they were surely nearing the end of the game.

Yet the man played stubbornly on. Marching straight toward the alien base, no longer trying to hide the trail. Though each new blizzard dimmed the trail, the cold snow held scent enough to mark it. However handicapped, the Defender felt no pain. When he found a worn-out rawhide boot, black and hard with frozen blood, he knew the man was suffering.

One night, seeking shelter from a cruel north wind, he lay against the bank of a dry ravine. The wind died, and the red gloom thickened. In the stillness, he heard limping footfalls and the rasp of heavy breathing. A wooden tool creaked and scraped above him, and gravel hailed into his face.

"So long, Defender." A hoarse croak of triumph. "Guess you thought you'd won the game. Could be you did, but you'll never brag about it. Not unless some damned idiot comes along to dig you out."

Blinded, powerless, he could only lie there listening. The rattling gravel covered him. Its frozen weight increased. The footfalls crunched away. He thought he could hear the wind's far whine and sometimes a brittle snap in the freezing earth. He thought that was all he would ever hear.

The African prison.

Scraps of it ran through his brain, ran through his brain till they grew unendurable, like the nonsense phrases from a broken phonograph record.

"You're goddam lucky." The man from the embassy gave him a pack of cigarettes and a thin sardonic smile. "Just three years. The ambassador says you should have been shot."

Cramping dysentery and toilets overflowing. Black men leering at a white man in trouble, never believing he had chosen to run the guns not for any reasonable hard-currency guarantee but in a moment of devotion to their liberation—a moment that looked lunatic now. The rats and the reek. Bad food and clanging steel. Harsh commands he had to obey. Bits of stifled kindness and acts of petty greed. Iron stupidities and arrogant hypocrisy. Killing sameness, today and forever.

"You're goddam lucky—"

Forever—

But the footfalls returned, dragging more slowly. The crude tool scraped, ceased and feebly scraped again. He caught an evil gangrene reek. Eyes brushed clear, he found the man. A haggard crimson ghost, with deep-sunk eyes and ice-rimmed beard, dragging him from the grave.

"Okay, Defender." A gaspy whisper. "I nearly made it. Got near enough to see the dome. Shining like silver, not a hundred kilometers off—on the other side of that damn canyon. No way in hell across it. So get happy, Defender. If you can get happy. But I—"

A fit of feeble coughing.

"I'm done for, but I've got one more job for you. Get back to the ship—you'll come alive when winter's over. Take a message—my last will. Tell the ship it hasn't failed. That took a while, but I remember now—"

Snowflakes whipped around them.

"Remember what we were meant to be." In the whistling wind, the wheezy rasp was hard to hear. "We got a bad break. Megan and Egan—her Eve to my Adam. When she fell for you. Born—we were born to love each other. I went crazy when I lost her. Sorry for it now.

"So tell the ship—"

The man sank down beside him.

"Tell the ship not to waste our genes. Program us again and let us love—love each other. Let us live to be—what we were planned to be. To tame the damned planet. To beat the robots if they get in the way. To build—to build—"

The rattling whisper died, and then the only sound was the howling of the wind.

On the heels of the next monsoon, he came downriver on another driftwood raft. Warned by the muted thunder of the waterfall, he went ashore above it and broke his way through another summer's jungle to look down across the canyon rim.

The ship stood where he had left it, rusted redder now and toylike from this height. The same driftwood stair still climbed its narrow hull to the birthcell, but the valley floor had changed. The system of ditches had spread. The gardens had grown into fields, golden now with ripened grain. He caught a wood-smoke tang from a mud-plastered oven below the cave and the aroma of baking bread.

Human sounds drifted to him. Laughter and the ringing of an ax. A baby's crying, quickly hushed. The whistling of a man at work in the lower field binding yellow sheaves. A murmur of soft voices—Eve's he thought and Egan's—the man barefoot in a puddle, treading straw into the clay, the woman molding it into fat red bricks for the sun to dry.

"Defender One reporting." He got no answer. "Defender One to Ship. Defender One—"

"Ship to Defender." At last, its sharp synthetic voice. "Report."

"I won the game—" He checked himself and shifted to its own robotic dialect. "Reporting assignment carried out. Fugitive human unit failed to reach alien base. Its death observed and verified. While still alive, it dictated a message to Ship."

"Relay message."

"Male unit stated delayed conviction that seedship project will not fail. Expressed confidence that colony will survive to populate planet. Revealed regret for malfunction, which it rated accidental and avoidable. Urged that lost units be reprogramed to salvage genes—"

"Reprogramed units already completed and released. Rated fully functional."

"I'm so very glad—"

"Ship to Defender One." Its brittle voice cut him off. "You will resume normal duty, assisting completion of total programed production of forty functional human units. Additional calcium and hydrocarbon feedstocks now required."

"Defender to Ship." He heard his own cold-toned computer. "New duty accepted."

Silently, his human selves were singing.

SIX

LETHAL AGENT

Trouble. He read it on their faces.

"Defender—" A man and a woman, still clad in the tan leatherlike stuff of the backpacks born with them. Shyly, they stopped a dozen meters away. "Defender, may we speak to you?"

Over three of Mansphere's years, the ship had given birth to forty colonists, all its programed gene pool. They had learned to tend it. Now no longer needed for anything important, he tried to keep apart. Today they found him building a terrace wall to hold more garden soil in the steep upper canyon. He dropped his trowel and walked down to meet them. They were the youngest couple, only a few months old and not yet sure of themselves. The man stopped, and the girl shrank uneasily back.

"Why not?" He shook his head, smiling wryly at her. "I'm no monster, no matter how I look."

"You're wonderful."

He saw her staring, afraid of him, yet fascinated by his shining golden height and the umbilical cable running from his navel to the bright-winged power pack the ship had made for him from the last few liters of the special Defender feedstock brought from old Earth. If she realized his naked sexlessness, her eyes didn't pause.

"So—so splendid! So powerful!"

Her admiration hurt him, recalling too much tragedy.

"But not human, remember," he reminded her quickly. "I'm only a tool of the ship, my brain more computer than anything organic. Though I do have scraps of human recollection." And, he added, trying to break their awe, "Bits of both of you."

"I was named for Jayna Rablon." Her eyes grew wider. "Do you know why?"

Jayna. He nodded, remembering. Jayna, that blazing midsummer day when she returned from the yacht cruise with her Texas oil tycoon to look for him in Albuquerque. He was in the lab, still groggy from too many hours under the scanner. Security wouldn't let her in, and she called from the gate.

"Marty, darling! Can't I even see you?"

The breathless contralto recalled her, the way she had been that dreadful afternoon she left. Perfumed and glowing from her shower, sailing their wedding picture to shatter on the bedroom wall and opening her robe to give him one last taunting glimpse of her naked loveliness before she left with Crowler.

Walking out to meet her now, he felt so weak and strange, so breathless in the desert heat, that he knew he must be having another reaction to Tomislav's isotopic mix. Emotions spinning, he couldn't help hating her or crazily hoping she was home to stay. At the gate, she darted eagerly to throw her arms around him.

"Marty! Marty—"

The scent he remembered rose to haunt him with all he had lost. Her lithe body flowed against him, her hot tongue thrust between his lips. He wanted her desperately, but in a moment she was pulling away.

"Darling, this is Hubie."

A gangling, yellow-bearded youth he despised on sight, Hubie nodded at him warily, not offering to shake hands.

"Hubie's my attorney," she told him. "And a very dear friend." She reached back for Hubie's hand. "Since I got away from your old friend Crowler." Her ripe lips curled. "That bastard! Screwing every whore he could coax on to the yacht."

Sliding her arm around Hubie, she stepped back and cocked her perfect head, inspecting him with the dispassionate concentration of a child pulling legs off a grasshopper. The kiss had smeared her vivid lipstick. She smiled through the smear, with a flash of perfect teeth.

"I'm so happy for you, Marty." Her voice rang brighter.

"We've been reading all about you in the *Wall Street Journal.* About your computer patents and all the GEECO millions you'll be raking in. With hints about your secret project here."

He backed away, blinking at her. He couldn't talk about the project, but it was all—it ought to be all that mattered to him now. Feeling giddy, he wanted to sit down.

"We won't ask what you're doing here. Not if you want to be reasonable. But we're still married, honey bun, don't you forget, and I've come for what is mine." She glanced at Hubie with a kinder smile. "If you don't remember Hubie, he used to work here."

"Summer jobs while I was getting my law degree." Hubie had pulled away to drop uneasily back behind her. His voice was a husky squeak. "With the contractors installing all your hush-hush lab equipment."

"Darling, I know you still adore your precious honey bun." He still felt quivery with longing even when he knew she was taunting him. "I felt you tremble when I kissed you, and I know you want to treat me right."

"I was hoping—" he whispered. "Hoping—"

"If you really wanted me, you should have taken lessons," she murmured. "Lessons from Hubie."

Hubie flushed and shook his head, retreating farther.

"Too late to think of that." Her eyes were violet, wide and scalpel keen. They stabbed back at Hubie. "But I can tell I'm still your baby honey bun." Lazily intimate, her breathy voice caressed him. "Besides, Hubie knows enough to fuck up your precious project if you try any chicken-shit tricks."

Swaying giddily, he blinked at Hubie. "You can't blackmail me."

Hubie gulped and shrank again.

"Now, honey bun, don't talk dirty." She shook her head, smiling at him tenderly. "You don't know how. Not like Hubie can—"

She reached again for Hubie's apprehensive hand and pulled him up beside her.

"Think about it, honey bun." She might have been back at home in Kingsmill while he was just a teaching assistant, trying to extract forty dollars for a sale at the Fashionette when his lunch money wouldn't last till payday. "Would you want a lot of stories in the press and on the air about how your noble foundation isn't really designing L-5 habitats but shooting at the stars with rockets full of synthetic men?"

Hating her and hating Hubie, he felt lightheaded and not altogether rational. He needed a double Scotch to counteract the scanner mix in his brain. Her red-smeared smile seemed to waver in the breathless air, a mocking mirage. The guard had taken his arm to help him back inside, but the old hunger for her was still a burning fever in him.

"I've got—I've got lawyers, too." He had to lean on the guard, and his own hoarse voice seemed to come from far away. "Maybe—" He blinked at her unsteady image. "Maybe we can work out a settlement. If you'll give me—give us a few of your precious cells for genetic analysis."

A little ruefully, he grinned at the girl.

"Some of your genes did come from a Jayna I knew," he told her. "But they've been improved. Immensely improved!"

"Did you—" Awed, the man was gaping at him. "Did you know me? Galen Ulver?"

"I've bits of his mind in me. Stray recollections the scanner picked up, along with the know-how about fusion propulsion they were recording for the computer. An old man then, with a bad heart."

His eyes on the rugged, deep-tanned giant before him, the Defender recalled that bald brown elf. Spry enough in spite of all the years when Megan first brought him to the lab but afterward nearly always ill from the scanner mix. Warned to quit, he refused. Because he had come to love her, and the others on the project. And because it was his only way to space.

Shuffling into Megan's Albuquerque office.

"I was glad to give you what knowledge I could, but you can't want my genes."

"But we do." He loved her voice and her grave smile. "We know you, and we all agree."

"May I—may I sit down?"

"Why of course." She waved him into the chair beside the shimmering stellarium. "Galen—" She eyed him sharply in a way she had, one eye half shut. "Is something wrong?"

"Something you don't know." He nodded awkwardly. "Something I don't tell anybody. About my father."

"Does it matter?"

"I told you—told you how my mother brought me up." Her quick concern made it even harder to say than he'd thought it would be. "The hard times after my father left us. But he—the man she married—hadn't been my actual father. My father was black."

He saw her greenish eyes go wider and cringed from what he thought she must think.

"My mother had attended a little fundamentalist college. She had two male friends I know about. A black athlete—the token black, I guess—and a white student studying to be a minister. She got pregnant by the black. They must have been in love, but of course they couldn't marry. Not then. Not there.

"She went to the white student for help. For money to get an abortion. He married her instead. More out of idealism, I imagine, than actual love. Tried to claim me when I came, but too many people had seen her with the black, and I wasn't all that white. People talked, and I guess the would-be minister lost his calling.

"He went north and left my mother to bring me up. She did that—nobly, nobly!" His voice caught. "With two hard strikes against her. I told you about the polio when I was six. Rough times for both of us. Used to fight with my crutch when the kids called me nigger.

"I survived." Painfully, he grinned. "With her brother's help after she died. Got out of the hills and into engineering, where I hoped people wouldn't know or care what my father was. I learned to walk—and dreamed of flight to space. But I guess I never got over the other. Not down inside. It has crippled my life. And it's why—"

He had to gulp.

"Why you won't want my genes."

"Oh, Galen—" Laughing, but with tears in her eyes, Megan came around the stellarium to kiss him. "That's one more reason we do. Ivan says we need a wider pool."

"You can be proud," he told the brown giant. "Proud of all the genes that other Galen gave to you—and all he did to help mankind replant here."

Waiting to see what they wanted, he felt a glow of pride

in them. Since that first unlucky couple, there had been no more malfunctions. All forty were magnificent, more hardy and more handsome than their long-lost creators. Saner, too, since they had begun to find themselves, living together in a leaderless consensus that sometimes astonished him. Until today, he had seen no unhappiness.

"Defender—" Still too hesitant, they stepped a little nearer. "We speak for the colony, and we've come to ask for help."

"If I can help," he said. "But have you asked the ship? It has programs for most problems."

"The ship isn't human." Frowning, the girl glanced back to where it stood just above the broad line of red mud the monsoon flood had left. A fragile metal shell, scarred from space and fire and a million years of time. "It never says much."

"It's always busy with the program for whatever it's making in the assembly cell," the man added. "With us all done, it's ready for livestock now. And books, as soon as we have safe places to keep them. But we've no room for livestock here."

He turned to gesture across the narrow fields, now patterned green and gold with growing crops and ripened grain, sloping sharply up from the river bank to the rust-red cliffs and the wide white curtain of the great waterfall.

"The canyon has been a good beginning place, but we're already tilling every meter of it, down to the lake. That's why we need you—to help us get out. Some of us, anyhow. Onto new ground, up above the cliffs, where floods don't come."

"I can try." He hated to quench their eager smiles. "But that thorn jungle—it covers nearly everything."

"Which is why we need you."

"Not much I can do about it." He had to shake his head. "It's ugly stuff that loves the monsoon rains. Not native, I think, to the planet. The invaders must have brought it, maybe as a weapon. The thorns and the rotting leaves are poison."

"We'll fight it." Eyes resolute, the man looked up at the far green rim above the cliffs. "It's pretty tough for stone tools. We need metal. We know how to work metal—and lots of other technologies. But we've found no ores."

"None here." The Defender shrugged. "Scarce, I imagine, everywhere. I haven't seen any surface deposits. Probably used up by the natives before the robots murdered them."

"There will be metal." The stubborn brown eyes returned to him. "Metal the natives used, left where they died—unless the city was looted." The girl caught his hand, and they stepped a little toward him, straight and sturdy and determined. "We want you to guide us there."

"If the ship agrees—" He raised a golden hand to temper their shining joy. "But the jungle will be cruel."

The ship agreed and even improvised a quick program to fit them with heavier boots and gloves and headgear, shields against the thorns. They packed food: bread from the community kitchen, nuts and dried fruit, all grown from plants adapted to the planet and their needs. Working by the night's infrared, he salvaged metal from empty fuel tanks to make a water can and machetes.

At sunrise, when he could unfold his stubby wings to catch new energy, he led the way up the canyon and around the fall, following a perilous trail. Not entirely natural, it still showed traces of what must have been a scenic drive when the planet was alive. They turned north along the rocky brink, where the soil was washed thin and the cruel-spiked jungle sometimes broken.

The thorns had turned green by then since the monsoon, veiled in delicate fernlike sprays of young growth and splashed with enormous scentless purple blooms. Last year's leaves, rotting everywhere, were a foul black carpet that set Jayna and Galen to wheezing till they masked themselves against the evil reek. Blood streaked and swollen where the thorns had caught them, they hacked and hacked at each new barrier with a cheerful determination.

He led the way where there was sun and spreading space for his flightless wings, but when the jungle grew too dense for him, they forged quietly ahead. At ease with him now, they spoke of all their eager hopes for Mansphere. His human half found a cautious joy in their human fellowship, though since the tragedy of Eve he had been afraid to let the colonists get too near.

Two days out, the canyon walls closed in toward a floor of great blue boulders, brighter and harder than any natural stone. Fragments of a dam, he thought, which must have been shattered by missiles from space—natural erosion could never have crumbled the material so utterly. The jungle pressed closer there, but they found a way to push north through it, along a half-clear avenue that must have been a buried road.

At dusk on the fifth day, with the jungle turning crimson to his infrared vision, they came to an enormous object towering a hundred meters out of the spiky tangle off the road. Unmarred by the attack from space and all the millennia since, it was an egg-shape stood on end. A dull yellow-red by daylight, it shone golden after dark, like that strange rectangle he had found on the stormy eastern cliffs.

Galen and Jayna, feverish and worn, stopped to sleep beneath that luminous ovoid, but he spent his little store of power to reach the source of another golden glow. What he found was a second level strip, longer and broader than the one by the sea, most of it buried under the debris of time and ruin. An airfield that had served the city?

Next day, beyond a boulder-rimmed crater lake where the humans drank and bathed and refilled the water tank, they entered outskirts of the murdered metropolis. Mountains of its broken stuff, shining white and midnight black and sapphire blue, all gemstone hard. The sad remains of shattered walls and towers jutting out of the tangled spines like the broken bones of some leviathan.

"It must have been a splendid world." The girl had paused to regain her breath, a sort of wary awe on her red-wealed face. "What killed it so terribly dead?"

"I can't imagine." He had been afraid to frighten them, but looking at her, listening to the ring of Galen's whetstone on the worn machete, he knew they were strong enough to face reality. "The space missiles did harm enough, but I can't guess what sort of missile would kill everything." He shook his head. "The only animal life I've seen is in the sea."

"Do you think—" The man squinted sharply at him. "Do you think we're in danger?"

"Perhaps." He had to nod. "You've heard about the other Defenders? They flew this way three years ago, sent by the ship to learn what they could. They never returned." He paused again, recalling their bright-winged splendor. "We never knew what happened to them."

"The robots are responsible?"

"They call themselves Attack Command."

"Should we expect attack from them?"

"I talked to one robot—talked in a way—but it told me very little." He shrugged. "They've been sitting there at their base for twenty thousand years, waiting for whatever it is they call the Master Builders. I hope they keep on waiting."

"If they don't—" The man tried his blade on a green thorn twig. "We were never promised paradise."

He turned to the girl. They stood a long time looking into each other's eyes before he took her blade to sharpen it.

"All they ever promised us—" Smiling solemnly, she looked up at him. "All we ask for is a chance."

That night, he picked up a signal from space.

Rising, fading again, the signal grew slowly stronger until at last he knew it was a modulated beam, transmitted on a frequency the robot disk had used. The source hung motionless among the westward stars. Sliding down with them into the crimson jungle, it was gone before dawn.

When the humans woke, he told them.

"The orbital ship?" The man frowned gravely, undismayed. "Calling the robot base?"

"Something farther. Out toward the stars." He added, "We've heard nothing from the ship since I was on it. I believe we left it dead."

The girl rubbed sleep from her swollen eyes.

"We came for metal," she said. "Let's look for it."

His magnetic sense soon found it, lying beneath broken stone and the muds of long millennia and last season's foul leaves, most of it buried deeper than they could dig. They built little cairns of bright rubble shards to mark the largest masses.

"We'll come back," the man said. "More of us, with better tools and some kind of vehicle, as soon as we can build one."

The girl was cheered when she found a layer of charred twigs and ashes under the rotting leaves.

"The jungle has burned." She rose to face its spiny tangle with a red-scarred smile. "Touched off by lightning, I imagine, in dry springs before the monsoon comes. A way for us to fight it."

Now and then, bits of metal lay within reach. Small objects, most of them broken and corroded, all of them puzzling. A few were whole. A graceful thin-winged creature in flight, shaped of a silver-white metal harder than their machetes. Three heavy golden disks, strangely stamped, that must have been coins. The figure of a woman—a tiny copy of the statue he had found when he crossed the city before—cast in some hard copper-red alloy, unbroken and exquisite.

"Lovely." The girl's blistered palm cradled the statuette. "Too precious to be melted down."

"Human." The man bent to stare, awe in his eyes. "Human as we are." He looked at the Defender. "Do you think—"

"Cousins." The Defender nodded. "Children of another ship, one that reached here I couldn't guess how long before us."

"Nothing—" Whispering, the girl shook her head. "Nothing to tell us how they died. All of them, so suddenly."

Eyes dark with dread, she looked at the Defender.

"A riddle we've failed to solve." Watching her, he saw a surge of quiet reliance, stronger than her fear. "It looks as if they had no chance for defense. The missiles must have been loaded with something very deadly. I've begun to doubt that we'll learn much about it here."

"At least we're getting metal." The man grinned, a little grimly. "If the weapon's anything that can ever strike again, we've been warned."

Before sunset, the signal clattered again, stronger. Rising in the east, crawling fast across the sky, dropping like a stone into the reddening eastward dusk.

"Here?" The girl had watched him follow it, her grave eyes still unafraid. "Already?"

"In orbit now." He nodded. "Calling down. Most of the signal was gibberish to me, but it kept repeating one phrase I know from the disk. 'Attack Command.' "

Silently, she turned to the man.

"The things that sent the robots?" He peered into the darkening sky and swung to squint at the Defender. "Does this mean they're finally here?"

"Perhaps." He shrugged. "I'll have to find out."

"If you go there—"

The girl caught his arm. They had never touched before. He shrank from her fingers, afraid she might awaken more of Martin Rablon's hopeless devotion to that older Jayna than he could handle now.

"We'll go with you."

The man was reaching for his machete and the water tank as if to march at once.

"I wish you could," he told them. "But it's two thousand kilometers, most of the distance across a bare plateau where you couldn't find food or even water. I'll have to go alone."

"If the other Defenders were lost—" The girl came closer, and her nearness sent a shudder through him. "Isn't this very dangerous for you?"

"No—no matter." He tried to restore his computer control. "I'm a Defender. Expendable. With very little to lose."

"Shouldn't—" He heard the tremor in her voice. "Shouldn't we ask the ship?"

"It's out of reach." He shook his head. "Out of radio range, down in that canyon. The trip back to ask would take too many days."

"Defender—"

The girl's scratched and swollen arms were suddenly around him, her mouth on his. Her odors wrapped him, sharp with her sweat but still intoxicating. Swaying against her warm flesh, he felt a stab of pain where his penis should have been.

"I wish—" she whispered. "I wish you were human."

Afraid to say what he wished, he squeezed her briefly and let her go, turning to grip the man's calloused hand.

"I wish," the man said, "that we had been Defenders."

"We're what—what we are," he muttered. "Programed a million years ago. For bigger things than we're apt to wish for."

"We—we'll remember."

Half blind until his senses adjusted to the red-clotted dark, he blundered toward the road. Looking back when his vision had cleared, he found them standing hand in hand, peering after him. The man waved, and he heard the girl call, almost in Jayna's voice:

"Come back, Defender—"

In low orbit now, the object crept across the sky three times that night. Its signal clattered and paused, clattered and paused. In the pauses, he supposed, the robots at the base would be answering, but they were out of his range. Once again, he caught the phrase "Attack Command," but nothing else he understood.

His power ran out before midnight, and he had to wait for the sun. Even then, the thorns tearing at his wings, he had to keep them half closed. Starving for power, he was two days reaching the ancient avenue that he and the disk had followed north. Five more retracing it, until the jungle thinned beneath the rim on the highlands he had to cross.

Out on the open plateau, he made better time. The days were still long, the sky commonly cloudless. Spread wide to the sun, his wings caught surplus power to recharge the backpack and let him tramp on far into the crimson nights.

Pushing always on, he listened to the orbital signal. It ceased and came again, ceased and came again. Lower now, the object crept faster across the sky. Its orbit tilted suddenly, letting it swing north to the latitude of the robot base.

Then the signal separated. One source remained in the tilted orbit. The other, weaker but very busy, dropped fast until he lost it beneath the north horizon. A few days later, that happened again. A few more days, and yet again.

The falling sources must be landing craft, sliding down toward the base. The Master Builders, he imagined, somehow delayed for many thousand of Mansphere's deliberate years but here at last to claim their conquest. Wondering about them one cold red dawn when he lay waiting for the sun, wondering what they might be and whether they could be beaten, he remembered Olga.

Her funeral. A wet winter day, cold for La Jolla. His own parents dead and hers unable to come. She had never been well enough to make friends there, and the service was private. Jewish, for her parents' sake. He hardly heard the words. All he could feel was a numb gratitude that her suffering was done.

Afterward, dreading the empty house, he walked down to the beach and stood staring at the breakers till the drizzle had soaked through his coat. Thinking how Olga would have scolded him for getting chilled, he stopped at the Lighthouse for a glass of dry sherry, and a steak sandwich he left on his plate. On impulse, he phoned Megan from the booth outside to tell her he would be back at the lab next day.

"Not yet!" she protested. "Ivan, please. You've been through too much. You need at least a little time—"

"I need the project," he told her. "It's all I have left."

In the house at last, he tried to write Olga's mother, tried to sort through the things she had left in her bedside desk, tried to read the diary she had kept until her crippled fingers failed. Awake half the endless night, he woke late next morning from a dream that he was God.

Reigning in some high heaven where the angels behind him all sat silent, bent over row upon row of computer terminals. He sat on a diamond throne, robed in snowy ermine, splendidly crowned with jeweled gold. The crown was too heavy and lined with stinging thorns. Blood oozed down from them to clot his flowing beard. It felt stiff and sticky where it dried.

Olga and Roger knelt on a mat of thorns far below his throne, praying for their lives. Roger was only seven, young bones showing through the worn-out Dodger T-shirt he wouldn't quit wearing. His little hands were raised and trembling, cruelly torn and dripping blood on the thorns, his huge eyes desperately imploring.

His prayer was the multiplication tables, up to twelve times twelve, each table run into one breathless sentence, the way he had shrilled them out when he came running home from his third day of arithmetic. He was begging to stay alive so that he could be a scientist like his father.

Olga was young and well and wonderful, alluring in the snug yellow sweater she had worn the first day he saw her in that biology classroom at Union. She was crying but not for herself. She had seen the blood from his own crown of thorns, and she prayed for him, chanting the old prayers from the siddur that her cantor father had *mutched* her to learn.

"Should we die in this misery, *chas vesholem*! Save us, Father, that we may save you."

He stretched his hand out to bless and save them with the healing virus he had created, but his arm changed as he raised it, stiffening into a scaled and taloned reptilian limb. He wanted to pray for them and himself, but there was no other God to hear him, and his voice had become the senseless clatter of a computer-driven printer.

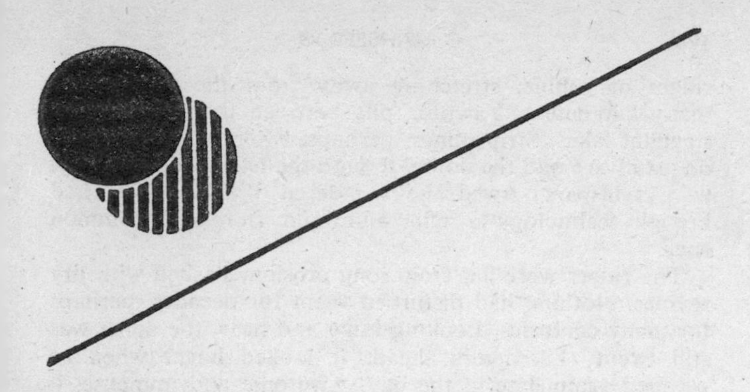

Pushing on, he veered far westward to avoid the chasm that had stalled his first effort to reach the robot base. The river was a long lake where he reached it, held behind an ancient dam that was somehow still unbroken. He rafted across the lake and turned east along the canyon rim toward the base.

It rose over the rocky horizon at last, a pale silver moon still hazy across a hundred kilometers. He hid that day in a dry arroyo, wings spread wide to drink the sun, and crept on through the dim crimson night, keeping warily low.

Before sunrise, another lander sped from the west. He heard the loud clatter of its signal, but even there he caught no answer from the base. At first a dark fleck in the milky dawn, it swelled silently and fast. It was suddenly gone, fallen toward the silvery dome, before he heard the sonic boom and then its dying shriek.

The craft's signal ceased, and he heard nothing more from space. It had been the sixth craft to land. Recalling the six empty housings on the orbital craft he had explored, he thought it ought to be the last of this new armada.

He followed a ravine down to a steep shelf a few hundred meters below the rim, where he was under cover. Half the day, he crawled and scrambled on toward the base, across treacherous gravel slopes and sheer cliffs that fell giddily to roaring white water. At noon, he climbed to look over the rim.

What he found was stark desolation. Mountainous

ridges of rubble, stretching away from the canyon for many kilometers. Yawning pits between them, filled with stagnant lakes. Strip mines, perhaps, where the robots had dug stuff to build the dome, though the naked rocks he saw were feldspars. Awed, he wondered if the robots had brought technology to refine aluminum from such common rock.

The ridges were flat from long erosion, slashed with dry ravines. Nothing had disturbed them for decades, perhaps for many centuries. Looking huge and near, the dome was still twenty kilometers ahead. It looked huger when he climbed again, late in the day. Awesome and immense, it ballooned into the sky just beyond a gray-paved strip three kilometers wide. Five of the landing craft stood in a row at the edge of the strip, thick-bodied machines with stubby wings. The sixth, drawn closer to the dome, seemed toy-small beneath it.

He had expected intense activity, unearthly aliens and teeming robots busy unloading the fleet and preparing to take possession of the planet, but he saw no movement, heard no sound, overheard no signal, not even from the orbital starcraft.

Clinging at the top of a narrow rock chimney, he looked for a way to get nearer, but the level pavement stretched unbroken for many kilometers in both directions, with no cover anywhere.

He waited, watching. A narrow doorway stood open in the base of the dome near the last lander, but nothing emerged and nothing entered. The silence, the total inaction, began to seem ominous because it was so baffling. He was almost relieved, just at sunset, when he saw movement.

A bright glint sliding out of that last lander.

His eyes telescopic, he made out a mirror-surfaced tank-shape riding a thick block of some duller metal down a narrow ramp. Like a railway tank car, he thought, except that it had no wheels. It crept slowly toward that doorway and vanished at last into the dome.

He climbed out of the chimney. Veering a little so the lander screened him from the doorway, he walked out toward it. Nothing stopped him. Nothing moved until, half across the strip, a second tank-shape descended the ramp.

He dashed to overtake it. Recalling a skill from those

hard years when Don Brink had learned to ride the rails before he learned to fight, the Defender ran beside the vehicle, caught a jutting flange, hauled himself aboard. Gliding silently down a red-shining track, it carried him toward the dome.

Into air with a dreadful taint.

He crouched behind the tank. It was slick metal, cold to his touch, almost black by infrared. Inside something was stirring. Something throbbed like a pump. Something hummed. Something wheezed like escaping air. Something clanged, clanged again.

Still clinging, he was carried into darkness.

Into death.

The odious malodor that Don Brink had learned too young and never learned to endure. His human feelings reeled from recollected nausea, but his computer control kept him hanging to the tank. Sliding on, it swept him into a dim and dreadful shadowland, lit only by the glowing red track.

The track branched, branched, branched again. When his eyes adjusted, he counted many hundred tanks, spaced as far as he could see along the branching tracks. They all had opened, the top of each hinging upward to uncover a sort of berth surrounded with dark mechanisms.

They had contained men and women. Sleepers in those berths, who had awakened only to die. He found them everywhere. Sprawled across the berths. Fallen on the shining tracks. All bloated, distorted, glassily staring and terribly still.

The block-shape stopped. Gas hissed. A strange hot scent washed the evil reek away, but only for an instant. The black metal behind him throbbed like a beaten gong, slid abruptly upward. A harsh shout, and a living man lurched off the berth.

A big man, hard faced but seemingly human, in strange battle gear. Uniformed in mottled brown and green, harnessed with bristling devices that must be weapons. A rifle-like device in his hands, sweeping toward the Defender.

The Defender dropped under the rim of the carrier block, rolled toward the nearest corpse. A woman's, her breasts strutted hard, blackened nipples bursting from her green-splotched jacket. He scrabbled for her weapon.

"Control Program to Defender." The toneless words froze him, spoken only in his mind. "You will not fight."

The man sprang after him off the block.

"You will not initiate combat with any inhabitant. You will not resist hostile action."

The Defender tried to wrest the weapon from those cold fingers, but his own hand was paralyzed.

"Natives display advanced technological culture," the machine inside him ran on, silent and inexorable. "Consequently, they are protected. Control Program prohibits any violence against them."

"Defender—"

Staggering for balance, the man swung the weapon toward him. The Defender dived behind the corpse. The weapon followed. A double purple flash, a double crash. The projectile exploded against the floor behind him. Flying fragments stung him.

"Defender to Control—"

The man stumbled blindly nearer, and he tried to flatten himself.

"Attack Command is not protected." He groped for human logic. "Because it isn't native. These aliens are invaders. We got here before—"

"Correction, Defender." The program cut him off. "Their robots were already here. Quite possibly they were here. We lack information for resolution of logical dilemma—"

He quit listening.

The man had dropped his weapon. It discharged again when it hit the red-glowing track. The projectle shrieked away to blaze against a distant wall. The man goggled and gasped, clutching at his throat. Frozen for a moment, he toppled forward, kicked twice, and lay still in a bright-red puddle of his own excreta.

An instant of stillness before the echo crashed back from walls he couldn't see, crashed again and yet again to reveal the vastness of that black chamber before it died. The human in him was giddy with illness, overpowered by too much death. Shuddering to a wave of human terror, he saw that the dome had become a dreadful trap, even for him.

If his power gave out, here in the dark—

In a moment, with his computer self in control, he was

climbing back into the open tank on the block-shape he had ridden, using every sense to study it. The berth was pliantly padded, still faintly glowing with the warmth of its passenger. Some strange-odored gas was still whistling softly from beneath it.

He turned away to stare into the dark, grappling with a monstrous irony. The invaders must have crossed space in these machines, sleeping through centuries, perhaps through millennia. Awakened at last to take over the world their robots had won—now dead forever.

He shivered and moved on.

What had killed them? Something very sudden; his attacker had lived hardly twenty seconds outside the tank. Something silent, invisible by infrared. Something unforeseen. Armed for battle and here inside their own fortress, they had been taken by shocking surprise.

Were others coming? Looking back at the distant doorway, he noted no movement. Was yet another starship on the way, with another armada of landers? No more signals had come from space, but there had been none till this last craft was in orbit.

He pushed deeper into the reeking dark. Row upon row of the open tanks, all identical. The invaders lay where they had fallen, most of them many days dead, hideous now. He heard no sound, saw no movement, met no robots, discovered no clue.

Where were the robots?

Conquerors of the planet, exterminators of its human civilization, waiting through the ages for their builders to arrive—had they also died? Or malfunctioned, perhaps, to destroy their own creators?

Pushing on, and on again, through thickening crimson darkness, he found no answers. The glow of the tracks had dimmed, as if the system had been turned off, until all he could see was a tiny island around him, lit by his own body heat.

That room was enormous, too large and too dark to let him see its full extent. He came upon enormous cylindrical pillars towering till he lost them in the gloom. He blundered into lofty walls of some gray aluminum alloy, reaching up and out as far as he could see.

Wasting too much time, draining too much power, he searched for corridors that might take him farther. Several times he found a dark track that ran straight against the wall, as if into a door he found no means to open. At last, at the brink of turning back, he stumbled on an oval opening in the base of a pillar.

Stepping past a monstrous, bloated thing, he was inside a circular shaft that ran upward into darkness. His own dim glow showed ladder rungs spaced for human climbing. Already too far from where the sun could come, he climbed.

On another level, eighty meters up, he came out into another silent space, dark as the one below. Dim shapes loomed around him. Tools of war, when he was near enough to make them out. Low-crouching armored things like trackless battle tanks—propelled, perhaps, by gravity mirrors, as the machines he fought on the orbital starcraft must have been. Long guns and ugly missles not much different from those Don Brink had known so long ago.

The odors of death were different here, laced with the lethal peach-pit scent of hydrogen cyanide. He followed it out of the armor, into rows of wheelless gravitic transports stacked with ammunition and lighter weaponry. On one black avenue, he caught a scent that froze him.

Megan's lilac, very faint.

That led him aside, and he found the lost Defenders. They had fallen side by side, golden arms embracing, fragile wings flattened to the floor, all color gone. Strangely peaceful in his pale glow, their faces woke old recollections. A half smile of Megan's, gravely wistful. Wardian's half-ironic grin. They were cold when he bent at last to touch them, stiff and still as the dead on the level below.

Wardian, a million years ago.

Lean and athletic in the trim yellow jumpsuit. Just in from hang gliding because the wind had become too high. They were in the Albuquerque lab, waiting for the staff to prepare the scanner. He had boiled water in the little kitchen off the lounge to brew *yerba maté*.

"Like to try it?" Brink passed the gourd to Wardian. "I learned to like it years ago, in a time that was pretty grim for me. The aftermath of a misplanned ccup that got nipped in the bud. I was hiding in Asuncion, with next to no money and a wound in my shoulder. Most of my friends dead or in jail. A Guarani girl taught me the taste—"

He watched Wardian's cautious pull at the silver *bombilla.*

"A taste I'll never get." Wardian handed it back and went to the kitchen for tomato juice. "If you've never noticed, we're an odd lot." He turned to look at Megan's grave, green-eyed smile in a big photo she had let them hang above the door. "When you think of all the ways we've failed and all we hope to do."

"We've all failed. Too often." He nodded, savoring the hot *caa-cuys* and feeling close to Wardian. "I was beaten when she found me, washed up and hopeless. A pretty unlikely accident that she ever picked me for this peculiar game."

"The greatest game there'll ever be." Wardian opened the little can and lifted it as if for a toast. "Though in the nature of the case we'll never know the final score."

"Win or lose, I love it."

He enjoyed Wardian. Enjoyed Tomislav and old Galen Ulver. Even Marty Rablon. And Megan, most of all. After a life of hard conflict, of too much mistrust and too many betrayals, he had found something strangely good in the way they were all sharing themselves to create the Defender—that splendid future fighting man he couldn't quite imagine and knew he would never live to meet. An odd lot perhaps, but in a way the scanner was welding them into one. He pulled on the *bombilla.*

"Life rolls funny dice." Wardian frowned absently at his silver-mounted gourd. "I never expected the freaks of fate that put me here. I should have been a business man, watching the Dow and voting Republican and fretting about the GNP."

He nodded companionably, not needing to speak.

"I'd grown up shy of women." Wardian glanced up at Megan's photo with a wry headshake. "Burnt by my own innocence when I was a kid and taught by my dad that they'd be poison. Steered clear of them till I met Debbie. A better sort—or seemed to be. We were college juniors when we met. She'd had two or three unlucky affairs, but she convinced herself that I'd be different.

"We fell for each other. Hard. Her people were wealthy. Banking, mining, oil—my dad had worked for hers, surveying mining properties. They knew I had nothing, but that didn't matter to her. Maybe not to him. He'd made his own way up, and I guess he saw his early self in me.

"Her mother had older money, though I think not much. Philadelphia Mainline. She was cool to me at first, but Debbie commonly got what she wanted. She wanted me. That Christmas, she took me with her parents for two weeks at Angel Fire. I taught her to ski. She made chances to teach me sex. I loved it and thought I loved her.

"At Easter, she took me home with her. An old farmhouse out of Philadelphia her folks had rebuilt into a mansion. We talked to her parents. Her mother wanted us to wait till we graduated. Her father said he trusted her. If I'd change my astronomy major to business, he'd give me a chance in his companies.

"We shook hands on it. Her mother kissed me on the cheek. Debbie had me in her room that night, and I thought we were in heaven." He sighed, gazing at Megan again. "It all blew up the day classes ended. Her mother wanted me back in Philadelphia at a formal reception to announce our engagement. Debbie was delighted, and I felt happy enough—or thought I did till she said I had to cut my hair." He shook his head, with a quizzical shrug. "I said I wouldn't.

"Surprised at myself. A silly row when I look back at it. Not just about the hair—it really wasn't all that long. I felt torn up and sorry for Debbie, but I couldn't help the way I felt. She cried and kissed me and tried to get me back into bed. I'd loved her—but maybe not enough. When the showdown came, I couldn't pay the price."

Wryly, Wardian shrugged again.

"No haircut, and here I am. Used-up astronaut and defeated space explorer. Overaging pilot. Part-time playboy. When I was on the way to be an oil and coal tycoon." His brown face was ironic as he grinned at the gourd. "If Debbie's dice had come up seven . . ."

He unlocked the stiffened embrace and moved his arms around Defender Two. She was clumsily rigid, her half-metallic body nearly too heavy for his drawn-down power. Stumbling under her weight, he took her back to the shaft, down again to the dreadful lower level and all the dead invaders.

The reek of hydrogen cyanide on the upper level had solved the riddle of how they died. Harmless to him, its odor masked by the charnel reek here, it was thick enough to kill anything organic. Yet puzzles enough were left. What had turned the robot fortress into this appalling trap? How had these new invaders been lured inside?

The doorway was a far shard of brightness. He labored toward it, reeling under Defender Two. Too heavy for him, she felt too stiff and cold to live again. The tiny light mocked him, drawing farther away, and farther again, but he stumbled out at last into clean air and sunlight.

Morning had come. Dimly surprised at the time, he staggered on for another hundred meters, upwind. Beyond the lander, he laid her on the edge of that wide airstrip. Her lifeless wings were too stiff to spread, but he opened his own and dropped beside her.

Noon had come before he stirred and called to her. She made no response, but her golden limbs felt warmer, and her wings were pliant. He stretched them out to catch the sun and went back into that cavernous tomb. Nothing had changed. He found the shaft again. Climbing back to the second level, he brought Defender Three down through the horribly dead and out into the sun.

The rest of the day he lay beside them, drinking precious energy. His human elation shadowed with a human dread, he tried to keep his senses tuned for surviving invaders. For their robots—which should not have been harmed by cyanide. For signals out of space.

Nothing. Nothing but another fleeting reek of death once when the wind shifted. No robot emerged. Nothing moved or called from orbit. When Three's wings had warmed, he roused himself to spread them wider. The sun went down, and the silent world turned crimson.

"Don—" Megan's breathless-seeming whisper. "Don?"

He found her rising beside him. Alive again, luminous, lovely. Her body shone with its own warmth now, a rosy shimmer reflected on her half-spread wings.

"Meg—"

She was Megan to him, no longer Two. Trembling, he reached to take her in his arms, but she was turning away. She had found Defender Three.

"Mack! Mack, are you all right?"

On her knees, she gathered up the limp-winged body to kiss the lifeless face. Wardian's, Roman nosed, frozen with his old grin.

"He'll be—okay." The words came hard. Seeing that naked golden maleness, he flinched and shivered. "All he needs is more sunlight."

"You brought us out?" The new Wardian still in her arms, she looked up at him. "You've grown wings?"

"The ship modified the retranslation programs to grow a power source for me—"

"The ship?" She shook her head, staring. "Still alive?"

"When I left it."

"We thought it was lost." Her eyes opened wider. "And thought you were when we saw your gravitic flyer falling into space."

"You were free? The robots hadn't caught you then?"

"They never did."

"Three years—" He frowned at her, astonished. "Since

you left the ship. I imagined you had been captured or destroyed."

"We heard you—" Awkwardly, she hesitated. "Heard you calling, but Mack said we shouldn't risk an answer—by then we'd seen too much destruction, and we thought the killer things might be listening. But we did go back. We really did, close enough to look. All we saw was the monsoon lake. We thought the ship was drowned. Gone."

Her roseate hand rose impulsively to stroke his arm.

"I'm sorry," she whispered. "Dreadfully sorry for the pain we must have caused you. Mack said we were malfunctional Defenders. Malformed by that old damage to the ship's computer, though in a different way than you are. Perhaps—perhaps we are. We should have kept on searching, but I guess we didn't care enough. Except for each other. Can you—"

She reached out to him imploringly.

"Oh, Don, I hope you'll try to understand."

"Megan—Megan—" Her hand was golden velvet, her touch electric to him. Peering at her luminous loveliness, he couldn't feel accusing. "Actually, I suppose we've done well enough. The ship floated. I hauled it out of the water. Up to the depot where you cached the oil nuts. All the colonists have now been born."

"If you feel bitter—" Staring down at the body in her arms, still lax and dark, she drew it closer to her own shining warmth. "Can you remember what it means to be in love?"

"I remember," he told her. "Too well."

"If you blame us—" Her bright voice broke. "I guess you should. Because we *were* malfunctional. But we were happy, Don. Terribly, terribly happy. So happy not to have the burden of the ship. We were gods! Immortal gods, with all the planet for our own. Having each other, we needed nothing else."

She smiled down at Wardian, murmuring tenderly:

> The soul selects her own society
> Then shuts the door
> I've known her from an ample nation
> Choose one
> Then close the valves of her attention
> Like stone.

Her eyes came back to him. "That's how we felt—"

"Don't grieve." He tried to grin. "If you've really killed all the invaders and stopped their robot armies, nothing else can matter much—"

"Killed?" Frowning, she stared at the lander and the dome. "You're sure?"

"All I saw. They were carried into the dome still sealed in their transport pods. The pods opened there, and they died. I think of hydrogen cyanide—"

"Mack's work." She looked keenly up at him, her warm voice falling. "Maybe I should say your own work, Don, because Mack had so much of Don Brink in him. That was the last hope we had, and not a strong one."

Very gently, she laid the slack-limbed body back on the pavement. Sighing, she turned to kiss him lightly. Her cool lips left him chilled and quivering. Bathed in her faint scent, he ached with memories of Megan.

"Don!" she whispered. "Dear Don! It's a dreadful thing, when I love you so and feel how much you hurt. But you must try to understand what Mack meant to me. Emily said it better than I can:

> Yet never met this fellow,
> Attended or alone,
> Without a tighter breathing
> And zero at the bone—"

Her glowing fingers rose to stroke his face, to touch his eyes and stroke his nose and linger very lightly on his lips.

"Remember, Don," her Megan voice begged him gently. "Remember you're in Mack. Galen is. Ivan is. And Marty. Loving Mack, I was loving all of you. I guess it doesn't help to tell you, but that was the best of our happiness. Discovering so much of ourselves in each other.

"Don't you see?"

"I'll try—try to see."

She held him briefly against her, then drew slowly back to look at him again.

"How'd you get here, Don? Without the flyer—"

"On foot. A long trek."

"If you hadn't, we'd have been trapped there." He felt her shiver. "Forever."

"The colonists need metal," he told her. "I came out with two of them—a couple who call themselves Galen and Jayna—to look for metal in the old city. Hoping, too, to learn what killed it."

"No evidence there. Or anywhere outside this base. Not that we could ever find, digging into a hundred different sites. The same cruel story, repeated everywhere. The planet was attacked from space. No warning so far as we could tell. Nor time for any effort at defense. All land life was wiped out by some weapon we couldn't imagine then.

"A tantalizing puzzle." She shrugged rosy shoulders. "It occupied us all those years. Not that we felt much urgency about it, because we were so happy in each other. Expecting to live almost forever, with all the planet for our own. Aware of no real danger—

"Not till we heard the signal—"

"The invaders?"

"Still far out." She nodded, with a sad glance at Wardian. "So faint at first we couldn't be sure it was a signal. All gabble, of course, even after it was stronger. The end of our honeymoon. I wanted to look for an island where we could live in hiding, but I told you Mack has a lot of Don Brink programed into him. He said we had to tackle the robots.

"We found the canyon and followed it to a point where we could watch the dome and listen in. When we knew the alien ship was headed here, he said we had to get inside. We waited for a cloudy night. Climbed out of the canyon and flew low to the dome.

"Nothing challenged us, and we landed on the crown of the dome. The robots were talking to space through a signal dish there, but they didn't spot us. We kept low and dived down an airshaft. Nearly blundered into a robot gliding out of a control center they have just under the dish. A pretty desperate time!"

He felt her tremble.

"The place was dark. Our power ran out, and of course we couldn't risk going back outside for sunlight. At first, we were able to tap into the power lines to recharge ourselves, but the robots detected the loss. They cut off the lines we were using and came to hunt us. We had to live in hiding, eking out the little energy we found ways to steal.

"Yet I guess we were lucky, at least in a way. Except

around the dish and the control center, those upper levels were pretty quiet. Storage spaces. Hangars and munitions depots. Most of the robots were down below. Busy, I imagine, preparing for the landings. With a lot of luck and a bit of Don Brink's skill, we got into the arsenal where you found us.

"They came after us when we had to tap another circuit. A dreadful time, Don. We could barely move because they cut the power before we'd got enough to help. We could sense them cruising in the dark to run us down, but we hid inside a big thing Mack said was a gravitic transport. And they failed to find us. Because we were getting so cold, Mack said, so near run down that we weren't radiating.

"When they were gone, we dragged ourselves out to look at all those horrible weapons. The same type that were used to murder the planet, Mack thought, still kept on hand for anybody else. All of them dreadful enough, but the worst were the cyanide bombs. Hellish things, when Mack found what they were."

A kind of horror hushed her voice.

"The way they kill! Mack took one of them apart, far enough to find out that. It was loaded with a killer catalyst. A heavy, persistent gas that would be stable for days out in the air. When it's activated by any radiation, even infrared, it combines carbon dioxide and atmospheric nitrogen into hydrocyanic acid gas. Even in the human lung."

"So that was it?" he whispered. "The lethal agency?"

"Those missiles must have been scattering it all around the planet." She nodded. "For the wind to sweep everywhere—turning the air as people breathed it into a quick-killing gas."

"I see." He grinned bleakly at the dome. "And you released it against the invaders?"

"Mack's plan." Her luminous smile was fixed on Wardian, her fingers caressing that rigid patrician face. "We listened in as the starship dropped into orbit and the landers began to separate. The first one came in. Watching from the upper level, we saw the automated gear begin hauling the passenger capsules inside.

"We saw them opening. Armed men and women reviving from sleep, tumbling out to take over from the robots. Mack said we had to stop them. Of course, we didn't have to worry about the cyanide, but they had other weapons that terrified me—"

He saw her bright face tighten.

"I hated Mack's plan. I had to, Don, because—because you know we're forbidden to kill. But Mack said he was malfunctional enough to do it. Anyhow, of course, stopping robots isn't killing. The first trick was to keep them from warning anybody. What we did wasn't easy because we'd both drained our power too far. So far I thought we could never be revived.

"The robots never caught us—credit Don Brink for that. We set a bomb to stop their main computer. That knocked down a flying thing Mack called a servo-robot. We reprogrammed it to talk the aliens into the trap. Dragged ourselves back to the arsenal. Mack was opening valves to flood the place with the cyanogen catalyst when I blacked out."

A shadow of terror lingered in her eyes.

"We never expected you to come—" She clung to him, whispering desperately. "Or to see light again." Her shining mouth sought his, and the lilac scent was suddenly more than he could bear. "If we had any way to thank you—"

Trembling, he turned away.

She said no more, and they waited for the sun. Lying beside the reborn Wardian, she listened at his chest, touched him to sense his temperature, finally spread her own wings to cover him. The cooling world faded into redder shadow, and he sat watching the stars of Mansphere, cold and still strange to him. Before the sun was up, he heard her startled whisper:

"Don! Who's that?"

He saw an alien aircraft diving toward the dome.

If invaders were left alive and he was forbidden to fight—

Triumph snuffed out, he turned to watch the landing craft. It was a stubby-winged jet, like the one he had flown. It touched down silently, one hundred meters across the strip. A man jumped out, a woman behind him. The man was another invader, clad in motley brown and green, harnessed with arms. The woman—

Jayna!

No prisoner, she wore a bristling belt slung with a pistol-shaped weapon. She paused a moment, staring in wonder at the dome, and ran to overtake the man. He had discovered the Defenders. Falling flat, he leveled a long gun.

She dropped beside him, weapon drawn.

The Defender walked on toward where they lay. Staring at him, Jayna whispered to the invader. He shouted at the flyer, and a golden-glinting object darted from it. The disk-thing they had brought from the orbital ship. It dived and stopped, hanging in the air between them.

"Flight Commander Donbrik to Defender One," its sharp inhuman staccato rattled abruptly. "Flight Commander Donbrik requires you to halt where you are and kneel to acknowledge his authority."

"He has no authority."

The invader barked again, with an imperative gesture.

"Defender One, you are to halt," the disk clattered. "If you disobey, the flight commander will open fire."

He walked on.

"Donbrik, don't!" He heard the girl's whisper. "Not yet—"

The invader had fired. Senses sharpened, the Defender saw the little puff of glowing red vapor, the spinning bullet creeping ahead of it. He accelerated his left wing to deflect the bullet and heard it whine away toward the dome.

He walked on.

The invader was about to fire again, but Jayna pushed the gun aside. Scrambling to her feet, she holstered her own weapon and ran out to meet him. Tanned browner since he saw her, she still wore the leathery stuff from her birthkit. The red welts from the jungle thorns had healed. Lithe and lovely, flushed with excitement, she was suddenly the Jayna that Rablon had adored a million years ago.

Trembling, he stopped.

The invader had come to his feet, rifle still ready. He muttered something at the disk. Gabbling, it dived into the Defender's face.

"Flight Commander Donbrik to Defender One. Flight Commander Donbrik informs you that he is not afraid. He has facts from the woman. He is aware that you are not a god. You are a machine. A service robot, not designed for combat. The commander requires your service now."

"Tell the commander I don't serve him."

The disk swung in the air to chatter at the invader. Scowling at the Defender, he waved the gun and rapped an answer.

"The commander requires obedience. He informs you that machines can be stopped."

"Tell the commander we've stopped his own machines—"

"Defender—" Not listening, the girl pushed forward to interrupt him. Her cool voice was Jayna's, cruel music to him. "Don't quarrel with the flight commander. Just let me tell you about him."

The invader had followed her forward. A lean, compact man, brown and fit, with an air of wary competence that he had to respect.

"He's the leader of his people, here to claim Mansphere—"

He watched the invader swing to peer at the other Defenders. The reborn Wardian was rising, rainbow wings alive again. The new Megan had bent to aid him. Golden, godlike, they stood for a moment face to face, absorbed in each other, then flowed together, wings closing to cover their hungry nude embrace.

Aching inside, he looked quickly away.

The disk jangled the invader's language. Scowling at them, the invader listened till it stopped, then grunted something at Jayna.

"Tell them, Defender." She grinned. "Tell them we've changed the rules here—if you can get their attention. Flight Commander Donbrik knows what they are. Robots, built to serve mankind. He'll have orders for them. He doesn't want them screwing, and he expects to be obeyed."

"Expects Defenders to obey?"

"You will obey. All of you." Her grin was gone. "Flight Commander Donbrik has come to take the planet over for the star masters. The ancient ruler race. They are children, I believe, of another seedship that reached their world so long ago that all they have is legends about it. The commander is named for Don Brink. A mythical hero to them."

"Your friend's no hero here."

Scanning that hard brown face, the Defender found nothing familiar. Yet, a little wistfully, he thought the original Don Brink might have liked being hired to conquer planets.

"How did you meet him?"

"He was scouting the planet when he saw us from the air. Galen and me. We were back near the ruins where you left us, cutting a trail through the jungle. At first, he thought we were survivors of the old civilization. Possible enemies. He sent the talker to spy on us, and finally landed to tell us who he is."

"And you surrendered to him."

"A dreadful misunderstanding." Shrugging impatiently, with a pout of momentary pain, she was the Jayna he recalled. "Galen wouldn't give up. I tried to hide after he was killed, but the talker ran me down. Donbrik was pretty rough with me at first. But now—"

A lilt he remembered lifted her voice.

"He's kinder to me now, since I've convinced him that our races must be cousins."

"Kinder? Have you forgotten what they did to our other cousins here?"

"Please—" She looked hurt. "Wait till you understand."

"I think I do," he told her. "It was his quote ruler race—his robots—that murdered the old civilization—"

"It was war." She shrugged. "The star masters were fighting in their own defense. Anyhow, you can't blame Commander Donbrik—not for mistakes made so many thousand years ago."

"Or for killing Galen?"

"Don't be cruel." A shadow brushed her face and vanished. "I did love Galen. What happened to him hurt me dreadfully, but he'd asked for it. With only that machete, he should never have fought. I did grieve for him, and at first I hated the flight commander. Till I knew him and the history of his people.

"A tragic history, really." She sighed and shook her head, smiling sadly at the invader. "The star masters. Even their name seems ironic now, because they've suffered such dreadful disasters. But it's a proud history, too. They were conquerors once."

"They shouldn't have been." He scowled at the scowling invader. "Don Brink's genes weren't engineered into the seed for conquest but only for defense—"

The invader yelped abruptly at the disk. Hovering lower, it jangled again.

"It's translating," she said. "The flight commander wants to know what you're saying."

"Nothing he'll be happy about—"

The invader barked, and the disk swung its dark face back to him.

"Flight Commander Donbrik to Defender. If you have information, the commander requires it now."

"Later." And he told the girl, "Go ahead—if he'll let you."

"He will." She swayed a little where she stood, to let her hips and shoulders touch the invader's. "He's a hard-nosed bastard, but I've learned to cope. I can keep him reasonable so long as you don't get reckless."

He showed his empty hands.

"Making trouble would be stupid." Her eyes had grown innocently wider, in a way it hurt him to recall. "Because you couldn't hope to win. I think you're brighter than Galen."

She raised her voice above the rattle of the disk.

"Really, Defender, we're lucky Donbrik came. Because

he can share with us. Share the civilization of the ruler race. They can lift us out of barbarism and make things easier for all of us." She swayed against the wary-eyed invader. "He's so very good to me."

"I'm sure he is."

"Don't be mean." She made a fetching face. "If you'll just listen to the history—"

"I was listening."

"There was no malfunction in their seedship," she said. "His people were thriving on the world where it had fallen. Happy and peaceful for many thousand years—until they were attacked by creatures from another star. The raiders were dreadful brain-things that lived in robot bodies. The humans were nearly wiped out, but the survivors learned from the raiders. Learned to build robots.

"And learned to be warriors—men like the flight commander."

Listening to the disk, the invader nodded at her with bleak approval.

"In the end, they beat the brain-things. Extending their defenses, they conquered the planets of a dozen other stars—"

"Including Mansphere?"

"It had a high technology. It was therefore a possible enemy."

"He admits the sneak attack?"

"He calls it an unlucky blunder." She shrugged. "The expedition set out. No news came back. His people never knew the reason, not till he got here. Talking to Attack Command, he has turned up evidence that the native scientists lived long enough to strike back with some new weapon that killed the colonists as they landed."

"Good enough," he muttered.

"Defender, please—" Imploringly, she caught his arm to pull him nearer the invader. "We've got to understand the flight commander and his unlucky people. They're fugitives now, because of another dreadful blunder. Another attack, which they considered necessary to secure their defenses against another sun system.

"Maybe human once, its people had engineered themselves into something else. Into angels, he says, and terrible demons. The demons hit back with fighting robots and copied weapons. The commander says his own people were wiped out. All except his own ship. He was in flight to occupy one of the new planets they thought they had conquered. After the disaster, he changed his course in space to come here. A flight they weren't prepared for. Too long for the ship and his people in their transleep capsules. A desperate risk, he says, but the only chance he had to keep the ruler race alive.

"That's why, Defender—" She clung to his arm, her Jayna voice catching and quivering in a way he remembered. "Why we must understand. They didn't come to conquer anybody. They're only looking for a safe refuge—"

"A pretty ruthless way of looking. When your new hero murders Galen and fires on me." He frowned at the invader. "Is he alone?"

"Alone?" She gestured at the empty landers by the dome. "He brought many hundred people. Enough to secure the planet and establish their civilization."

"Does he have other scouts still out?"

"None." Her head lifted proudly. "He was brave enough to go all alone."

Grimly pleased, the invader leaned to meet her swaying shoulder.

"You can tell him now. Tell him he has made his last blunder. His transleep passengers are dead in the dome. Killed by their own world-murder weapon. Tell him he really is alone—"

She recoiled from him, staring.

"Flight Commander Donbrik to Defender One." The disk came down to buzz around his head like a vast, angry insect. "The commander informs you that your foolish falsehood has not deceived him. He knows your fantastic statement cannot be true because he inspected the fortress ahead of his disembarking people. He found it secure, and he ordered the carriers taken inside where they could be opened safely—"

"Tell him to look."

Squinting sharply at him, the invader growled an order at the girl. She darted away toward the dome.

"Jayna, stop! If you go inside, you'll never come out."

She ran on.

"Get her back," he snapped at the invader. "She'll die—"

The disk cackled. Staring after the girl, the invader ignored it. The Defender had turned to follow when he saw her stop. She came staggering back, wheezing for breath.

"A horrible—horrible stink!"

The invader bellowed an order at the disk, and it flashed past her and on into the dome. Kneeling, he leveled his rifle to cover the open doorway and the other Defenders. Still clothed in shimmering wings, they stood gloriously remote from everything else. Even when the fitful wind brought a breath of death from the dome, they seemed unaware of anything outside themselves.

At last, the disk emerged. The invader rose, barking questions. The rattle of the disk seemed to quaver and hesitate. The invader stiffened, blinking at the dome and the bright-winged Defenders. For a long time, he stood frozen. Then he shook his head and whispered something to the girl.

Bent in a fit of coughing, she seemed not to hear.

Looking hard at the Defender, he lifted one hand in a slow salute and marched silently toward that dark doorway.

"Commander! Don't—"

She stumbled after him, gasping something in his language. He stopped and turned, staring at her blankly. She flung her arms around him, and they stood a long time talking. The disk drifted back and forth above them, darted away toward the dome and the other Defenders. Still wrapped together in iridescent wings, they aroused themselves to call something that stopped it in the air.

"Don!" They beckoned him to join them. Trembling with too much emotion, he walked unsteadily to where they stood. "Thanks, old boy." Speaking with the clipped voice Brink had known so long, the new Wardian thrust out a strong gold arm to greet him with a hearty handshake. "Megan tells me you've saved the ship and got the colony safely born."

"The thanks," he said, "should go to you."

"No matter now." Wardian shrugged and paused to smile at Megan. "Looks as if our problems here are settled. I imagine you'll be going back on duty with the ship.

"As for Megan and me—"

"We're staying, Don." Eyes glinting green in the early sun, she shone in more than the first Megan's loveliness, and he longed for her. "At least for now. To clear out the catalyst and set the robots to cleaning up the carnage."

"Then we'll want to look over the loot." Wardian gestured at the landers and the dome. "With all the history and technology of the invader race to learn, that's enough to keep us happy."

"Oh, Don!" Her Megan voice stabbed through his heart. "We love you so—"

She opened a rose-glowing wing to sweep him into the circle of their wings. Her gold lips touched his, and the odors of their sex washed him in a wave of too-human heartbreak. Reeling to it, quivering and giddy, he heard her far-seeming murmur:

"If you must leave—" The velvet wing pressed him closer to her fluid power. " 'Parting is all we know of heaven, and all we need of hell.' "

She let him go.

"Carry on, old boy." Wardian leaned again to clap his shoulder. "When you need us, we'll be ready."

Their wings had shut him out again, and he stumbled uncertainly back to Jayna. She was leading the invader toward the flyer, holding him by the hand as if he were a bewildered child.

"You win, Defender." Her cover-girl smile was bittersweet delight. "The commander's ready to admit he's lost his expedition and the planet, though I don't think he understands quite how it happened. He wanted to kill himself. The last duty, he says, that a defeated warrior owes his people—but I've persuaded him that we're going to be his people now. I'm taking him home in Galen's place.

"And don't say I shouldn't."

The Jayna he recalled, sleekly cajoling.

"Really, Defender, he'll make us all stronger. Of course, he's shaken now, but he's tough stuff. He'll soon be okay. He can help us learn to use the gear his people brought. If trouble comes again, we may need a warrior."

"If trouble comes—"

He paused to frown at Donbrik. Shuffling beside her, shoulders sagging and eyes on the pavement, the invader looked harmless. But what of his conqueror genes, mixed into the tiny gene pool of the colony?

"Trouble will come," he muttered, his joy of victory once more diluted. "It will always come."

Aboard the flyer, he vented mass-inverted water to lift them for the long flight back to the colony. The dome dwindled as they climbed, a tarnished silver coin dropped beside the gray landing strip and the black slash of the canyon. He turned south toward the colony.

Jayna had revived the invader from his daze of defeat. In the seat behind him, they were making vigorous love. Listening to their breathing, he yearned again for all he had been born without. Yet, as he watched the empty planet rolling back beneath them, that old pain faded.

For Mansphere was alive again. With its major mysteries solved and its major hazards conquered, the human seed was firmly rooted, the colonists heirs to two worlds. Exciting infants still, just awaking in their cradle. He thrilled with human pride in their cosmic promise, ached with a human pity for all they might suffer, relaxed at last to upwelling human joy. When things went wrong—some things always would—he would still be their Defender.

Glancing back again toward that endless empty strip, he recalled another empty starport. The launch facility, ten thousand centuries ago, its vacant miles spread across a high mesa in western New Mexico. The historic Dos Lobos ranch, which old Luther Raven had bought for a tax shelter and finally left to the seedship project.

An autumn weekend, with the lab shut down. Marty Rablon was away with his lawyers and Wardian had gone hang gliding. Megan had driven him up from Albuquerque, along with Brink and Tomislav, to see the first seedship mockup. The scanner mix had been nearly too much for him, and he was glad for a day away. A day with her, riding in the front seat beside her.

At the old ranch headquarters, just inside the gate, they stopped for a lunch of *chili* and *frijoles* and *tortillas* with wiry old Jesus Aranda and his withered woman. *Mojados*, they had come up from Chihuahua to work for *El Señor* Raven. Most of the staff was away, and Jesus rode along to show them the new road to the launch complex. Standing on the pad, the mockup was a thin yellow pencil, dwarfed by the fatter auxiliary drive-mass tanks and the cranes around them.

"That toy!" Don Brink blinked in startled scorn. "You're really telling me it can fly to the stars? On plain water?"

He tried to explain hydrogen-fusion propulsion, so much

more efficient than chemical rockets and safer than any fission system.

"The seedships have to be small," he added, "because we have to launch so many of them. One a day. Maybe two, when we get going. At least a thousand before we're done. Most, of course, will be lost. Maybe all, unless we're lucky."

They parked near the pad. Megan got out with a camera to take pictures for Ben Bannerjee. The altitude was too high for Tomislav, and Brink's knee was bad; they waited with him in the car.

"Pretty dismal odds."

"The odds are always—always dismal." Tomislav was wheezing for his breath. "For seed or genes or people, in the competition for survival. That's why nature has to be so prodigal, sometimes so cruel."

"I guess I ought to be grateful." Brink looked hard at the biologist, who had never really wanted his mind or his genes in the computer. "And grateful to Megan, if it's why she took me on the project. I know I've seen my share of ugly odds. Spent my life playing hard games against them." He looked back at the tiny ship, his scarred features softening. "And I've loved it. We're a fighting kind, we humans. All we need is a fighting chance."

"But fighting—fighting isn't all." Tomislav had to gasp for air. "A lesson you had better learn, Mr. Brink, if you really hope to continue fighting. Aggression has sometimes been useful, but too much of it has eliminated species. It's about to eliminate mankind now; that's why the project matters. Altruism is a far stronger factor for survival.

"Our Defenders will be programed for altruism."

"But don't forget—" Don Brink shook his head, with an impish grin. "Your altruists may have to be defended."

ABOUT THE AUTHOR

Jack Williamson began writing science fiction in 1928, before it got that name. With time out for service as an Army Air Force weather forecaster during World War II and a more recent career as a college English professor, he has devoted his life to science fiction, and he says he has no regrets.

A Southwesterner, he was born in Arizona of pioneering parents who took him to a Mexican mountain ranch before he was two months old, moved from there to Pecos, Texas, and then, the year he was seven, brought him by covered wagon to the Staked Plains of Eastern New Mexico, where he and his wife, Blanche, still live.

The best known of his thirty-odd novels is probably *The Humanoids*. He has been honored by the Science Fiction Writers of America with their Grand Master Nebula Award, and he has served for two terms as president of the organization. He taught one of the first college courses in science fiction and has edited a guidebook for science-fiction teachers.

Now retired from teaching, he writes on a word processor. His next work, he says, is to be an autobiographical book about his own adventures in science fiction.